Thanks for everything!

The Ledger

A Novel

Lloyd Holm

FFP

FOX FARM PRESS

FOX FARM PRESS

This book is a work of fiction, set against the background of actual events. The characters, however, are entirely fictional and are products of the author's imagination or are used fictitiously. Any resemblance to persons, living or dead, is entirely coincidental.

ISBN: 978-0-9847564-1-4

Cover design by The Fast Fingers Book Formatting Service
www.thefastfingers.com

www.lloydholmbooks.com

Printed in the United States of America

To my wife Gretchen,
for her love, inspiration, and kindness.

"Virtue cannot separate itself from reality without becoming a principle of evil."

Albert Camus

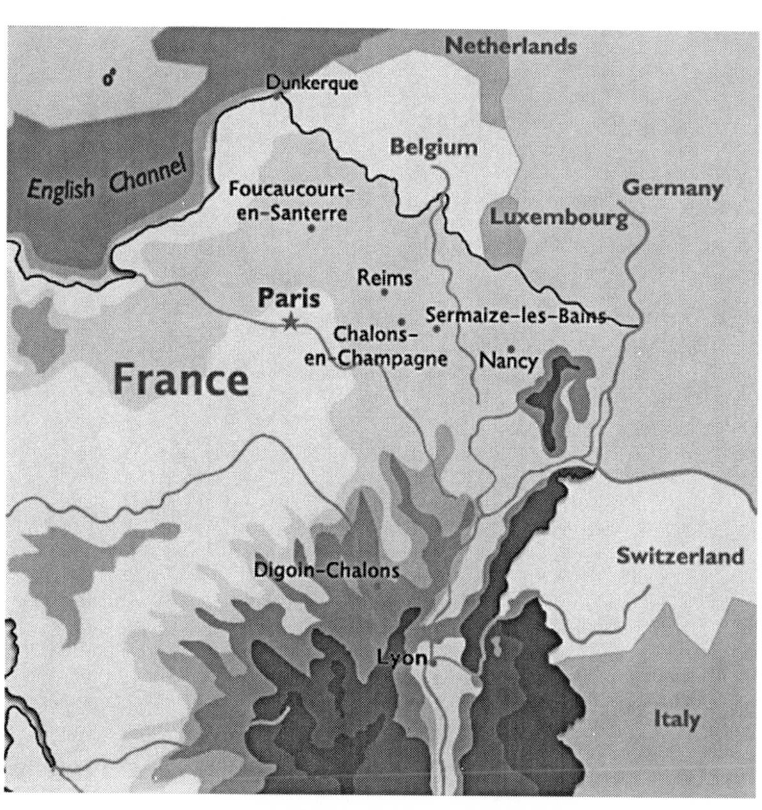
Netherlands
Dunkerque
Belgium
English Channel
Foucaucourt-
en-Santerre
Germany
Luxembourg
Reims
Paris
Sermaize-les-Bains
Chalons-
en-Champagne
Nancy
France
Switzerland
Digoin-Chalons
Lyon
Italy

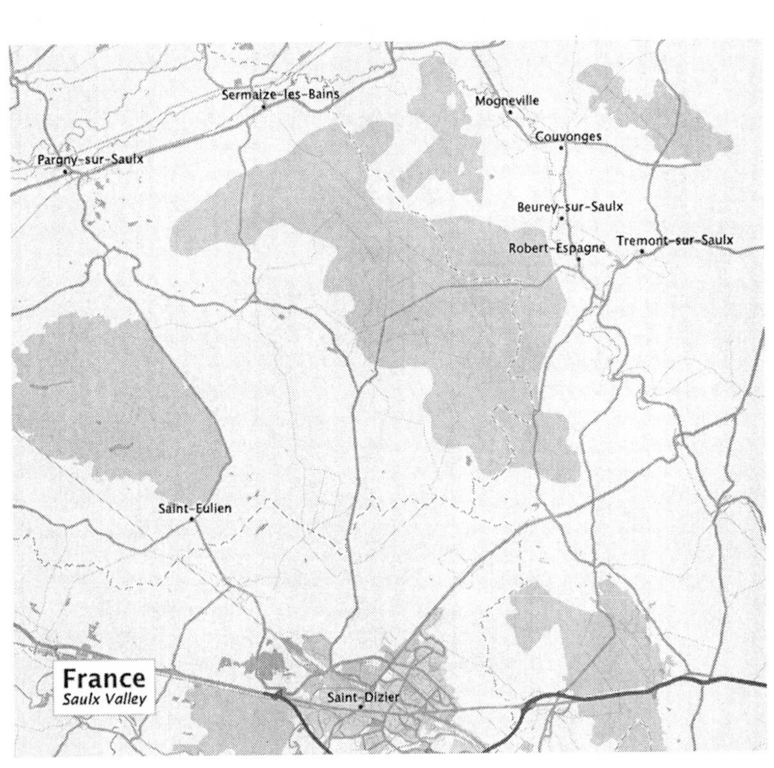
Sermaize-les-Bains
Mogneville
Couvonges
Pargny-sur-Saulx
Beurey-sur-Saulx
Robert-Espagne
Tremont-sur-Saulx
Saint-Eulien
France
Saulx Valley
Saint-Dizier

CHAPTER 1

Paris
December, 1982

Paul tiptoed down the darkened hall when he came to the open door of Hans Krüger's study. He glanced in to see Mr. Krüger standing at the window, absorbed in thought. Hmm ... three a.m., yet the man still wore the same clothes he'd worn at dinner. Paul watched his future father-in-law, erect and resolute, bathed in a shaft of soft moonlight.

Hans Krüger wasn't at all what he expected, but then Paul hadn't really known what to expect. The family photos Christine shared gave few clues about her father, and despite Christine's obvious love for the man, she seemed to know very little about him.

As for Paul, he knew three things. One, he knew he and Christine were in love and engaged to be married. Two, he knew the silent man at the window fought in World War II as a Nazi soldier. And three, Paul knew Nazis killed Jews.

Transfixed, unaware of Paul studying him, Mr. Krüger hadn't moved. His breathing was slow and rhythmic. But then for no apparent reason he raised his shoulders and winced, closing both eyes as if trying to keep some painful thought at bay. A noise from elsewhere in the house failed to disturb his trance.

Paul pushed back from the doorframe and continued on to the bathroom. There he somehow felt safe and far removed from the questions that were sure to be asked the next day. Already he knew his responses:

Yes, Mr. Krüger, I plan on finishing my thesis on time.

Yes, Mr. Krüger, I do plan on teaching at the university level.

No, Mr. Krüger, I have never really thought about living in France.

No, Mr. Krüger, we have not discussed having a family.

Yes, Mr. Krüger, we have only known each other a year.

Yes, Mr. Krüger, I know Christine was brought up in France and I am an American.

There was also the big question, the one that was sure to be asked, and Paul didn't know how to deal with it. The issue that caused him constant anxiety, the same one that had provoked more than one argument with Christine.

Yes, Mr. Krüger, I am Jewish, and now and then I do attend shul.

At last Paul opened the bathroom door and retraced his steps to the guest room, glancing into Mr. Krüger's study as he passed.

The room was empty.

CHAPTER 2

Paul yanked the car door shut. The turmoil fermenting within him since their arrival from the States two days earlier began to simmer. He gripped the steering wheel but didn't start the engine.

"Christine, I don't get it, things seemed to be getting off to a good start. And to think I was even beginning to forget about last night—"

"Look," Christine said, "I don't know what's going on. Maybe nothing. Maman never seemed displeased before." She unfolded the map on her knees. "Even if something is going on—which I question, I don't think you need be concerned."

Paul set his jaw.

That's what you think. "I have every reason to be concerned." He let go of the wheel with one hand. "Tell me if this doesn't make sense. Why are things different now?"

She said nothing, studying the route to her grandfather's home in Sermaize-les-Bains.

Still confused, he started the car. "It's your father. Or maybe me? That's it. It's me."

"I think you're imagining things."

No, you think I'm paranoid. "It's your father, after he sized me up. And you can bet he's influencing your mother. I'm telling you, I'm not imagining anything."

"Next right." Christine pointed to the sign at the corner. "I've always known how Papa is, but I can't believe he would do that."

"So I'm an American and I'm marrying his only daughter." Paul shook his head. "No, I know what it is, I've always suspected it. It's my last name."

For a moment Christine pursed her lips, as if deciding what to say. "It has nothing to do with your last name." Still distracted, she turned her head to check the road signs. "Careful! Take the third road off this roundabout."

"Come on." He leaned into the turn. "You're the one who told me your father was a Nazi." I can just see his arm thrust out in a Sieg Heil! salute as his heels clicked together.

"What?" She raised her voice. "I would never say that. You know very well he was a *German* soldier. I would never use the word Nazi about my father." Her shoulders heaved when she exhaled. "Never!"

"You said you didn't know anything about what your father did in the war. Look how aloof he is. Don't you see, he's hiding something?" Admit it, he still has no use for Jews.

"Papa's not hiding anything and he wasn't a Nazi. Since you brought it up, most people don't know you're Jewish, even if they did, they could care less. And you don't have to say with every little insult, 'They know I'm Jewish.' "

Paul slammed his palm against the steering wheel. "That's not fair."

Christine startled in response to the outburst, then resumed. "Paul, trust me, you get sensitive. But none of this is because you're Jewish, not in the least."

"Okay, let's assume you're right. It still doesn't explain your father's behavior." When her voice broke, Paul turned to see her fighting back tears.

"Maybe I should listen to Maman. Maybe we shouldn't get married."

Paul pulled over to the shoulder, stopped the car, and pulled the emergency brake. "Where did *that* come from?"

"Maman mentioned it once on the phone, long time ago." She looked over at Paul and added before he could respond, "It was her, *not* Papa."

"Great, now it's both of them."

Christine sat straight. "Can't we just enjoy ourselves?"

Paul sighed. "Sure, I'd like nothing more, but it won't help my frustration one iota."

"Fine." Christine bit her lower lip and stared straight ahead. "You needn't take it out on me, or anyone else for that matter, especially Papa. If he was a Nazi, like you think he was, and he hates Jews, then why did he marry Maman?"

Paul glanced over at Christine. "Your whole family's Catholic."

"We were raised Catholic, but Maman is half Jewish. I told you that in Chicago."

Paul reached over and brushed away the lone tear rolling down her cheek. "Honey, I'm sorry. You're right, maybe I am too sensitive—"

"*Maybe*?"

"Okay, I am too sensitive."

She looked over, relaxed her shoulders and smiled. "Thank you."

Easing back onto the autoroute out of Paris, Paul headed northeast toward Reims. At length Christine placed her hand on his as he shifted the Citroën into fifth gear and said, "I don't like it when we quarrel." She lifted his hand to press her lips to his fingertips. "After all, we'll be living in America. It's my life, my decision, my engagement. And *our* wedding."

Paul grinned. Now that's more like it. "If you're trying to distract me, it's working."

"What if I am?"

"Then I'm all for it. Like you said, we need to do what *we* want to do. Besides, you're twenty-seven years old, not seventeen and in love for the first time." Paul glanced over his shoulder, then passed a truck. "I guess that old saying is true,

'A son is a son 'til he takes a wife, and a daughter's a daughter the rest of her life.' "

"Very cute. I've never heard that before. I like it."

Paul nodded, then scanned the horizon before looking over at Christine. "It's amazing how much the French landscape reminds me of the drive from Rockford to Chicago, even the toll booths."

Christine folded the map and put it away. "Do you think your parents will ever see it?"

"Of course, and they'll love it, I promise."

"Paul?"

He hesitated, then replied, "Yes?"

"What did you and Papa talk about last night?"

"What did *we* talk about?" She can't be serious. "*We* didn't talk about much of anything."

"It wasn't bad was it?"

"Are you kidding me?"

"I wish I had prepared you better for Papa. Really, what did he ask? What'd you tell him?"

"I told him about my research, how I hoped to teach at the university level, and with a little luck, maybe score a book out of my thesis."

"That's not so terrible."

"No, it's not. But then, silence. Total silence." When he looked to Christine her face told him she'd experienced it herself, that she knew what he meant. "I didn't know what to say, so I just sat there."

"Did he ask you anything else?"

"Just two questions. He asked if my Nuremberg Trial research dealt with any particular war crime. Then without even waiting for my answer, he asked if I'd ever come across the name Karl Beck. Both questions seemed well thought out in advance. They had to be. After that, nothing." A big Nazi nothing.

"I wanted you to like Papa so much." Her voice sounded defeated.

"It's not that I dislike him, I just met him."

"I'm sure things will be better when we get back to Paris." Christine shifted towards Paul and scanned the dashboard. "How's our fuel?"

He looked over and smiled. "We're fine. Just relax, we'll be to your grandfather's before you know it."

The once heavy traffic and distractions had lessened as they continued toward their destination. Paul appeared pensive. Christine turned around and reached into the back seat pulling two soft drinks out of a cloth sack. She handed one to Paul and said, "You want to ask me something, don't you?"

Paul smiled. "How'd you guess?" He assessed her facial expression before continuing. "I've been thinking, in 1939 your father, he'd have been twenty-five, so he wasn't just a young recruit when Germany invaded Poland." Paul didn't wait for a response. "It's entirely possible he was an officer."

"Possibly," Christine said, "but I don't know anything about what he did or where he fought."

Paul shook his head in bewilderment. "How can you not know?"

"That's just how Papa is. He would never talk about it. I asked him once, years ago when I was a little girl. We had a school assignment to present something about the war, but even a topic that simple would cause a problem.

"You see, there were French who were sympathetic to the Nazis, they aided them in many ways. Collaborators, that's what they were called."

"Those women whose heads were shaved?"

"Yes." She rotated the half-empty can in her hand and continued. "I didn't even know if Papa had served in the war, but he would have been old enough. All I knew was he had grown up in Germany.

"Anyway, at the supper table one night I asked him if he fought in the war. When Maman looked at me, it was clear I'd said something wrong. Then she looked at Papa like she was scared. I told him my history class had an assignment about the war and I thought he might be able to help me. With that, a weird stillness came over him.

"Maman rushed about, gathered up the dishes like she does when she's nervous. In an odd voice she said, 'More wine, Papa?' He just sat there. After a moment he shuddered and flinched, as if he had a tic. He looked down at me and said, 'Mon ombre'—that was my nickname, means my shadow. He said, 'Mon ombre, war is a terrible thing. I pray you never have to experience it.' He had a far-away look I had never seen before, and after that I knew I must never ask him anything about it again. And I never have."

"But you know so much about the war." Paul slowed to let a car pass. "Where did you learn it all?"

"Reading books, magazine articles, things like that."

"What about your grandfather, did he fight in the war?"

"Grandpère fought in World War I, but he was too old for World War II. He has never talked much about the war, just enough to say what a terrible toll both wars took on Sermaize-les-Bains. All of France, for that matter."

"And your paternal grandfather?"

"Papa's parents are dead. They were both German. I'm pretty sure his father fought in World War I."

Before anything further could be said, the rural countryside gave way to the outskirts of a town, a few abandoned sheds and an end to the barren trees that had lined their route for the last few miles.

"Here, take this turn." Christine indicated to her right. "That building's new, used to be a farm."

Paul made the turn. "Just how much English does your grandfather speak, anyway?"

"Oh, he can keep up a decent conversation. I'm sure he understands more than he lets on."

"Well, he wouldn't be the first in the family to do that, now would he?"

She smiled at him then turned back toward the window. Within seconds she pointed, "There it is! That house, there, the one on the left."

CHAPTER 3

"Oh, I'm so excited to be here again! Look, he's watching out the window for us!"

"Wait up. Let me stop the car before you jump out!"

As Paul came to a halt and before he could even set the brake Christine was out of the car, running up the walk and into her grandfather's waiting arms.

"Prends garde, ma p'tite, tu vas me bouleverser!"

She laughed in delight. "Grandpère, knocking you over's the last thing I'd want to do." She kissed him on one cheek, then the other, as Paul followed her from the car.

André Ferrand's stooped posture and precise movement suggested his age, but the smile on his face was as young as a boy's. His features were as crisp as his recent haircut, his short beard trimmed and neat. No scruffy, unkempt fuzz. Nor did his vigorous voice suggest eighty-seven years.

Christine grasped his upper arms and took an appraising look at him. "You don't change, Grandpère. Still wearing your favorite blue sweater?"

"Eh bien, why not? It's good as new."

He drew her to him for a prolonged embrace, as if that would lengthen her stay, then pulled back to admire her. "Ah, Christine, you're the portrait of your mother. Such a beautiful woman."

"Wait, Grandpère, before we go inside, I would like you to meet my fiancé Paul Rosenbaum. Paul, this is my grandpère, André Ferrand."

Paul seemed to feel he should make a slight bow. "It's a pleasure to meet you, Monsieur Ferrand."

"And you also, Paul. Welcome, welcome to Sermaize-les-Bains."

The old gentleman turned toward the house. "Come, children, let us, how do you say? Go inside away from the cold. We have some hot chocolate and pastries."

After a few steps André gave Christine's arm a squeeze. "Eh bien, ma chère, how long are you staying?"

"Oh, Grandpère, you always ask that the moment we arrive. You see, Paul, my grandfather would ask 'How long are you going to stay?' before we even got into the house, and Maman would get so mad! Grandmère would scold him."

"But, ma p'tite, don't you remember, I would just smile and say, 'I ask, Elsie, so we know for how much time we shall be able to enjoy their visit.' "

She nodded. "I remember." He was guiding her through the front door, motioning for Paul to follow. "For now, though, as much as we would like to stay forever, I'm afraid we must head back to Paris tomorrow, probably after lunch."

"Oui, magnifique. Wonderful. I have put away a special bottle of wine just for your visit. Come, come, sit down, make yourselves comfortable."

Paul joined Christine on the sofa as the old gentleman took a chair that fit him like a glove. He commenced to study Paul and note his mannerisms. His slight nod and the look on his face told Christine her grandfather was already forming a favorable opinion. But then why should he not? Paul had such kind eyes, such a gentle way.

She felt far more comfortable about this meeting than she had about Paul's earlier meeting with her parents. When introduced, Paul had looked the old man in the eye and given his hand a firm shake. Her grandfather would like that combination of courtesy and straightforwardness.

Just then an older woman appeared in the door from the dining room with an inquiring look on her face.

"Ah, Mme. Moreau," André said. "Mes enfants, here is the good Mme. Moreau. She helps me with meals from time to time." He nodded to the smiling woman. "Oui, nous sommes prêtes. Now that we are ready, she will bring us some refreshments."

In moments Mme. Moreau reappeared with a tray bearing a pot of hot chocolate, a plate of madeleine cakes, three cups, and three crisp linen napkins. With a second nod from André, she poured out the chocolate and passed cups and pastries around.

After the visitors had thanked her, she left and Christine's grandfather leaned back in his chair to rest his feet on a small ottoman.

"Now, Paul, tell me about yourself. How is your acquaintance with my Christine?"

Christine said, "He means how did we meet." She smiled at her grandfather.

"Yes, yes. How did you meet? I am sorry for my English. It has been some while since I speak it, but it will get better as we converse."

Paul glanced at Christine. "Should I tell him about the ad?"

"Sure, go on. That's how we met."

Paul lowered his chin and took a deep breath. "You see, sir, Christine and I are both studying at the University of Chicago. My field is history, and as you know, Christine is studying business. Well, I was riding the campus bus to the library one night and there was this beautiful woman in a white sweater sitting across from me."

André nodded, eyes bright. "Yes, yes, I understand."

Pleased with her grandfather's interest, Christine gave Paul an encouraging glance.

"I noticed she was reading a French newspaper, and there was a French magazine poking out of her backpack."

"Backpack?" André looked to Christine. "This is what?"

"Sac à dos, for wearing on one's back."

"I see. So what was the magazine, *Paris Match*?"

"Yes, that was it. That's when I figured she was French."

Paul took a sip from his chocolate then continued. "Anyway, we got to the library and she stood up to get off the bus. I had been staring at her, and when she looked at me, I just froze. I kind of smiled and looked away, embarrassed, and she got off the bus."

"You said nothing? Then how did you meet her?"

"I know. I felt stupid I hadn't said anything. So I followed her into the library and looked around for her, but I couldn't find her anywhere. Not at any of the tables, the study carrels, nowhere. Then the idea hit me. I took out an ad in the student newspaper, *The Maroon*."

"An ad? I do not know this word."

"An advertisement," Paul said.

"*Ah,* oui, un advertisement."

"That's it. I went to the newspaper office and took out an advertisement for the following week."

Setting her cup aside, Christine reached into her purse for her wallet and retrieved a small folded and worn piece of newsprint.

Paul's eyes widened. "Hey, I didn't know you kept that!"

"And why shouldn't I? It changed my life." She handed it to her grandfather.

"Eh bien, this is written in French." André seemed surprised. "Did you, how do I say, Christine? Spy it right away?"

"Oui, Grandpère. I saw it right away. I always read the paper every week to improve my English. It was a surprise to see something written in French, so imagine how intrigued I was to realize it was intended for me!"

André took the paper and perused it, looked over at Paul, then smiled. Out of courtesy to his guest, he translated it into English as he read it aloud.

> "To the beautiful French woman in the white sweater on the UC campus bus Monday night: I am sorry I was too shy to follow my smile with a hello. I would like to formally apologize and introduce myself. Meet me where you got off that night. This Friday at 8:00? Please be there."

"Alors, Christine, after you read it, what did you do?"

"It wasn't a difficult decision. I met him there, and we talked. I liked him, and he asked me out. We've been going out ever since, and then on October sixteenth he asked me to marry him."

André gave a wistful sigh. "Such a romantic story. I wish your grandmère were here to know this, she would smile as I smile now."

The door from the dining room opened again, and Mme. Moreau reappeared to offer more cocoa and pass the madeleines again. She seemed pleased to see that the atmosphere had become quite cozy.

"Anything else, Monsieur?" she said to André.

"Pas maintenant." Not at the moment. She retreated to the kitchen, the soul of propriety and housekeeping excellence.

Satisfied that Paul and André would go on talking,

Christine stood up and gave Paul's knee a soft squeeze as she rose. On the table by the couch she observed a group of framed photographs, arranged in a precise semi-circle. Then she walked over to the wall to study more photos hung there, most of them in black and white.

"Grandpère, I never knew you had so many photos."

"Oui, but while your grandmère lived they were put away. After she was gone, I déterrer, Christine, what is this word?"

"You dug them out."

"Oui, merci. I dug them out. They recall for me all our times together, the bad as well as the good."

She held one photo up to inspect it like a jeweler would inspect a watch, then turned it over but found no clues to what it portrayed. "This photo, it's horrid. Look." She held it out for him to see. "Something terrible happened. What was it?"

The picture showed a solitary, erect chimney projecting through mounds of rubble and jagged sections of wall from several collapsed buildings. Not a living soul, just devastation.

The old man shook his head and sighed. "That is Sermaize-les-Bains in the early part of la première guerre mondiale. World War One, as you say. That is what happened here in the famous battle of the Marne."

She carried the picture over to show it to Paul. "Honey, look. Grandpère, is this far from here?"

He inclined his head northeastward. "That direction, not far, perhaps one kilometer, maybe two."

She shook her head as she set the photo back on the table. "What a dreadful, dreadful thing. Was your home demolished?"

"This house was, yes, but we did not live here then. Your Grandmère Elsie lived with her parents on their farm at the edge of town. We had not married then, and I was in the armée, fighting the boches. Perhaps two hundred and fifty kilometers north of here, on the Somme, near Foucaucourt-en-Santerre. We dug deep trenches to fortify ourselves against the Kaiser's troops."

"I've read about those trenches," Paul said. "A nightmare for sure, having to live in mud day and night."

"Not charming, no," André said. "One could surely say that. You see, the Germans rolled into France expecting to win Paris without a fight. But we French were heroic. The English, too. Our armies arrested the Kaiser's troops and held them back for a very long while."

Christine had picked up another photograph. "Isn't this a photo of a German soldier? Why on earth do you have it? And in a frame, too."

He took it from her and gazed at it for a long while before he said, "That, Christine, is your Grandpère Krüger. You can see, he's in his uniform."

"But, why do you have a picture of him? Your soldiers were fighting theirs."

The old gentleman cocked his head like a pert robin. "Christine, how is it you do not know of this?"

She shrugged her shoulders.

"I think I need to tell you and Paul these things that you should know. But, for now I have, I have … how do you say, rambled. Yes, that's it. I have rambled, like an old man. There will be plenty of time later to tell you all."

He said this in such a way that Christine knew it would be worth the wait.

"Very well, then, we'll wait. By the way, Grandpère, I congratulate you on your English. You're doing very well."

"Thank you. I have a much better feeling about it now." He put up both hands as if horrified at himself. "But what am I thinking? I haven't asked about your wedding."

"Oh, Grandpère, Paul and I are so excited."

Another tilt of the head, eyebrows up. "Vraiment?" Really? "Your words say you are excited, but I don't hear it in your voice. Why would this be?"

"Truly, we are excited, but Maman and Papa are not so excited."

André looked puzzled. "Have they removed their support?"

"No, but they make it very clear they're not pleased, and we don't understand. Before we came home, Maman seemed fine."

"Your papa? Is he not fine also?"

Christine shook her head. "Not at all. We didn't talk about it much while I was away, he seemed happy for me, but now—"

"What happened, ma chère?"

"He … well, he doesn't seem to like Paul." She paused, then continued. "I don't want to be angry at him, but he has no right to act like this. I'm not a child. I can make my own choices."

Struggling to hold back her tears, she took a deep breath hoping that would help, and when her grandfather began to speak, she sat back to listen.

"I suppose it became real for them, ma chère, when they met Paul. Perhaps it was then they knew, this wedding was more than talk. They do not know yet that they have nothing to fear. They will know soon, you see, because I know this myself."

Relieved at her grandfather's confidence, she sat a bit straighter.

"And you must comprehend that your papa loves you. It has been difficult for you to know him, I understand. He is not the man you might think he is. Now, before it grows late, why don't you and Paul make a little promenade? Move your legs after your drive. I will help Mme. Moreau with these cups."

Paul stood up. "I'd like to help, if I may."

"No, no, you young people go, enjoy the fresh air."

"Merci bien, Grandpère." Christine hugged the old gentleman and rested her head on his shoulder for a moment to savor the clean lemony smell of his soap. Then, after she kissed him on the cheek, she and Paul picked up their coats and headed out.

"Don't walk too long," André called after them.

André Ferrand tried to help Mme. Moreau in the kitchen, but she shooed him out, telling him to sit himself down and relax.

"After I get these cups and plates washed, I'll be on my way home," she said. "I've left the cassoulet in the oven, and a salad. Oh yes, and bread. I've even ground the coffee, you need only boil the water and pour it in the cafetière."

"Shall I lay the table, then?"

"Not even that, Monsieur. It will all be done, I assure you."

He went back to his usual chair, sank into it, and thought about Christine and his son-in-law Hans. He thought of how much he missed his Elsie, how alone he'd felt ever since that fall day when they'd laid her to rest beside the church.

Christine had been Elsie's favorite, always seated next to her grandmère at meals whenever the family came to visit. The passing years had hastened her growth, it was hard not to think of Christine as a little girl. What advice Elsie would give about the engagement, her papa, the wedding—if she were here? So many times he wished she were.

How had Elsie Ferrand done it? Famous for the advice she gave, everyone sought her out, yet all she ever did was to listen and nod. Never a cross word passed her lips and not one word of advice either. Yet every child and grandchild would come to her for counsel and leave convinced she had guided them through their troubles to the very solution they sought.

"It will all work out for the best"—that was her trademark response. He smiled when he thought of her wrapping a galette in a napkin and slipping it into the pocket of each of the grandchildren before the long ride home. He went back to the kitchen and, before Mme. Moreau could interfere, took two of the sugar cookies from the crock himself and wrapped them in a napkin, hoping he'd remember to slip them into Christine's and Paul's coat pockets in the morning.

When the ringing of the phone in the sitting room startled him, he went to answer it. "Allo? Aimée, is that you?"

"Oui, Papa. Ça va?" How are you?

"I'm quite well."

"How are you getting along? Is there anything you need?"

"No, Aimée, Mme. Moreau is here today. There is plenty to keep us busy."

"Are they there yet?"

"Yes, we've had a pleasant visit. They just went out for a little promenade."

"What do you think? Do you like him, this Paul? Do you think it will be good for Christine to marry him?"

André knew better than to commit his opinion on such a matter. "What do *you* think, ma fille?"

He heard her sigh over the wire. "I'm afraid it is not such a good idea. He's from America and she hasn't known him long enough, only a year. I want to like him, truly I do. And yet—"

"What is the opinion of Hans?"

"That's a problem also. Hans is not at all happy about a wedding, especially now. He won't tell me what it is he doesn't like, but you know how he is when he makes up his mind about something. I think perhaps he's afraid we'll lose her forever if she goes to live in America."

"Alors, Aimée, Christine is an adult, quite grown-up in fact. Is it not true you want her to be happy?"

"I do, but unless Hans will accept it, I fear we may drive her to do something rash without us. Please, will you talk to her?"

"Give her advice, you mean, as Elsie used to do?" He was smiling to himself.

"Papa, I'm serious."

"No, Aimée, I will talk *with* her, not *to* her. Come now, what rash thing can she do? If she marries him, she marries him, that's all." He softened his voice. "Aimée?"

"Oui?"

He hesitated, not sure what to say, then chose his words like a stonemason choosing the next stone for a wall. "Aimée, do you remember that August day in 1944?"

"Mais oui. How could I forget?"

He paused for effect before saying in his gravest tone. "Eh bien, your maman and I, we accepted Hans."

Just at that moment, Christine came breezing through the back door with Paul in tow. Without a change in his tone or his inflection, André waved them into the kitchen and continued his conversation. "Yes, Aimée, they arrived before lunch. They have just come back from their promenade. Yes, I will tell them to drive with caution. Oui, I love you, too."

He replaced the phone on its cradle and said with a smile, "That was your maman. She said she loves you and that you must drive with caution. Now, after we sit down to our meal, I will tell you a story, all the things you should know. And before I commence, I will unhook the phone and get a blanket for my legs. But for now our stew is ready to come out of the oven."

CHAPTER 4

The supper over and coffee finished, André brought out a bottle of brandy and poured each of them a small glass. "My old friend Jean-Claude presented this to me last Christmas. Something told me to save it for a special time, and now it is the special time." He raised his glass to his guests. "Santé, mes enfants, and many good wishes for your marriage."

"Santé," they echoed, taking their first sip.

André Ferrand settled into his chair, lifted his legs and smoothed the edges of the blanket before he began.

"I had been in Lyon during the summer of 1914. It was a wonderful time to be young. I was nineteen, enjoying life. I knew your grandmère already, but we were not in love, at least not that I knew. Disquieting events were happening all across Europe, yet I was without a care. It is interesting, over the many years since, that the causes of the Great War have been analyzed from every angle. But at the time it was not so simple."

"It must have all been quite confusing," Christine said. "I always had trouble keeping it straight in school."

"It's obvious you know far more about it than we do," Paul said. "After all, you were part of that war."

André smiled. "As historian, then, you would consider me un personage historique?"

Christine laughed. "Historical, yes, Grandpère, but not ancient history."

"For that I am grateful, ma fille. So, with all of the alliances and treaties between Austria and Germany, Russia and Austria, Germany and Russia, France and Russia, Serbia and Russia, it *was* complicated. And the alliances changed every ten years or so according to the projects—the territorial projects, you see—of whoever was the ruler at that time. It was all for the nobility, forget the common man.

"Life went on. Nobody could see it for what it was, nobody was in a position to stop it. And now the historians think they comprehend it all, but it's a curious thing about these historians—they are never there to stop the terrible events that are rushing forward like a train.

"So in this case, one might say the locomotive had been built. It was operating under its own power, and the tracks had been constructed, but there was no engine driver, no one to control its speed. The first curve in the tracks—the assassination of Archduke Franz Ferdinand and his wife—this is what made it depart the rails. Most people believe that was the start of the Great War."

Paul said, "That's what I was taught."

André shook his head. "Too simple, I fear. It's as if you say one makes bread of flour. Everyone knows, one makes bread of flour, but it is not so easy. Just to put flour on the table, that does not produce bread an hour later. One needs much, much more. So it was with the start of the Great War."

As André paused for breath and adjusted the blanket on his legs, Paul and Christine both said, "Please, go on."

"Very well. The assassination in June of that year alarmed the nobility, and they continued to be alarmed through the summer. It was the match to the powder cask that was Europe in 1914, but the cause more profound was the complicated alliances. That August, Austria-Hungary declared war on Serbia, because the assassin came from Sarajevo, and then all the alliances and treaties came into play.

"No one could stop it, and in effect no one wanted to. Everyone thought it would be a short war. Home before winter. Why not?" He shrugged. "After all, we must support our friends. Austria-Hungary was for Germany and Italy, while Russia and France were for Great Britain. You see, it was to be a simple game of chess.

"And it could have worked, this plan of the Germans, but so many things conspired to defeat them at that time and over the years after. Germany's position on the continent, its various alliances, required a conflict on two fronts, both in this first war and the war to follow."

He took another sip of brandy. "After the declaration of war, the mobilization commenced. I enlisted in Lyon, attached to the 99th régiment d'infanterie, part of the 28th Division. It was a gay time. We trained, we marched, we saluted, we kissed the girls. And we looked splendid.

"Oui, Christine, your grandpère cut a fine figure in his uniform. Why not?" He gave his head a confident little wobble and touched his beard. "I was as handsome then as I am now."

She laughed. "Well, naturally!" She took Paul's hand and smiled at him.

"When it was all over, over for good, I believed I would return home to be with my parents in Sermaize-les-Bains"—his eyes sparkled—"and perhaps chase your grandmère." A smile came to his lips every time he spoke of Elsie, as if he were with her somewhere in one of their shared memories. He still wondered how he'd managed to go on after such a loss.

He shifted a bit in his chair and cleared his throat. "But I fear I am boring you young people with this long lecture."

"No, sir, not in the least," Paul said. "Please, go on. Hearing someone who was there tell about it is far better than a history lecture."

"Alors bien, I must believe what you say. But the war was not ending as they had promised us. At the front we had seen too many friends die, unimaginable horrors. We were just kids, you know, so young. I remember one evening in November when it all became so real. It had rained, and rained, and rained even more. The trenches had become un marais—Christine, what is this word I want?"

"A swamp."

"Yes, thank you. A swamp—mud, filth, a sewer of contagion. We tried to make a floor of wooden planks, but that was useless. We never had enough wood to conquer that sea of mud, and the rain continued day and night.

"We could only huddle together with the cold settling among us like an unwanted guest, when my friend Pierre grumbled, 'Do you suppose our general is as comfortable as we are?' I replied, 'You may be sure he is. But poor fellow, he won't have so many little friends like we have. And even if the general did have these little friends, I don't think they would be eating the same thing as ours.' Everyone laughed at my joke, but deep inside we were in despair. You see, our little friends were the rats. They would feed on dead soldiers beyond the wire in No Man's Land. We could see them run about among the bodies, hunch down to nibble, sit up again, look around, then return to their repast of cold flesh."

Christine shuddered and brought her hand to her mouth. Once the nausea passed, she said, "Ugh! What a horror! How could you endure it?"

He shrugged. "One did what one was required to do. The first time a soldier sees this, you know, he feels such a wave of nausea that, depending upon when he ate last, he might lean over and add to the filth and stench in the trenches. Sometimes a rat would run up a sleeve or pant leg of the dead, and you would shiver and shake your own arm or leg as if the rat had come for you. But the war went on around us, and after a time we ceased to notice these horrors."

Christine, still shivering, snuggled close to Paul for the warmth of his body, and he put his arm around her while the old man relived his nightmare. The only sound was the ticking of the clock.

No longer aware of his audience, André was staring through a window in time. "You never dared raise your head from the trench to watch the rats, at least in the light of day, for then a German sniper might add you to his tally of dead Frenchmen. Yet after a while, too brief a while, this seemed almost normal. We knew that the death-feast never stopped, even if we didn't look. That was bad enough, but hearing it at night, mon Dieu—my God, it was terrible."

With that André seemed to come back to the present.

"Ah, Christine, ma chère, I regret so much having to tell you such stories, but you are a child no longer, and you will comprehend your two families' history only by hearing this. I hope you will forgive me."

She shook her head, unable to speak. When he saw her use the sleeve of her sweater to dab at her tears, the old gentleman brought out a clean linen handkerchief and handed it to her. "You will forgive me, won't you, ma p'tite?"

Without a word, she nodded and sniffed, then gave his handkerchief back.

"You see, the image that the rats' noise would bring forth was frightening, those horrible squeaks, especially when one was trying to sleep and a rat ran across your leg or your chest. Envision, if you will, that if you were fast asleep when this happened, you would awaken in a cold sweat, desperate to beat the vermin away. You would touch your arms and your legs, hoping no rat had found its way to your living flesh.

"In sitting around a makeshift table one night with my comrades, I said, 'Before there was war, and long after this war, there will be rats.'

"Pierre spoke up. 'Did any of you ever see a rat before this war? I never did. Perhaps on occasion in the city, but never so many. I swear, there are more rats than there are boches.' I said I had seen many rats, because I was a farm lad, and rats always tried to get in to eat our grain, but Papa kept barn cats. 'Exactly what we need here,' I said, 'some very large, very hungry French cats. Then we would conquer les boches!'

"One of the other men said, 'Where do you suppose they came from, these rats?' Somebody else answered, 'From Germany. They brought the rats with them. Something that filthy could only come from les boches.' I remember that evening so well because it was the first time we had discussed the rats in such a way. War made us act and see things differently. The filth that the rats represented had become a part of us. Oh, at the time, we did not see it so, but looking back, it is all so plain to see.

"Then Toothy spoke up." André chuckled. "We called him that, you see, because he had such formidable front teeth, like a rabbit. 'Why don't we—les boches and les français— take our rats and train them? Put them in the trenches and have them fight the war. I can be the general of my division and Fritz over there can command his troops. Whoever wins the battle of the rats is declared the winner of this war and we can all go home!'

"Another chimed in. 'Not so funny, mes amis, because isn't that what our generals are doing with us? Aren't we in the trenches while they remain safe in their headquarters, a fine chateau somewhere behind the lines? Yes, we poilus, we are the rats of this war. We are the ones shooting each other and devouring each other. We are the ones being ordered about here and there, and for what?'

"We all nodded in accord. Our corporal, who would soon succumb to pneumonia, attempted to stop this talk, but he was coughing so, he could hardly make us hear. 'Look here, my men'—cough, cough—'such talk'—cough, cough—'will get you sent over the top.' With that, a blanket of silence descended and we contemplated our fate, what we had to lose with this war, and our loved ones at home.

"Some of us—me for one—even dared to think about a future. A mere three months before we had thought we would soon be traveling home, but when the days dragged on, we knew it was a foolish hope. I tell you it was this knowledge that brought us true despair."

The clock chimed—eleven. "But what am I doing, keeping you young people up so late? We must go to bed, finish this story tomorrow."

"Oh, no. We wish to hear the whole thing," Christine said.

Paul nodded in agreement. "It'll be worth staying up all night just to hear you tell it."

"Well, then, if you insist." André smiled. "Not often do I have a reason to sit up all night. I thought those years were long past. So, we shall continue, yes?"

"Don't worry yourself," Christine said. "Just tell all there is to tell."

"Eh bien. By the time the snow fell, victory had eluded us and no one would be going home soon, at least not for Christmas. After the battle of the Marne the lines were established. Following the Germans' first push into France, the fortifications on our front proceeded in a straight line from Amiens to Chantilly, just north of Paris, and from there, northward to the coast of Belgium where the Yser debouches into the English Channel."

"Dayboosh?" Paul said. That was how André had pronounced the word.

"He's thinking of déboucher, a French word," Christine explained. "The river's mouth."

André nodded. "The mouth of the river, yes. That is how close les boches came to fulfilling their objective. But we French fought with such bravery, for we were defending our homeland. The Kaiser was thrown back, still not defeated. And so this long-endured battle line and entrenchments were established east from Vimy and Loos down to Gommecourt and Albert to just west of Noyon. From Noyon, the front extended east to Verdun."

As the old man explained it, his arms flew left and right pointing in the directions of the towns, as if doing so made it all clear.

Paul shook his head. "I wish we had a map. Verdun, though, I've heard of that."

"Too many details, I know," André said.

"In fact," Paul said, "I think we drove all through that area on our way here."

"Ah, you did, and more. You're sitting on the front, right in that chair. The German advance had arrived at this very place, then pushed a bit south from Chantilly toward Paris. Like in the photograph Christine asked about, you can see why Sermaize-les-Bains suffered such great damage.

"At that time our town had twenty-seven hundred citizens, about what it has now. Of nine hundred homes, just thirty or so remained intact. The German advance had been stopped right here. Yes, this was the leading edge of the battle"—

when he pointed to the floor, the young people glanced down expecting to see barbed wire—"before it was pushed north to Reims.

"I would get news of home from time to time, mostly second hand. After the first shelling of Sermaize-les-Bains, word from home was sporadic, but by December we had more hopeful news. The citizens of Sermaize-les-Bains had begun to rebuild and clear away the rubble before winter. My parents had taken in two children from the town until their papa could repair their home."

"So," Christine said, "did you ever fight near Sermaize-les-Bains?"

"No, no. By this time the 28th Division and my regiment, the 99th, were entrenched about two hundred and twenty-five kilometers northeast of here, just west of Peronne by the village of Foucaucourt-en-Santerre. I never made it this far south."

Paul yawned and André's bright eyes took note. "Mes enfants, you have been very patient for this old man. In any case, enough is enough. We must retire for the night now, and if you consent to stay a bit longer tomorrow, we can conclude our story then."

"You're right, Grandpère, much as I hate to admit it." Christine was yawning too. "We are tired. Jet lag, then the drive here earlier today, the fresh air—let's soyez sage, as Grandmère used to tell us when we were children. Be good and call it a night."

"Sir, what about those dirty dishes?" Paul said. "May we take care of them first?"

"No, no, Mme. Moreau will see to them in the morning when she comes to prepare our petit déjeuner." He waved them toward the stairs. "Go, sleep, dream. You will know all tomorrow."

CHAPTER 5

"I can't believe how well I slept," Christine said as she came downstairs. "I guess it's because I'm back here in this house where I've had so many happy visits."

"The *co-co-ri-co* did not disturb you? My neighbor keeps these chickens, you know, and always before the sun rises the husband of these chickens must announce his importance to the world."

She broke into gales of laughter. "Husband of the chickens—what a delicious expression!"

Her grandfather felt a bit sheepish. "Eh bien, you know I am out of practice with this English."

"You're doing just fine. It struck me funny, that was all." She followed him into the dining room where the breakfast table was laid.

He pulled out a chair for her. "Paul, he will descend soon?"

"Right now he's shaving. He insisted we not wait for him. Being here always brings such an appetite. May I do something in the kitchen?"

"No, no, sit down. Mme. Moreau will bring us whatever you like."

After Paul had joined them and breakfast was consumed, he said, "Now, Monsieur Ferrand, we're ready for the rest of your tale. I hope you're able to continue."

André inclined his head a bit, a modest performer. "If you are sure?"

"Wouldn't miss it for the world," Paul said.

"In that case, let us return to the softer chairs." Once all three were back in the places they'd occupied the night before, André took up his recollection again.

"Let me see now, where were we? Ah, oui, in the trenches, and the rats. Do you know, sometimes I still dream of those rats? Unbelievable. Across from us, you see, between the trenches was No Man's Land. It was littered with the bodies of countless comrades, soldiers from both sides—Germans as well as French. On the other side of this zone of death, the 20th Bavarian Regiment was dug in beneath their parapets, just as we were beneath ours.

"At last, though, the fighting stopped. No longer were our officers giving us orders to charge over the top. Artillery shells flew from time to time, most often after an observation plane flew over, but to us it seemed that the generals on both sides no longer knew what to do. I'm sure they knew *how* to do, for they had become most expert at sending our boys into battle, but *what* to do—that was where they were lost. So combat stopped, everything at a standstill."

Paul said, "Could you ever leave? Go home for a few days?"

"Passes were available, but not long enough to benefit. No, we could not escape. And just when we thought this temporary peace might endure, more artillery shells would start to fall onto our line. It was so frightening we began to wish that if a shell were to find us, it would do so mercifully, no long agony to endure.

"The worst was when a shell struck two or three meters in front of the trench, for then it would shake the ground and collapse the earth around the trench. If one of our poilus had dug himself a—this word I don't know, Christine, un cocon—"

"A cocoon," she said. "Almost the same. We understand."

"Very well, then, if he had dug himself a cocoon in the wall, when the earth collapsed it would swallow him up to suffocate, unless his fellow soldiers reached him in time. And the noise would render one deaf, to wait was pure torture.

"I remember after one such attack Toothy asked us, 'Do you suppose you are aware of it when a shell lands on you?' He was always asking such questions. Someone said in a monotone, 'If that happens, Toothy, we'll never know, because we won't live to tell.' Then Toothy said, 'But, do you hear it?' Pierre had the answer for him. 'I'll tell you what, Toothy, if it happens that you are dispatched in such a lucky way, we can discuss it in detail fifty years from now when I join you.' Yes, it's true, we could even joke in a situation like that."

Christine had a question. "Did you ever get letters?"

"Now and then. Mail was always something to look forward to. As December drew on our thoughts were of home and our loved ones. Some of us received Christmas items and food, cheeses and candies. And some had letters, letters that were read and re-read day after day. Photos would arise from someone's pocket, and soldiers would pass them around and gaze at them, wishing they were at home. On the 17th of December our officers attempted an offensive, but with little effect. We moved the wire a bit to the north, perhaps a meter or two, but the trenches remained in the same place. It was insane. I kept thinking of my poor parents, so fearful for me, and our town in ruins.

"By the 21st, nothing had changed except the cold was even more profound. There was snow on the ground. The advantage of this was that it reduced the foul odors and froze over the mud, at least in places, but for us it was another form of a more miserable existence. The 24th was a Thursday. Mail delivery was always poor early in the week, but better by Thursday and

Friday. So as the mail and some parcels reached us our spirits rose a bit. Lads were exchanging photos and offering cigarettes.

"Everyone seemed to know there would be no fighting that day. No orders came down from above, and we had long ago learned to keep watch for the battalion messenger. The look on his face and the size of his pouch told us what we should expect. That day the rumormongers had nothing to pass on. We had an extra ration at noon, and it seems to me the weather became less glacial, although the years may have softened my memory of this. Some of us played cards, the rest passed the time as best we could.

"And then, after our evening ration when things began to grow even quieter, we thought we heard the soft notes of a Christmas carol. It was in German, 'stille Nacht, heilige Nacht.' In English, I think this is 'Silent Night, Holy Night.' A few brave souls among us peered up over the trench, and one shouted, 'Fritz, your singing is killing us!' A clear reply came over the top, 'Jawohl, Frenchie, we will kill you, but not tonight.'

"Toothy was not known for taking risks, but he had crawled up the parapet, and when he got to the top he cried out, 'Look at that! Incredible!' Now, you must know that one never saw a man standing above the trench. Never, for it meant sure death. Oh, you might see him crouched down running at you, but never standing. What we witnessed, to this day, is unimaginable. Not only were Germans standing up, several of them were setting illuminated candles on small fir trees stuck into the mud above their trench. The boches—these very ones we considered to be savage animals—were grouped around their trees, admiring them, singing in those hushed tones.

"No one in our trench said another word aloud. Murmurs and whispers went up and down the line faster than an epidemic until someone again was bold enough to yell, 'Fritz, have you a Christmas gift for me?'

"One German soldier looked across at us and waved. He actually waved at us! Pierre, astonished, scrambled up and waved also, then slid back down. It was impossible to believe he had escaped a sniper's bullet. And then, almost as if there was a maestro among us, we also began to sing songs of Christmas, songs that reminded us of home, of beautiful holidays gone by."

"Christmas carols," Christine prompted.

"Oui. Our courage rose and so did the force of our singing. The Germans stopped their singing to listen, and when our carols ended they applauded and sang 'stille Nacht' again. We applauded also and shouted a few comments about singing off-key, and then someone sang the first notes of 'les anges dans nos campagnes' and we all joined in."

Christine, her eyes shining, said, "Oh, yes, in the States they call that one, 'Angels We Have Heard on High.' "

André nodded, his own eyes misty. "We could hear the Germans applauding. We looked at one of our officers, as if their manual might describe what was happening, but they just exchanged glances with one another and shrugged. Several of us found the courage to perch on the parapet and gaze out to see one brave soul carrying a white flag in one hand and a flask in the other. He was walking toward us across No Man's Land, picking his way between the bodies, yelling in broken French, 'Don't shoot! Don't shoot! I only want to wish you a happy Christmas!'

"Pierre, Toothy, and I jumped out of the trench and began walking toward him. He froze for an instant, and as he turned around, we expected to be cut down by machine-gun fire. Ready to fall flat in the snow, I remember feeling faint when he waved his arm with the flag, signaling his comrades to join him.

"And with that, making our way around the dead soldiers, we met half way. We had left our fears behind us in the trench. The German uncapped his flask and offered us a drink. Toothy ran back to the trench, and our comrades tossed their tin cups to him. By the time he returned, three more Germans had joined us, each carrying his own flask."

André Ferrand stopped talking because a rapt silence had settled over the room, Christine and Paul sat transfixed. A small tear had worked its way down Christine's cheek.

"You are unhappy, ma fille?"

Christine waved off his concern. "No, no. I'm fine. Just being silly, you know how sentimental girls are."

Paul put his arm around her and pulled her close. "She'll be fine, sir. A tender heart, that's all."

The old man nodded. "So we continue, bien? For that moment, we didn't know what to do. The Germans examined us, we examined them right down to their boots. I could see that the German boots were superior to ours and seemed drier. Their uniforms, like ours, were caked with mud and even appeared a bit warmer.

"One of these Germans seemed older than the rest. I thought he was an officer, but upon closer inspection it surprised me to see he was an enlisted man, like us. Pierre, the portrait of sociability, said, 'Thank you for the schnapps.'

"Another of the Germans offered us bread. When I realized we had little to offer, I ran back to the trench, careful to avoid the dead bodies and the shell holes. Other men were climbing out of the trench to join us, so I stopped a couple of them and sent them back for cheese and wine to offer and share. When we rejoined the group, now much larger, one of the

Germans began to hum 'stille Nacht' and by the middle of the first verse, we were all singing or humming.

"Truly, I wish you could see this for yourself, because it was so beautiful. The look in the eyes of all of the soldiers, German and French, was that of tranquility and peace. After this, we commenced to converse. Most of the Germans spoke some French, and some of us could speak a little German, so one way or another we managed. I had never imagined that I would converse in friendship with these men, and I'm sure they must have felt the same."

Taking care then to focus his gaze upon Christine, he went on. "And with that, a very proper and neat soldier, the older one I had remarked, came over to me. I thought he might be preparing to salute, but when he saw I was not an officer, he extended his hand to shake mine, looked me in the eye, and said, 'Joyeux Noël. Je m'appelle Konrad Krüger.' "

Eyes wide, mouth open in surprise, Christine stared at her grandfather. No more tears. "So that was when you met Papa's father? When you got his picture?"

"Not then, but after the war. He sent me his, and I sent him a picture of me."

She struggled to take in the revelation. "But you were enemies. How—"

"Enemies until then, yes, but from that moment of peace and afterward, friends. I then wished him a happy Christmas also and told him my name. I offered him some cheese and bread. We conversed more, and I liked him. I could tell he liked me. We spoke about ourselves and about our families. He was twenty-six, he said, married to a beautiful woman. He showed me her photo."

"And that was my grandmother Krüger?"

"It was." André was pleased to see Paul reach for

Christine's hand and keep it in a tender clasp. "Konrad, your other grandfather, went on to explain that his wife Greta was enceinte, the baby due any day. He had not seen her since August, nor heard from her for some time, but he felt sure she was well, for she was living with her parents until her confinement."

"I know Papa's birthday is Christmas Eve. So it was that very day. Do you know when, what time, he was born?"

"I believe later that evening, perhaps around ten."

"And why is it I have never heard anything of this? Never, not once." Now Christine sat at attention, stirred, not angry, but enthralled. "I suppose I shouldn't be surprised, Papa has always been secretive about things. I apologize, Grandpère, I don't mean to interrupt. Please go on."

"He asked about my family. I told him about my parents, our farm, and he asked if I had a sweetheart." An engaging light had come back to his eye.

"So, what did you tell him?"

"I said, 'No, but I have someone I like very much, and I write to her when I can, on those nights when I have a candle.' I told him she was eighteen and very pretty. I said I had not asked her to marry me because her father was so terrifying."

Paul guffawed. "Believe me, I identify with that. I hope he became less terrifying once you were married."

"As you see," André said, smiling, indicating the pleasant rooms around them he and Elsie had shared. "But let us return to our sheep, as we say in France. The other soldiers were conversing also, the French singing more songs of Christmas. 'Il est né, le divin enfant'—Christine, you used to sing that when you were a tiny girl."

She was humming. "'Un flambeau, Jeannette, Isabella'—did you sing that too?"

"I'm sure we must have done. In any case, because our curfew was approaching, we started to drift back to our separate trenches at the same time. Hands were shaken, tin cups refilled. It no longer seemed cold. One of us said, 'let's meet here tomorrow to bury our dead.' At that one of the Germans spoke up. 'Ja, and respect our Christmas.'

"After the last of the adieux we descended into our labyrinth, our hell in the earth, soothed by the wine and schnapps and warmed by the astonishing events we had seen. I assure you, there was not a one of us who didn't think or dream afterward about what had just happened. I found myself wondering later about Konrad and his wife, whether he was a father already, whether it was a boy or a girl. He had said that if it was a girl her name would be Gretchen, if a boy Hans. Greta wanted a boy, Konrad wanted a girl.

"After such an evening, sleep came easily to us all. The next morning I awoke excited about the day. The burial details were assigned, and we ascended the trench onto No Man's Land. The digging was easy, for our sergeant had chosen the deepest shell crater as the tomb for our dead. One by one, we placed these mutilated and rotting corpses into the hole and filled it with dirt from the sides of nearby craters, that was the hard part.

"The Germans were finishing their burial detail about the same time while a German and a French officer conferred for a moment, close enough for us to hear. The French officer said, 'Shall we return in thirty minutes and perform our own ceremonies?' But the German officer objected, 'Nein, let us all attend each other's ceremony, in thirty minutes.'

"The officers returned to their respective trenches and informed their troops of the planned service and ordered the men to clean up as best they could. The men trudged out of the trenches on both sides and assembled in facing lines on either side of the German grave. They had made an appropriate marker with a German helmet on it, one of the Kaiser's helmets with the point on top. The French soldiers considered that helmet a prized souvenir, but this time no one would dare to touch it."

André shifted his shoulders a bit. "We are sitting so long, I am having a cramp."

Paul said, "Shall we stop now, sir?"

"No, no, let's come to the end. So, do you know, for the remainder of the battle and entrenchment, that helmet was never disturbed? The German chaplain read his verse and said some words, and our chaplain did the same. This was all repeated at our grave, save that instead of a helmet, we placed un havresac—"

Christine nodded, "Yes, a knapsack."

"This knapsack, yes, containing some fresh soil from behind the lines. This was Toothy's idea to make a memory of our soldiers having died to defend French soil. After the funeral service honoring our fallen comrades, I sought out my new friend and wished him a happy Christmas again. A thought came to me as we stood talking, and I said, 'Wait right here. I have something for you.'

"Running back to the trench, I found my kit and returned with a sausage and bottle of wine that I offered to him. 'This isn't much, but I want you to have it for your Christmas supper.' I could see that your Grandpère Krüger was moved. I felt a little embarrassed when he responded, 'But I have nothing for you.'

"It was at that moment he removed his knife from its fourreau—" André searched for the word, frowning.

"Sheath," Christine supplied.

"Thank you. He inspected his greatcoat and its buttons and choosing the brightest one, he cut off the second button from the top just like a butcher cuts a chicken leg. Regarding it further, he held it in his palm a moment as if to impart something special to it, then presented it to me. 'For you.' "

Christine's eyebrows made peaks. "A button? From his uniform?"

"Mais oui. But you must understand, this was a very special gesture. The buttons on the Kaiser's uniforms were brass, of a very high quality. They were most impressive, embossed with an ornate crown. The poilus treasured these buttons at such times as they could cut one from a dead German's uniform.

"And in a very serious tone, Konrad warned me, 'My friend, should you be captured by our troops, take care you are not found with this in your possession. If this should happen, you would be shot then and there, for they would assume you had defiled the dead. In any case, I want you to have it. Just take care.'

"I made a protestation. 'Your gift will last forever, and my gift to you will be gone by tomorrow.' That didn't bother him at all. 'What you say may be true,' he said, 'but the memory will be with me,' and he struck his clenched fist against his chest, 'forever.' I knew that he meant what he said, for I felt just the same.

"We shook hands once more, lingered for a bit, smoked several cigarettes. We talked of our lives and plans. He told me of his business as a book publisher, we spoke about his baby wondering if it had been born. He reached into his pocket for a stub of pencil, tore off a bit of the sausage wrapping and wrote his address. 'After the war,' he said, 'we should exchange greetings. There is no reason we shouldn't continue to be friends.'

"I took his note and did the same with my parents' address here in Sermaize-les-Bains. With our friendship thus established, we spoke of the war and the folly of it all. I said we had been told it was to be over by now. 'Oui, mon ami, you also?' he said. The Germans had told their troops the same, but that the French would capitulate in the first weeks of fighting.

"As the day was ending and the two groups of soldiers were separating, Konrad clasped my hand one last time. I tell you, I shall never forget how firm his grip was. 'Mon ami, let us pledge never to let this happen again to our countries. I know we are only two soldiers, and we may not even survive this war, but I owe it to Gretchen or Hans not to allow this to happen again, ever.'

"I returned his handclasp. 'On my solemn oath as a Frenchman, I promise to do what I can never to fight another war, ever.' And he too gave me his promise. It was almost as if we had sealed this pledge in blood.

"With that, we returned to our comrades, our war, and the carnage that didn't end until 1918, by which time eight million soldiers had died."

Paul and Christine sat mesmerized. Christine's eyes were bright with tears, her tissue saturated and wadded into a ball. The clock ticked the minutes away until Paul broke the silence. "Did you ever receive a letter from him?"

"Yes," Christine said, "who wrote first?"

CHAPTER 6

Berlin
Sunday
16 February 1919

[*This letter and all subsequent ones translated from the French*]

Dear Monsieur Ferrand,

I am writing this letter not knowing if you survived the war. I am well and think of you often. Please respond, as I am most anxious to learn of your disposition.

If perchance this letter finds its way to your loved ones, I would like them to know you were a fine soldier and a loyal Frenchman, and that we met under unbelievable and trying circumstances on Christmas Eve of 1914 in No Man's Land near Foucaucourt-en-Santerre.

I still remember your gift with sincere fondness and I shall always hold Christmas Eve in my heart.

I pray you are well.

With amicable respects,

Konrad Krüger

Sermaize-les-Bains
Saturday
8 March 1919

Monsieur Krüger, mon ami,

It was with the greatest joy that I received your letter Friday last. Since my return home, I have been very preoccupied. You see, my father died of influenza last year, and I have been quite busy aiding my mother with the chores of the farm and arranging for her needs. It has been very hard but she is a strong woman. I believe God meant for me to survive the fighting in order that I could be here for her. What else would explain my good fortune?

You should have seen the look on my mother's face when she saw I had received a letter from Berlin. After I told her the story of Christmas Eve in the trenches, she said she had heard something of this but did not believe it for a moment. I fear she is very bitter about the war, so much death and destruction, even my father's death which she believes was also a result of the war. You see, my mother has friends whose sons did not return from the fighting, so one can understand. Perhaps your mother has such friends also. She looks so much older than when I left in 1914. We were not the only casualties of the fighting, do you not agree?

When I was demobilized I was happy to learn that my young friend Mlle. Blaisé still had a place in her heart for me. You may recall how I told you I entertained these hopes while I was away. As soon as I found myself at home again I called upon her. I wanted to throw my arms around her and hold her close, but her daunting father, old M. Blaisé, refused to leave us alone. You may remember I said I was terrified of him before the war, but now not quite so much. He must have been a soldier once, because he knows what such emotions are. I have not asked Mlle. Blaisé to marry me yet, but I hope I will find the courage to ask this of her father soon.

If you will be so kind, please inform me of your family, your wife, and whether you are now the father of a boy or girl. I also want to know of your work and all aspects of that. For me, I have been asked to join my cousin at his bakery. He needs the help, because his brother, my other cousin, died at Verdun. I am not sure what else to do, but I will stay here for a while and aid my mother on the farm also. It is a noble calling, and it is good to be able to provide food for one's family as well as for others. I have considered establishing a poultry farm, for as you know, there is always a market for both chickens and eggs.

Again, please know how happy I was to hear from you and learn that you survived the fighting. Please convey my most respectful wishes to Mme. Krüger. Perhaps one day we shall meet.

I remain, with the most cordial regards, your friend,

A. Ferrand

▪▪▪▪▪

Berlin
Saturday
5 April 1919

Esteemed Monsieur Ferrand,

Here too there was true happiness to receive your letter. Since I posted my last letter to you in February I have been most anxious to learn of your fate. My wife also had very much desired to know you were safe. It is a strange thing, one I cannot begin to explain, yet every day when I returned from my office my first question was always whether there had been news of you.

Now, I must enlighten you about all that has happened. After the war's end and my release from military service, many times I wondered whether the day of my return to Berlin would ever come. The fact that I had survived the influenza, however, led me to believe that I would, with continued good fortune, return to my wife and to our little Hans.

Yes, I hasten to assure you, it was a boy, born on Christmas Eve. Do you remember how we wondered there in No Man's Land whether this child had come into our troubled world, and whether it would be a girl or a boy? I still hope for a Gretchen one day, but my wife is most happy with her Hans. I too am grateful that he is well and strong, after the privations of wartime. Perhaps you may think me foolish, but I shall say that he is a remarkable child, handsome, and quite intelligent.

While I was gone my wife took great care to make sure Hans knew who I was, showing him my photograph, speaking often of "Papa," so that when I returned, he was not at all afraid. Although a bit shy at first, he soon let me take him up in my arms. It was then that I knew the true, deepest feelings of a father's heart.

At supper the first night I was home, he looked at his mother and said, "Why Papa sit in that chair and not over there with my bear?" He is always thinking and asking questions. At first they were questions for my wife, but by the second day they were for me also. Things I had never thought of, such as, "Why is the sky blue?" Or, "If they are called sea gulls, Papa, why are they by the river?" His mother would often take him to the zoo, so he asked if I had ever been to the zoo. I told him I had, and he asked if I would rather ride a one-humped or a two-humped camel! Later on he asked, "How tall is the tallest mountain?" I am afraid I will have to go back to the gymnasium to renew my education, just to keep up with him.

My friend, do not fear Mlle. Blaisé's father any longer. After all you have been through, you surely cannot be afraid of a single unarmed man. If she is worthy of you, as I believe she must be, then you will soon overcome the challenge of asking for her hand. To me your affliction has all the appearances of love, my friend.

I believe your plan for a poultry farm is a sound one. Regardless of the state of the economy, being able to produce some necessary thing is the secret for success. I fear the turmoil in this country will be difficult for many, perhaps including me and my business. People do not require books as they require chickens and eggs. One day I may be forced to send you a shipment of books in exchange for some fresh country eggs!

It has taken a while for us to get back to normal. If my family is any example, soldiers' wives require a time of readjustment. It is our good fortune that little Hans helps to keep us on a routine. In spite of what is required, it is reassuring to me, as I'm sure it is to my wife, to have our family reunited. At night when I put Hans into his bed and he says his prayers, we include you.

I hope you are well. Write and tell us of your progress with this fierce ogre who has it in his power to grant you Mlle. Blaisé's fair hand.

This letter comes to you, my friend, with my most respectful wishes,

Konrad Krüger

Sermaize-les-Bains
Friday
11 July 1919

Monsieur Krüger, my good friend,

I am so happy to learn of your Hans. I feel sure he is his father's image in all regards. Whom does he resemble most, you or his mother? And does he spell yet, or perhaps compute his numbers? And these questions, one wonders how he thinks of them.

The spring and summer here have been warm, so that every day we see progress in the recovery of our region. Farmers are filling in the trenches, so perhaps by next year they will be able to plant again. It is sad, though, the scars will always reveal themselves. I hope one day it will be possible to go from village to village in France and not know what happened to our country. But each day it improves. One sees the amazing ability of nature to heal herself.

Much celebration is planned next week on Bastille Day. Sermaize-les-Bains has planned many festivities, and I will be taking part, with Mlle. Blaisé. She is most pleasing to look at and it gives me much pleasure to do so. Her black hair is cut short, exposing a charming nape. She is almost of the same height as I, not even a centimeter or two less. And she is timid. It took weeks for her to be at ease when we would talk, but now that she knows my heart, she is much less so.

I attribute her timidity to the fact that she was adopted as a little child. This may be why her second mother, Mme. Blaisé, is so protective. I have learned that Mlle Blaisé was orphaned almost in infancy, in Revigny-sur-Ornain, when her parents, Polish Jews, both died. The priest there wrote to our priest in

Sermaize-les-Bains, Father Feuillerat, who agreed to take the little one to the home of M. and Mme. Blaisé, parishioners of his who had no children but yearned for one. Mme. Blaisé fell in love the instant she laid eyes upon her, and since then this dear child has never left her side, raised as her own.

You will congratulate me to know I finally summoned all my courage and asked M. Blaisé for her hand. He was very cold at first, but then all at once he bestowed an enormous smile on me and boomed out, "André, my lad, what took you so long?" He then dug out a bottle of cognac, poured a glass for us both, shook my hand, and said, "I was beginning to think you did not want our Elsie." So we will be married in October. This may not seem like such big news to you, but to me it is enormous. And good.

My friend, I wish you well and send my sincere respects to Mme. Krüger.

A. Ferrand

▪▪▪▪▪

Berlin
Tuesday
20 January 1920

Monsieur Ferrand, my fortunate friend,

We took great pleasure in your recent letter and hasten to extend our congratulations on your marriage. I have every confidence your bride was as beautiful as they all are, and by now you will know great happiness. Please convey to her our warmest wishes for a long and happy union.

We have wonderful news also, for my wife is with child. In September she suspected as much because she had been feeling ill in the mornings since summer, so she consulted her physician who confirmed that she is indeed with child and can expect her confinement in March. He told her she should see him again if the baby has not arrived by the end of that month. Young Hans is not quite sure what will happen, although just last week he told his mother she must not think of bringing him a baby sister, as it is a brother he wants.

Aside from the joys of being a married man, how are things with you and your business endeavors? And how are events in France now that the Treaty of Versailles has been ratified? Still, I have to ask, what took them so long? As for Germany, I fear we can expect significant turmoil because of the drastic reparations imposed upon our country. At last food is becoming more available, so we hope that the political turmoil will lessen as a consequence.

I close for now, my friend, again with hearty felicitations on your wedded state.

Konrad Krüger

▪▪▪▪▪

Sermaize-les-Bains
Wednesday
22 September 1920

Monsieur Krüger, my honored friend,

I submit my apology for not writing sooner. We have been very busy. Like you, I am now a father, the joys of which I never knew existed. But before I continue, I must tell you about our wedding. It was a holy and beautiful occasion. We have made our home with my mother, who is thankful for the company and most thankful for the new baby.

A healthy girl, she was born a week ago and we have given her the name Marie-Aimée. As you know, her baptismal name must include that of a saint—but to us she will always be Aimée, nothing more. She is as pretty as her mother, but I fear that she shares my disposition. While I have yet to hold her, I look forward to this joy. She has a full head of hair, and when they said she had my nose, I regarded myself in the looking-glass and was grateful to see that I still am in possession of it. You will know about this, I am sure, but I find it amazing that such a small hand grasping one's own can deprive one of the power to breathe.

My poultry business progresses well, and our crops also have faired better than I had hoped through the summer. Harvest should commence soon and, with favorable weather, be complete before the winter rains.

If it is convenient for you to do so, please give us news of your Hans and the rest of your family. My wife joins me in hoping that all is well with Mme. Krüger and with you. We shall hope to hear from you when you find the time.

Sincere and most respectful wishes,

A. Ferrand

Berlin
Friday
22 October 1920

My proud friend Monsieur Ferrand,

Here we are all fine and so happy to learn of your news. My wife and I rejoice with you in your daughter's birth, hoping one day that we may emulate your achievement. Your Aimée sounds precious, a blessing indeed. Is it not amazing how much love such a small creature can generate?

I am grateful to report that Hans got his wish, for a small brother has come to join him, Peter by name. He arrived in March, on the 21st, to help us welcome the season of spring. In many ways he reminds us of Hans, yet he is his own person. As more time passes, his own personality becomes more pronounced. Unlike Hans, he is very quiet and watches everything that happens and makes cooing noises. I'm proud to say also that Hans watches over him and is very protective. When many brothers do not get along so well, this is a joy for us to behold.

Hans is now six years of age, progressing well with his schoolwork. He reads as well as a six-year-old should, and his mother and I can no longer spell words to communicate things we do not wish him to hear. Just yesterday after supper I was hoping there was pudding, so I asked my wife, spelling it backward. Hans thought for a moment then announced, "*Mutti*, I would like some pudding, too."

He remains fascinated by mechanical things. Since he was three, maybe four, whenever he spied a train or perhaps an airplane overhead, he would jump up and down and point with excitement. And inside our apartment, one must take care walking about for it seems his wooden train is everywhere.

Peter is fine now, as I have said, and I am thankful for that, but his birth was quite a worry for us. My Greta's labor went on for hours, almost two days, and then he had to be turned and brought forth feet first. She suffered great pains, losing much blood, and I was so worried afterward when she was forced to remain in bed for several weeks. Her physician, concerned for her future health, advises against any more children. This is a great disappointment to her, and while I continue to worry for her, with the passing weeks I am grateful to see improvement.

The political turmoil here continues. A coup was attempted that has led to a great deal of change. A workers' strike followed the coup, and although order now seems to be restored, in the subsequent elections the Independent Social Democrats made significant gains. With Germany's staggering debt from the war, I fear it will be some time before all is settled. Further, the issue of German troops in the Ruhr Valley and French troops in Frankfurt only stirs things further.

By all means, my fatherly friend, pay close attention as your Aimée grows. I can tell you that before you know it she will be underfoot and getting into everything.

Convey my kind regards, if you will, to Mme. Ferrand and a blessing for your dear daughter. Be well, my friend.

Sincerest and most respectful wishes,

Konrad Krüger

▪▪▪▪▪

Sermaize-les-Bains
Saturday
24 January 1925

Valued friend Monsieur Krüger,

I cannot apologize enough for neglecting my promise of writing, but allow me to explain, if only to relieve my guilt at this unintended slight. Many times I have taken the pen to my hand, only to be distracted without completing this overdue letter. It is not that you have escaped our thoughts. With each week that passes, I think of you. In our town there is a family whom we see at Mass with two boys the same ages of Hans and Peter. Whenever I see these boys, I think of the Krüger family, which makes me smile.

You will understand, perhaps, why I am late in writing, when I tell you that we have been blessed with another daughter. Joan-Claire was born on 20 June and is now six months old, able to sit up on her own and soon will be able to crawl wherever she wishes to go. Like your Peter, she is a quiet one. I believe that is because Aimée is at her side every moment, providing whatever she thinks her baby sister desires. And our Aimée, she likes to think she is the mother and, as a four-year-old, has become quite a little tyrant.

My wife is thriving, I am thankful to report, truly a wonderful mother and wife. It seems to me that her beauty increases with every year—no longer the adolescent charmer who won my heart, but with a more settled, womanly appeal. It is hard to believe we have been married now for five years.

Your last letter was interesting to read. The economy in Germany and the factions striving for political influence do nothing to settle the unease that is everywhere. Is there no end to it all?

Yes, the turmoil with the soldiers continues. The French troops who have occupied the Ruhr Valley since January 1923 remain there, and although we hear talk of their leaving, I do not put much stock in it. Reports of sabotage by the Nazis only make things worse. I must admit that even as a Frenchman I feel deep sorrow for all Germans. If Germany had prevailed in the war, I wonder whether France would have defaulted on her reparations. I ask you, doesn't a country have an obligation to its own citizens before its victors bleed it dry?

Your advice years ago about a poultry farm was very sound. I am relieved that I am able to provide for my family and others. Thank you.

Always with respectful wishes for you and your family, your friend,

A. Ferrand

Berlin
Friday
20 February 1925

Monsieur Ferrand, my loyal friend,

Yes, I too would like to write more often, but I also understand all the demands of work and family. I am equally guilty, as I could have written as well.

I congratulate you and your wife on the birth of Joan-Claire. I know how a second child can affect things at home, but on the whole, it is indeed a positive change. My wife wishes to be remembered to yours, with every good wish for health and the many happy moments that an infant can provide.

I share your concern regarding the Ruhr Valley. Already there has been an exchange of troops, and the unrest continues. On a positive note, the economy has stabilized as of late and there appears to be less tension in the air. Our business does well, but procurement of paper products continues to be a challenge. With the lumber exports required by the reparations, this may be an issue for some time to come. Frankly, I am surprised that the matter of Alsace has caused no more disturbance, but that may very well change in the future, and we would never learn of it until things are set into motion.

It is interesting, to say the least, to have an 11-year-old in the house. Hans is a fine young man, and his enthusiasm for mechanical things persists. There are few things he hasn't wondered about or taken apart. I am relieved he has now discovered the importance of keeping track of the parts and where they came from, as too often there was some leftover part that had not been installed in its proper location. I believe he will have a special aptitude for this, as he is very strong in mathematics and geometry. He continues to be very obedient and a pleasure to his mother Greta and me. His friends, the ones that come here to play, they, too, appear well mannered. As for Peter, he will be 5 years old in March, and he wants to follow Hans everywhere. For now, Hans is patient, but I cannot predict whether this will be so in the upcoming years.

I am afraid all has not been well with my wife. Ever since the birth of our Peter, she has suffered as some women do and, as you may recall, after Peter was born the doctor advised against more children in the sternest of terms. This alone has caused her unhappiness, and with each passing month she has felt weaker and more melancholic. With firm encouragement from me she consulted the doctor who diagnosed anemia and arranged for appropriate treatment. So now we begin to see improvement, and finally her color and disposition are back to normal. This is a great relief, for there was little I could do to console her, and her condition made caring for young Peter difficult.

My ardent wish is that you and all your household may continue to be well and prosper. Please know that even if our letters should become less frequent, our fondness for you and your family does not diminish in the least. That astonishing meeting in 1914 has brought a friendship we could not have believed possible, yet it is so. You have a special place in our hearts and we continue to wish you the best of everything.

In enduring friendship, yours with respectful appreciation,
Konrad Krüger

Sermaize-les-Bains
Saturday
4 April 1925

Esteemed Monsieur Krüger,

Your most recent letter caused us considerable concern for your dear wife. Knowing how any little trouble of my wife's affects me, you must have been worried about your own lady. My wife, Elsie, wishes me to extend her wishes for a speedy recovery. We shall hope that Mme. Krüger's regained strength will sustain itself. Your family is fortunate to have a capable physician. I regret to say our village is not so blessed. Our physician, Dr. Ganthier, is a cousin of the famous Louis Pasteur, but alas, he lacks the genius of his relation. We all joke that he must have been inoculated one too many times! Nevertheless, he is the one we must rely on, so we trust that no grave illnesses will present themselves here.

How our girls grow. Aimée dashes around as if propelled by a motor. She enjoys the outdoors and always wants to aid me in my chores. As for little Claire, she grows like a weed along the fence. She will attain one year of life in June, and already she is pulling herself up to stand. It amuses me to watch her arise to stand, but then something draws her attention and she releases her hold on the chair. When she realizes she is standing unassisted, down to the floor she goes. I am confident she will soon be walking everywhere like her sister.

I am glad your business grows. May it continue to do so.

Thank you for your letters, my friend, and please convey our affection and heartfelt prayers to your family.

Always your well-wishing friend,

A. Ferrand

Berlin
Wednesday
10 June 1925

Monsieur André Ferrand and the entire family Ferrand,

We hope this letter and card for Claire's first birthday arrive before the 20th. And we must not forget Aimée. Enclosed is a book about animals of the world our company published. The illustrations are wonderful. We hope she will spend many happy moments enjoying them, even if she is not yet able to read.

Thank you for your concern and prayers for my Greta. She continues to improve and I am grateful to say that her melancholy is less.

Our boys are well. Hans is gone for the week, camping in the outdoors with his Boy Scouts. He considers it a great adventure to sleep under the stars. I resist the temptation to dampen his enthusiasm by relating our military experience of sleeping outdoors.

I trust that your farm prospers. As you have never spoken in later years of your cousin's bakery, I assume you now give all your time to the management of the farm. It affords me pleasure to know your family is doing so well. Again, thank you for your kind concern for Greta, who asks that I tender her thanks to you as well.

With every good wish, André—I trust you will not reprimand me for the familiar use of your name after so many years of friendship.

As ever, with kindest respects,
Konrad Krüger

Sermaize-les-Bains
Saturday
23 December 1933

My friend Konrad,

Several months have elapsed since I last wrote to you, a delay for which I apologize, again it seems. Please forgive me. I regret I do not have an answer for you about what goes through the minds of the diplomats. Why is it they are never satisfied with the way things are?

Nineteen years have passed since we were soldiers in No Man's Land. How can that be? The horrid dreams I used to have are now less frequent, and Elsie no longer fears that I may shout or strike out at night in my sleep. That is a good thing.

How are your Hans and Peter? Is Hans not celebrating his 19th birthday tomorrow? He must be a fine young man. And Peter, he is 13? Do his interests follow those of Hans, or is he on a path of his own? It would not surprise me to learn that Hans is designing bridges and tall buildings by now. How proud you must be.

Aimée has 13 years as well, fast becoming a lovely young lady. Books and more books are her joy, for she loves to read. I feel certain we have you to thank for this. Of all her books, her favorite is the book about animals you sent her when she was four. It still sits on her desk. She must have read it 10,000 times, and in fact it helped her learn to read. To this day, she still looks at it from time to time. I can still see her on the divan, little legs sticking straight out, as she read it to Claire when they were quite young. I tell you, if she is not seated at the table by the window reading, she is in the swing reading. One day she should apply for a position with your business!

She could read all of your books for errors, and find them she would. She has a keen eye for detail and, not being shy like her mother, she would be sure to point them out. But perhaps your books do not have errors after all.

Claire and Peter must be similar in so much that they do. Is Peter as close to his mother as my Claire is to hers? She is very close to my wife Elsie, far more so than Aimée. I believe this may be so because while my mother, the elder Mme. Ferrand, was alive, this fond grandmother gave Aimée much time and attention, and in consequence my wife took care to see that Claire did not feel neglect.

It is with a heavy heart I must inform you that we lost my poor mother in November. She had developed dropsy and declined within days, dying in her sleep one afternoon. I am glad she did not seem to suffer. It has been most hard on Aimée, but in spite of her sadness she understands about life and death. We all miss her presence, perhaps I most of all, but we are truly grateful that she is reunited with my dear father after so many years.

And your own parents, are they well?

If losing a beloved grandmother wasn't trouble enough, our Claire recently suffered a terrible accident. While she and Aimée were playing in the barn, she fell from the loft where the hay is stored and struck her head, knocking herself unconscious. We rushed her to the dispensary where our Dr. Ganthier was able to save her life. Elsie was consumed with remorse, blaming herself for not being there to prevent Claire from falling. Poor child, for it was after she regained consciousness two days later that we learned her arm was causing her pain. Investigation revealed that it was broken above the wrist. The doctor said this often happens when someone reaches out to break a fall. She is now in a plaster cast for several weeks. I console myself with the knowledge that young bones heal fast.

The poultry farm continues to prosper, and our production of eggs helps sustain things. We have many loyal customers who appreciate our business. I cannot raise my prices, but I can limit my purchases, and this I must do until economic times change.

We wish you a joyful Christmas and many blessings in the New Year.

In friendship, with my most generous respects,

A. Ferrand

Berlin
Monday
9 July 1934

Esteemed friend André,

We were saddened to learn of your mother's death. There is little I can say to alleviate the grief you must feel, and the loss of Aimée's and Claire's grandmother must be difficult for them as well. I pray that her death was an easy one. I know your time with her can never be forgotten.

It also saddens me to report that the unrest continues in Germany. The future appears as stormy as the weather. With the man Hitler having become Chancellor through every kind of political maneuvering and chicanery, many hoped that would be the end of him by keeping him isolated, but he is a slippery one. I fear this is just the beginning of what promises to be some very bad times.

I cannot help feeling that this turn of events is most unfair. We survived the war and weathered the depression that has gripped the entire world, and now this. Many here believe

Hitler is the answer to all of the woes that seem to have been thrust upon our country over these past several years. And he is now the Führer. He may lead some of my countrymen, but not every German will be willing to follow that road.

While I am certain he is a man to be feared, my greatest fear is for our Hans and Peter. Hans is now almost 20 and well on his way in his engineering studies. But Peter is quite impressionable, and he seems drawn to this man. I cannot bring myself to admire Hitler or find anything pleasing about him.

When he comes on the radio, shouting and ranting, I do not hesitate to shut it off. His speeches attack Jews, social democrats, liberals, capitalists, and communists—in short, every group but his own. And his attacks are not merely verbal condemnations. No, his orations have a visceral component I find most unsettling. For the moment I shall continue to hope it is my age that renders me unwilling to accept this state of affairs, but I do not think that is the case.

You asked of my parents in your last letter. They are both in good health. It must be the fresh air in Bavaria that sustains them for they do not seem to grow old. I worry about them as well, however, just as I do about Peter, for they also are taken in by this Hitler. Peter is a child, so that I can understand, but for my parents, all I can do is shake my head.

In spite of this, we are all well. Greta is always busy attending to the needs of our family, and these days I am glad to report, she is quite healthy. My work with the publishing house is increasing, for more people wish to publish, and this I encourage.

We do not see Hans as much as we would like, just the holidays, as he is at the university. He does well, and his professors speak highly of his performance. He can manipulate his slide rule so fast I sometimes wonder that he doesn't set it on fire. Peter seems to live for those times when Hans returns, as he idolizes his older brother. It is pleasing to see the joy on Peter's face when he comes home from the gymnasium and there is a letter from Hans for him on the table. He tears it open and reads it aloud, and then reads it again and again.

Your Aimée is almost 14 and Claire is 10, I believe. The photos you send are charming. I try to visualize in my mind how delightful they must be and how much joy they have brought into your home. Girls would be difficult for me to comprehend for all we have known are boys. I sometimes wonder if there aren't too many men in the house.

Whatever the future may bring, I pray that you keep well, my friend. Greta and I send our kindest regards to you and to your Elsie. I fear that my letter may have been too gloomy, too full of ominous predictions, but I cannot be anything but honest. I often envy you, living as you do in the country away from the strife. Let us pray our two countries do not embark on a course reminiscent of 1914.

Yours always in friendship,
Konrad Krüger

Sermaize-les-Bains
Saturday
12 January 1935

My good friend Konrad,

Yes, your "friend" in Berlin is causing a stir in France, as is his friend in Italy. With talk in France of two years' compulsory military service, the atmosphere here also is tense. Many French people fear that Alsace will again be the battleground between our countries. I cannot see how the Treaty of Versailles has helped either country, but those who consider themselves so much wiser than the rest of us seem to be sealing our fate. What a splendid thing it would be if politicians could assume power without also assuming the mantle of arrogance.

I refuse to believe Hans is 20—and Peter the same age as our Aimée. Do you suppose Peter and Aimée would be friends if we lived in the same city? A farm girl and a city boy? Aimée continues to miss her grandmother a great deal. They were very close, and at the end it was Aimée who was there around the clock. As my mother slipped away, I am thankful we could all be there with her. One must rely on the coming of spring to renew our spirits.

My sympathies are with you in regard to your boys. We are thankful we have only girls to worry about, spared the profound concerns of a father with two sons. But perhaps these two old men are worrying too much. We must do our best to live in hope, despite how things around us may seem.

Thank you for the photos you send. It delights us to see your family. I try to the best of my ability to picture your surroundings there in the city. I pointed out to Elsie and the children how much Hans looks as you did when you were younger. Seeing him standing next to you brought me back 20 years. It may seem a bold thing to ask, but if you have a photo of yourself during your military service, I would very much like to have one. Not having seen you in person since then, I would like to have a memento of the brave young German who reached out to me as a friend.

With all kind regards for you, Konrad, and for your family, I remain,

A. Ferrand

▪▪▪▪▪

Berlin
Tuesday
25 October 1938

My esteemed friend André,

I have wonderful news. Our publishing company has a need for me to travel to Paris on business during the last week of November. I expect to depart Berlin on the 23rd and come to see you in Sermaize-les-Bains, if this is agreeable with you and your wife. The prospect of seeing you again and meeting your family is one I look forward to with great enthusiasm. I am not yet certain what arrangements I can make to travel from Paris to Sermaize-les-Bains, but I will investigate and let you know what the train schedule permits. Please do not go to any special trouble to accommodate me in your home, for I am able to make arrangements for my lodging in town.

As soon as I know a few more details, I will communicate them to you, but otherwise, relaying other news must wait until my arrival in November. I hope to arrive on the 24th.

Please be assured that I am eager to see you and your family.

In unfailing friendship,

Konrad Krüger

CHAPTER 7

Berlin
Friday
25 November 1938

My cherished friend André,

It is with a very sad heart that I write to you this morning. First of all, I must apologize for not arriving yesterday as we had hoped. I was looking forward so much to seeing you and finally meeting your dear wife, Aimée, and Claire. I hope you will convey to them my deep regrets for this change of plans, for I am as disappointed as all of you may have been.

Writing is the only way I could tell you about the events that have led up to this. Please believe me when I say my not coming was with your safety, and that of your family, in mind. When you have read what I have to say, you will understand.

Our letters these past 19 years have been a joy to read and to write. It has given Greta and me much pleasure to learn of your and Elsie's family and of Aimée's and Claire's progress. You must be very proud to be the parents of two such fine young ladies.

You know and understand my position relative to the events that have overtaken our Germany. I am afraid the situation will not improve for a very long time. From the moment Hitler came to power an overwhelming anti-Semitic attitude has prevailed among a certain element in Berlin. We are required to distribute anti-Semitic pamphlets to all our workers. I quote from one of these shocking publications: "A better future demands the systemic solution of the Jewish Question, not the organization of the Jews." You must believe me when I tell you I am not among those who harbor such thoughts.

I am certain you must have heard of the shooting of the German diplomat, Ernst vom Rath, in Paris by a Polish Jew on the 9th. The reaction in Berlin has been swift and terrible for the Jews. It distresses me to say that dozens of them have been murdered in their homes in revenge. Thousands more were arrested, and no one knows their whereabouts. Many synagogues have been destroyed. Jewish newspapers and magazines are shut down.

You will forgive me, I hope, if I explain some of the recent developments under Hitler's Nazi government, for your newspapers may not provide all relevant details. The Schutzstaffel or "SS" as it is known—the name translates to mean "protective squadron"—is an allegedly elite guard with numerous sub-organizations. One of these, the Geheime Staatspolizei, known as "Gestapo," is the government's secret police force.

Much of the intimidation being carried out in our country today is at the hands of this Gestapo. They investigate any publishing company that has published writings by Jewish authors, my company being no exception. The Gestapo presented to my office on Monday 14 November and demanded to see my files of "Jew writers." When I told them I never know the religion of our authors, they demanded *all* of my files. They took the files of three authors who had approached us with book projects, although we had not yet agreed to publish any of the three. The Gestapo insisted I knew they were Jewish. Again, I answered an author's religion is something I have no need to know.

André, my friend, I am afraid. Afraid for you, your family, my family, for all of Germany. For Europe, in fact, as this man Hitler's territorial ambitions have no bounds. And what he decrees for Germany, he will decree for all others.

Furthermore, one of our editors, a Jew as it happens, has not been seen since Thursday of that same week. No one else here was brave enough to go to his apartment to investigate, so I went on Friday myself. The Gestapo had someone standing at the entrance, and I was not admitted. I was told he no longer lived there. Only after harsh questioning and telling the officious policeman I was the man's employer, was I allowed to leave.

I tell you this because I fear for you and Elsie, as well as for Aimée and Claire. The Treaty of Versailles has done nothing to help your country, and if Hitler can regain Alsace-Lorraine, he will do so. If this happens, your family will be in grave danger. In view of your wife's origins, I believe even you as her spouse would be at risk. While our family has no known Jewish forebears, I even fear for Hans and Peter.

On the day I was to leave for France, before I left home, Greta warned me to be careful. She has never said such a thing to me before. I told her not to fret, that I was going on a business trip to Paris, nothing more, then visiting your family in Sermaize-les-Bains. No need for concern. Nonetheless, she begged me to be careful, even while dismissing her fears as "a silly premonition."

On the morning when I intended to travel I stopped by the office first to attend to some details and dictate a letter to a client. My plan was to return to our apartment, retrieve my suitcase, and leave for the railway station from there. As I left the office, however, I noticed a man whom I thought I had also seen earlier as I left our apartment building. This unsettled me beyond belief. I felt certain he must be Gestapo, yet I chastised myself for imagining such things. What could the Gestapo want with me?

But then I remembered how the Gestapo had interviewed me and confiscated those files, how I had gone to the apartment of a Jew and found myself questioned by the police. The Gestapo knew about all of it, and I'm sure they are already keeping detailed records, as we Germans are famous for doing. So I convinced myself that I was being followed and resolved to confirm my suspicions.

I stopped at a pastry shop I sometimes patronize and went inside. While waiting to be served, I glanced out the front window and saw the same man standing across the street reading a newspaper. Now, you and I both know, André, one does not stand on the public street to read the paper. More confirmation. I made my purchase and departed the shop to head for home. He followed. Gestapo, no question about it.

At that point I knew I could not go to Paris or Sermaize-les-Bains and risk having them find out I was associating with you and your family. No, France is not Nazi territory yet, but these people have a very long reach and an insatiable hunger to do wicked things. André, my friend, I am more afraid than at any time during the Great War. Do you remember how terrifying the shelling was, how hopeless we felt as we climbed over the parapet not knowing if we would fall dead in an instant? That was nothing compared to this terror, for now our wives and our children are in equal peril with us.

I burned all of the letters and photos you sent us. I am sorry to tell you this, but you must know. It is as if 20 years of my life have been stolen from me—no, rather a piece ripped from my heart. I did not burn them to hide the fact you are my friend. I burned them to protect you, because I have no doubt I am being followed and scrutinized. If our apartment were searched, your letters and your address would be discovered, and that could bring disaster on both our homes.

Germany is not a safe place, and I fear that soon France may not be so either.

My cherished friend, this must be my last letter to you, at least for a long time. When we first met and exchanged addresses on Christmas Day so many years ago, did you ever think we would be facing such another calamity? I could never have thought such a thing. I believed in our pledge to each other, I still do. I knew our promise was a solemn one, and I hoped millions of other young men would share our resolve. It is unfortunate events have spun far beyond our control, but in reality, we were never in a position to influence these events. I cannot bear to think man's foolishness led to this. What is wrong with a wish to live a simple tranquil life? Were we so absorbed in our own affairs we did not see and stop any of this madness? But how were we to know? Madmen arise like toadstools, unpredictable and full of poison, and the sane among us feel helpless to cut them down.

Let me make another pledge to you, just as I did that Christmas long ago. This, too, is a pledge I will do all in my power to keep. I pledge to you I will never forget our friendship, and if there is anything I can ever do to aid you and your family, I will do it. And beyond this pledge to you, I hope one day we shall be free to be open friends.

I urge you, André, do not send me a letter in return. Rather, send a postcard, but do not write anything revealing or sign it. And do not send it from Sermaize-les-Bains. When I receive it, I will know you received my letter. Send one every so often, then I will know you are safe. If the Gestapo should intercept my mail, they will have no reason to suspect a thing as I never completed my trip to Paris or Sermaize-les-Bains.

Respected friend, do all you can to keep you and your family safe. My prayer is that God may protect and bless you and your family. I pray also we may meet again one day.

Your devoted friend,

Konrad Krüger

P.S. In honor of our lasting friendship, with each Christmas Day that passes, Greta and I always have a special sausage and glass of wine. I am sure you know why.

André felt the blood rush from his face. When he finished reading the letter, his arm fell to his side and the pages slipped from his hand. They wafted back and forth before settling on the floor.

Elsie started up from her seat at the kitchen table. "What is it, André? You look as if you have seen a ghost!"

He leaned over the table to rest his bowed head on one hand, then raised up to look at his wife. "Elsie, does anyone here know you are Jewish?"

"Why do you ask? What is this? You have never asked me that question before."

"Here. Read this letter from Konrad."

She bent to retrieve it from the floor, then sat down to read it. As her eyes darted across the pages her face paled and her hands shook. She let her arms fall to her lap and scanned the kitchen walls as if seeking some answer there.

When no answer was forthcoming, she said, "No, I believe no one else knows. My birth parents and my adoptive parents are all dead. I am sure no one here knows."

"Perhaps an uncle you don't know of? Would it be recorded anywhere?"

"Oh, André, I have no way to find out." She began twisting a dishcloth between her hands. "Perhaps the files of the church in Revigny-sur-Ornain? I can't think right now. What on earth shall we do?"

He stood and went to her, raising her to her feet.

"Nothing. We shall do nothing but proceed with our ordinary way of life."

He drew her close. "What Konrad writes about Germany is happening there, but it is not happening here. We have no need to feel afraid. Germany's troubles are her own, France is a free country, thanks be to the good God. I am well, you also, the girls are quite well. And Mme. Elsie Blaisé Ferrand is as French as any Frenchwoman can be. Let us be at peace with ourselves.

"Now, is that a boeuf en daube in the oven I smell?"

CHAPTER 8

Two hundred and eighty-six days after the start of World War Two, on the 13th of June, 1940, the 3.Infanterie-Division rested to resupply and provide the needed maintenance their rapid advance demanded.

Ready for diversion, Hauptmann Hans Krüger and Oberleutnant Jacob Klumpfer sought out the only café in the village of Robert-Espagne and went inside to enjoy lunch. The waitress, her cool manner intensified by Jacob's boisterous entrance, showed them to a table.

After studying the menu, Hans, in perfect French, ordered pot-au-feu for them both and a glass of vin ordinaire for himself. She was on her way to the kitchen when Jacob, wanting a glass of beer, summoned her back with a whistle.

When she returned to their table, her face the picture of disdain, Hans said, "Mademoiselle, please excuse my friend. He is not accustomed to being in a civilized country."

Saying nothing, she went to the bar, brought Jacob his beer, and vanished behind the kitchen door.

"Damnation, Jacob, do you have to be such a lout?"

"Oh, your excellency, I beg your most humble pardon. I forgot I was dining with the nobility." He smirked. "Bet you'd like a glass of beer yourself, wouldn't you? But you're too high and mighty to ask for it."

The waitress reappeared with bread and a glass of wine for Hans, then made a second trip to the kitchen to bring their food and set it before them. Hans thanked her and inhaled the aroma. "Mmm. I hope this is as good as it smells." He watched her face in vain for a reaction. "I beg your pardon,

Mademoiselle, but your village is very pretty. Do you receive many tourists?"

"Not since September, and I doubt your German army can be considered tourists."

"No, I suppose not, but we will try our best."

In return for his courtesy he was rewarded with a hint of a smile, if a contrived one.

Just then four officers from the 386th Infanterie-Division entered the café. Without waiting to be seated, they took possession of the table closest to the kitchen.

Jacob glanced at the new arrivals and said in a low voice to Hans, "Did you notice how those four walked in?"

At that moment the oberst at the other table snapped his fingers to summon the waitress. "You serve potée?" It was not a question but a demand.

"I noticed," Hans said.

The waitress shook her head. "No."

The oberst leaned back in his chair and jerked his head toward Hans' and Jacob's plates. "But I see you have pot-au-feu."

"We no longer have any."

"Do you have choucroute garnie?"

Another shake of the head. "No. No *sauerbraten*, either."

By now he was sputtering with anger. "Then what can you serve us, aside from a surly attitude?"

She stood her ground. "Bread. And cheese."

"Bring it!" he snapped. "And beer."

The waitress had turned when he said in a commanding voice, "And make it quick!" He favored his comrades with a smug grin. "They'll have *sauerbraten* soon enough."

Hans had finished his meal and was gazing out the window onto the main street of the village when Jacob said, "D'you suppose our mail will catch up with us anytime soon? I'm expecting lots of letters, and I need to keep up with things." He gave Hans a jolly wink.

"Jacob, do you think of nothing else?"

"Oh, yes. If I'm not thinking of that, I'm thinking of when we might have some leave, and where we might go, and whom I might meet so I can get back to thinking about things like that. You'd do the same, if you had my opportunities."

Jacob glanced at the other table and lowered his voice. "I hear rumors we'll halt our advance about 350 kilometers south, in the Canal du Centre region around Digoin-Chalons."

"Makes tactical sense. But where would we go from there?"

"That's a good question, my friend. Yes, where, and when?"

"Your guess is as good as mine. But at the moment, I suggest we pay the bill and get back to quarters."

They were pushing back their chairs when the oberst at the next table sprang to his feet with an angry shout. "Mademoiselle!"

His chair skidded across the floor and upset a small table laden with plates, a pitcher of water, many glasses, scattering shards of glass and porcelain in all directions. Water sloshed over crusts of uneaten bread, gravy, and vegetable scraps.

From the swinging door of the kitchen the chef came at a run. The waitress, with no sign of emotion and no comment whatsoever, began to clear away the mess, ignoring the table of officers. When she looked up she saw Hans staring at her. He resisted the urge to bend down and help.

The chef looked about, not sure what to do. He wiped his hands on his apron, then approached the officers' table. "Colonel, what is the matter?"

The oberst said nothing. With the tip of his finger and thumb he lifted the cheese from his plate. A long string of saliva dangled from the cheese onto his bread. With that, the major at the oberst's side pushed his chair away from the table, clapped a hand to his mouth, and retched.

Incensed, the oberst reached out, grabbed the waitress by both arms, lifted her off the floor and spun her around to face him. Teeth clenched, he snarled, "Do you know I could have you shot for this?"

Defiance flashed from her eyes. Do it, I dare you, they seemed to say. Silence heavy as water filled the room. The oberst, still glaring, shoved her aside, seized his hat, turned on his heel, and left. The other three officers hastened out after him.

"Two weeks? Impossible!" Jacob shook his head. "Nobody gets a two-week pass. Nobody. I only got one."

"Well it seems obvious somebody does." Hans smiled as he lay back on the cot and clasped his hands behind his head. "Remember, I didn't ask for this. I keep telling you, I'm just a good soldier."

"A good soldier my ass. I didn't know you were so tight with the oberst."

Hans didn't mind the teasing from his good friend. He and Jacob had been close since the University of Berlin, even though they had little in common. An interesting contrast of personalities, Hans quiet and reserved, Jacob loud and outgoing, just short of obnoxious. Though well liked and a loyal soldier, he was untested in battle, whereas the 3.Infanterie-Division's initial campaign through Poland in

September 1939 had won Hans the Iron Cross 2nd Class, the Iron Cross 1st Class, and promotion to hauptmann. In spite of their differences, Hans was glad for the friendship.

Hans rolled onto his side. "Don't worry, Jacob." He knew he was one of the few who could tease Jacob with impunity. "If we run across some Frenchman hunting rabbits, a stray bullet may find your arm. Then you can get a *two*-week pass *and* a Black Wound Badge."

Jacob ignored the needling. "A whole week of glorious leave. You suppose we could make it to Paris? It's only 350 kilometers northwest of here."

"We'd have time, but I don't want to spend my whole leave in Paris. After all, I have two weeks." Hans sat up on the edge of his cot. "Hard to believe it was just a month ago we rolled into the Low Countries, and now a few weeks later Paris has fallen. Too easy, and without much of a fight at all."

"Easy?" Jacob punched up his pillow to prop up his head. "Sure, once we got out of Poland and the north of France, we made better progress. But easy? Oh, no."

"Come on, don't be so damn argumentative. When's the last time you heard gunshots? Hell, the last casualty report we filed was when Fritz came back drunk, fell, and split his head wide open."

"Fine, I'll give you that, but if it's been as easy as you claim, explain your waitress friend, the one in Robert-Espagne?"

Hans grinned. "The one who ignored you and smiled at me?"

"She's the one. Did you think he'd shoot her, that oberst?"

"On my last leave in Berlin, before Poland, Father and I went for a walk. I think he wanted to leave the house so he could speak of things my mother shouldn't hear. He said war was coming, and that it would change me. I insisted we were not going to war, that Hitler was fulfilling his promise to keep the Fatherland safe."

Jacob, still propped up on his cot, crossed his ankles and listened to Hans with interest.

"I assured him if war came, which I didn't expect, I would come back from it unchanged, maybe a bit older. My father shook his head. 'No,' he said, 'I feel it in my bones. Germany is going to war.' He thought it would be France. I had never heard my father sound so solemn, so grave. 'And when war comes,' he said, 'you will be changed.'

"And do you know, he was right? I too have found myself thinking, Why didn't the oberst shoot her? Perhaps she reminded him of a daughter. But after what my father said, I realize the oberst is old enough to have been in the trenches on the western front in '14. He must be fighting his second war." Hans stood when they heard several soldiers pass. "He was changed long before Poland. So yes, I am surprised he didn't shoot her, very surprised. Now let's get in line. I'm starved."

On their way to Paris Hans relaxed as he rode in front next to the leutnant who was driving them north from Digoin. Jacob and the other oberleutnant rode in back of the open car. Military traffic heading south often blocked their progress, as the trailing elements of the II.Armee Korps caught up with the 3.Infanterie-Division. For once Hans could enjoy the passing countryside with no fear of a firefight or skirmish. Before long he wondered where the springtime had gone. They'd been too absorbed in their advance into France to appreciate it.

From the back seat, Jacob shouted into the wind. "Hans, how did you talk Major Vogel into letting us have the Kübelwagen?"

“He owed me a favor. I promised we’d return it without a scratch.” He turned to fix Jacob with a stern look. “Do you understand? Not … a … scratch.”

The Kübelwagen was new to the German army and to the division. The first few had been deployed in the invasion of Poland, and as the division withdrew to invade the Low Countries, 125 more were shipped by rail to Belgium. The novelty of the new vehicle was not lost on the troops. Covering twelve kilometers for every liter of fuel, the Kübelwagen could travel 380 kilometers without refueling, achieving a top speed of eighty kilometers per hour. Thus, the four officers could travel to Paris in a day and, with the auxiliary fuel container, return to Digoin.

Six hours of constant travel had brought them to Saint-Dizier, their slower speed permitting easier conversation. After a short stop, the leutnant and the oberleutnant traded positions, as did Jacob and Hans.

Hans was consulting the map. “Look here, Jacob, why don’t we follow the route to Bar-le-Duc and stop in Robert-Espagne? It’s only sixteen kilometers northeast. D’you suppose that waitress would remember us?”

Jacob snorted. “Not me, your excellency, but you she would remember.”

The oberleutnant seemed interested. “You have met someone?”

Hans had to raise his voice above the noise of the Kübelwagen. “No, but the oberst did!”

Jacob nodded, though the leutnant looked puzzled. After a few moments he turned to Hans. “Hauptmann Krüger, how far is it to Sermaize-les-Bains?”

"Twenty-eight kilometers," Hans shouted. "With this open road, we should be there soon. You fellows can drop me off and we'll meet later for the drive back."

Eager to see Paris, Hans had entertained no idea of a detour to Sermaize-les-Bains, but the more he considered it, the more he realized how important it would be to his father. After all, his father had told him, "Hans, if you get anywhere close to Sermaize-les-Bains, you must make every effort to call on André."

By the time Hans turned twelve, it had no longer been necessary to say the last name. He felt he knew the entire Ferrand family. At first it embarrassed him, the way his father would have everyone sit down to listen as he read André's latest letter aloud. And after the reading, the story of the Christmas Truce was always retold, followed by an account of all the hardships the Ferrands had endured. By the time Hans turned sixteen, his father must have concluded either that his son had committed the story to memory, or that Hans was no longer interested.

But there was something about this Frenchman, this odd wartime friendship that fascinated Hans. In fact, the impression was a lasting one. Now and then he would steal into his father's study and open the drawer that contained André's letters. Curious, he enjoyed reading them again and again, studying the photos of the family. He dreamed of how wonderful it would be to live on a farm in the country, never have to ride the noisy trams, or climb flights of stairs to reach his home.

There had been a day once when he was with his father in the study, discussing Hans' future in the military. His father, looking for his letter opener, had pulled open the drawer that had always held the letters, but they were gone. Not wanting his father to know he'd rummaged through private correspondence, Hans feigned innocence. "Have you heard from André recently?"

"No, not lately." That was all his father had said, and for the first time a question about André had evoked no recital of the Christmas Truce. It was that same day when his father had urged him to make an effort to call on the Ferrands, should he ever be near Sermaize-les-Bains.

A sign announced the outskirts of town: SERMAIZE-LES-BAINS. Hans pointed to the right. "Follow this road and stop when you see the hotel. I'll get off there."

As Jacob pulled up at the café next to the hotel, passing citizens turned to stare—whether at German officers or at the Kübelwagen Hans didn't know. Heads came together, whispers were exchanged as Hans opened the door to get out. A brave child came closer and dared to peer inside the strange vehicle.

Hans, now standing beside him, squatted down and looked the boy eye to eye. "Would you like to sit in it?"

Terrified, the boy fled.

Jacob, who'd heard the exchange, guffawed. "Where's your charm today, Herr Hauptmann?"

"Your manners must be rubbing off on me." Hans hoisted his bag from the Kübelwagen's storage compartment. "And to think I was going to thank you for dropping me off here. Before I leave you, though, you must swear you will let nothing happen to this vehicle."

"Ja, ja, ja, ja. I swear it. On my mother's grave."

"Fine. I'll meet you at the Arc de Triomphe on the tenth, 1000 hours, German time."

Jacob was gunning the engine.

Hans wasn't ready to leave just yet. "The tenth of July, Jacob. Got it?" He looked to the oberleutnant. "Make sure you have him there."

"Yes, sir, Hauptmann Krüger." The oberleutnant snapped off a salute.

"If you're not there at 1000 hours, I'll wait until 1100 hours, and if you still haven't showed up, I'll take the train back to Digoin. However, I'm quite sure, gentlemen, you don't want me to arrive by train in Digoin to explain to Vogel where the Führer's Kübelwagen is."

Hans stood straight and smoothed his uniform before entering the hotel. The clerk, behind the reception desk was holding a telephone to his ear. When Hans approached the desk, the clerk raised a finger indicating it would be a moment. Hans smiled and looked about the lobby.

"How may I help you, Major?"

"Not Major. Hauptmann."

"I see." The man didn't repeat the title. "How may I help you?"

"I'd like accommodation, if you please."

"How many nights?"

"At the moment I can't say."

"Very well. Indefinite stay." The clerk made a note in the register, then turned it around and pushed it toward Hans to sign.

After Hans had signed he handed back the pen and looked up. "Would you be able, please, to direct me to the farm of Monsieur André Ferrand?"

The clerk glanced around as if afraid someone might overhear. "Monsieur Ferrand, did you say?"

"That's correct. I'm on leave and wish to call on him." Not wanting to raise unnecessary fears, Hans hastened to explain. "Yes, Monsieur Ferrand and my father are old friends, and it's on his account that I've come."

"Ah, now I see. Let me draw you a map. I'm certain you will find it is a pleasant walk, but if you prefer, I can summon a taxi." He busied himself with the map.

Hans waited for it, then picked up the map and the proffered room key. "Thank you. I think I would prefer the walk."

"Very well, sir. Do you require anything else?"

"One more thing. Do you know if Monsieur Ferrand would have a telephone?"

"Mais oui. On that side of town they now have telephones. Do you wish to call him?"

"By no means." Hans laid an elbow on the counter and leaned toward the clerk. "And I ask that you not call him either. I want my arrival to be a surprise."

His officious manner gone, the clerk became even more interested in Hans' signature on the register. "Yes indeed, Hauptmann Krüger, whatever you say."

CHAPTER 9

"Papa, Papa!" Claire shouted. "A German soldier! There's a German soldier walking up our lane!"

André Ferrand stepped in front of his daughters to peer through the window. As the stranger came closer to the farmhouse, father and daughters observed a tall soldier whose purposeful gait seemed non-threatening. He appeared interested in his surroundings, not hostile in any way.

With every step the stranger took André inched closer to the window. Aimée and Claire jumped when he exclaimed, "No, it cannot be!" and ran to fling open the front door.

"Hans! Hans Krüger! Konrad's boy! It can't be anyone else!" Heart racing, he pulled the startled and embarrassed young officer into the house.

Claire and Aimée edged forward, all ears and eyes.

Elsie Ferrand was coming from the kitchen. "What's all the excitement?" When she saw there was a German officer in her home, she gasped and swept her daughters behind her, a mother hen protecting her chicks. She'd heard a great deal, both in town and on the radio, about the German army's advance through France and she stood prepared to protect her brood.

Before André could salvage the situation to introduce their guest, Hans clicked his heels and with a slight bow extended his hand. "Madame Ferrand, I am Hans Krüger. It's my great pleasure to meet you and your family. My father, Konrad, sends his regards."

Elsie Ferrand regained a measure of composure, drawing in a deep breath then letting it out. "Forgive me, please. Naturally,

I was startled, a German officer, entering my home—" She accepted his handshake, her habitual courtesy returning. "I'm pleased to make your acquaintance, even though I feel I know you already." She shook her head as if incredulous. "But we had no idea you were a Nazi soldier."

"Elsie! Hans is here to meet us, not discuss politics." André took the young man's arm. "Come, Hans, sit down, tell us about your family."

Hans was looking for a chair when André urged Claire forward a few steps. "Hans—"

"Ma'm'selle." Hans was smiling. "This must be Claire. Much prettier than her photo." As she flushed with pleasure he turned to Aimée, who had come from behind her mother, and was about to offer her his hand when he stopped short, eyes wide.

"I b-beg your p-pardon, Ma'm'selle," he stammered, flustered. After raising his head from looking down he put his hand forward, "I'm also p-pleased to make your acquaintance."

She accepted the handshake. "Moi aussi." Me too. "I'm Aimée." She couldn't think what else to say.

He cleared his throat. "I'm Hans Krüger."

"Yes, yes, my boy," André said. "Come along. You've already said that."

Hans seemed to want to explain his awkwardness. "Monsieur Ferrand, and Madame." Unable to take his eyes from Aimée, he said, "If I may be so bold, I did not expect your daughters would be so beautiful. The photographs, you know, they were children—"

Claire and Aimée smiled at each other, flattered by such straightforward admiration.

"Very well," André said with satisfaction, "the introductions are complete. Now we must make ourselves comfortable. We've an enormous amount to talk about."

Elsie Ferrand indicated the best chair for Hans as the girls took seats side by side on the sofa.

André was beaming with pleasure. "Now tell us, Hans, how is your father? And your mother? Young Peter, too." His index finger shot upwards. "But wait, I'm forgetting my manners. We must offer you refreshments. Elsie—" When he nodded toward the kitchen she went out. Then he went into the dining room and was back moments later with an opened bottle of wine and glasses.

"Girls," André said, offering glasses around, "have I ever told you how Konrad Krüger and I became friends? It was on Christmas Eve of 1914. We were dug in, entrenched on the western front, both the Germans and we French. The space between us we called No Man's Land."

Aimée and Claire exchanged glances that said, Oh no Papa, not tonight.

Just then Elsie came back with a plate of small rounds of bread and slices of cheese, passing those around as well.

"I've heard this story many times, Monsieur," Hans said, "every time my father receives a letter from you. It's always fascinating."

"And the same here," André said. "The whole family always enjoys hearing me read those letters from Berlin, don't you, girls? Keeping up with your family's lives."

For the first time in years, André's audience listened in earnest as he carried his story to its conclusion. "So we know, Hans, you will be twenty-six in December."

André popped up out of his chair. "Elsie, where did you put the photographs? I know they're here somewhere." He rummaged in the drawers of a big bureau. "Ah, here they are." He brought out a bundle of photos, all of the Krüger family. Their frayed edges attested to having been passed around many times. André handed them round again and elaborated on the scenes they portrayed. He acted as if he hadn't observed Hans' stolen glance at Aimée and her immediate blush nor the aimless twisting of a loose tendril of hair over her ear.

Elsie noticed Hans' wandering interest just as he turned back to focus on André's remarks.

"Monsieur Ferrand," Hans said, "when was the last time you heard from my father?"

"It was 1938. Yes, November of '38. Your father intended to come to see us when he was to make a business trip to Paris, but he had to cancel at the last minute. We were quite disappointed, and since then, the end of '38, we haven't heard a word from him. It must be this war. Damn war!" he said. "Damn all wars."

"Ah," Hans said, "that was four years after I had left for the university."

Elsie wondered if Hans knew why the letters ceased to come. Who are you, Hans Krüger? Are you a Nazi? Do you have any idea who I am? Her heart nearly jumped out of her chest and onto the table when Hans asked, "Monsieur, were you born in Sermaize-les-Bains?" How clever. Who sent you, Hans Krüger? Probably the Gestapo. Yes, that's it, the Gestapo.

The conversation came to an awkward halt. Aimée and Claire looked about, not sure what to say, but before anyone else broke the uncomfortable silence, Hans got to his feet.

"I realize now it was rude of me to come unannounced and uninvited. I hope you'll forgive me, all of you. It's been such a pleasure to be here, but really, I must return to town. I've taken a room at the hotel."

"Rest assured, Hans," André said, "we would offer you a

room with us, except"— he shook his head—"we know how the neighbors would feel."

"That is most kind of you, Monsieur, but it wouldn't be wise for you or your family. We are beginning to hear of French people being called collaborators, and you don't want that label."

"No, certainly not. How long will you be staying in Sermaize-les-Bains? Perhaps you could come for supper tomorrow."

"I must be in Paris on the tenth. Until then I have no firm plans."

"Then we'll see you tomorrow evening. Six o'clock?"

"Thank you, sir. I'd be honored." He looked to Elsie. "Madame Ferrand, are you certain? This uniform, you know—"

She was about to speak when André answered for her. "We're looking forward to it, aren't we, my dear?"

Hans moved to take her hand. "Thank you for your kindness, Madame. May I bring something?"

"Your appetite," André said. "Just your appetite, my boy."

Elsie nodded, if not quite with enthusiasm.

Hans turned to the sisters. "Claire, Aimée, meeting you both has been a great pleasure. I look forward to tomorrow."

When André walked him to the front door, Hans said, "I shall be sure to tell my father about meeting you and your family. Thank you for your warm welcome. Good afternoon, Monsieur."

After a quiet meal at the café Hans went back to the hotel and asked at the desk for some writing paper before settling into his room. He took off his uniform coat, loosened his belt, and eased into the chair at the desk, ready to compose a letter to his parents. Before starting, he rearranged the blotter, paper and lamp. He stared at his pen as his thoughts focused on the Ferrands. There's no way they could know I read the letters. How old was I, six, maybe seven, when André wrote to father about Elsie? What difference would it make? He picked his fountain pen up off the table, glad he'd remembered to fill it with ink before leaving Digoin.

Sermaize-les-Bains
Friday
5 July 1940

Dear Father, Mother, and Peter:

I have so much to report, but as you can see, I am posting this letter from Sermaize-les-Bains! I am on a two-week furlough and was en route to Paris with Jacob and two other officers from the regiment when I persuaded Jacob to make a detour to Sermaize-les-Bains. Knowing how close to the town I was, I couldn't fail to fulfill your wish, Father. They dropped me off here and I will meet them in Paris. I am not sure how long I will be here, at least until after tomorrow. Regardless, I must meet Jacob in Paris on the tenth.

After I checked into the local hotel, I obtained directions from the hotel clerk—I know he was suspicious of my motive, so I explained the long-standing family friendship—and walked to their farm. Father, they were astonished to see me. M. Ferrand took little time in recognizing me from the photos you had sent. Mme. Ferrand was afraid—the uniform, no doubt—but a bit less fearful in the end. I can tell you M. Ferrand was most engaging, and I can see he has a subtle sense of humor. I can now appreciate why you have been friends all of these years.

Their home is comfortable and cozy. M. Ferrand has provided well for his family. His farm appears neat and trim in every way. The walk in the country was beautiful, reminding me of our student walking trips in Bavaria. Our visit was too short for me to learn about his farm, but I hope to do so tomorrow, as they have invited me to supper. It's a welcome change, being away from the war. I feel as if I have left it behind, at least for now. It concerns me though, that my presence could cause trouble for these kind people, their neighbors are sure to ask questions.

Father, I learned much about your friendship with M. Ferrand. I was surprised to see how many photographs you had sent them. They were very proud to share them with me and were all very interested in what I had to say about each one. M. Ferrand's recollection of my birthday was quite similar to yours, you'll be glad to know.

I shall post this letter in town, and since the censor won't see it, I can tell you our advances in the field have been rapid and successful. Our casualties have been few and the division is now in Digoin-Chalons. My promotion to hauptmann came through and the regiment takes much pride in my Iron Cross 2nd Class and Iron Cross 1st Class medals. I don't feel I deserve them, but the matter is not mine to argue. Mother, please don't worry. I exercise caution at all times.

The French, so far, do not seem too distressed by our presence. There has been but one instance of outright hostility that I have witnessed by a French citizen, a brave and feisty waitress in a small café. But for the most part these people are reserved. Since the armistice was announced in June there has been no fighting. While the French have not been engaging, they have been tolerant. It will be most interesting to see what we encounter in Paris.

Peter, you would be most taken with Claire. Very taken indeed! She is quite pretty, and she just turned 16. You would blush if you saw how she giggled when we were looking at the photograph of you, Father, and Mother on holiday. You had such a silly hat on your head. I don't remember having seen the photograph before; I think you were maybe 13 or 14.

Aimée is beautiful. It is difficult for me to describe her, but I shall try. She's quiet and poised, and very, very pretty. Her long black hair makes a striking contrast to her soft fair skin. She will be 20 in September and is employed, I believe, in Sermaize-les-Bains at the telephone exchange. I am more than eager to see her again, and if Mme. F. hasn't packed her up and sent her to the convent by my next visit, I look forward to knowing her better.

I think of you all often and miss you each and every day. I assure you I am safe, as I work toward our glorious victory. I will send some photographs from Paris. I wish I had brought a camera with me. Jacob insisted on bringing his, but there may not be enough film left in Paris after he has photographed all the mademoiselles. He has become a good friend and we do everything together—a good example of how opposites attract. Don't worry, Mother, I won't let him corrupt me. Father, I know you would like Jacob. He is always reading, and when his head isn't buried in a book he's making me laugh. He's quite a prankster. I'm afraid, though, one day his antics will land him in a fix.

I think of you often. Your devoted son and brother,

Hans

Claire and Aimée told their parents goodnight and left them sitting at the kitchen table.

"I don't understand why Maman was so afraid when Hans came." Claire was brushing her hair. "After all, his father and Papa are old friends."

"That's true." Aimée had turned back the covers on the bed and was undressing. "Do you think it matters?"

Claire laid the hairbrush aside, turned out the light, and climbed into the big bed the girls shared. "You're like me, you can always tell what Maman is thinking. When's the last time she wasn't happy to have a visitor? She was far from glad for this one."

"I know. Most people would have thought she was cordial, but we know better."

"Eh bien, but he is a German soldier, after all. An invader, in fact."

Aimée considered her sister's comment, then said, "Yes, but a very handsome one."

They were about to fall asleep when the unmistakable sounds of an argument drifted upstairs. The word "Nazi" could be heard but they could make out no other words, then "Nazi" again.

Claire sat up in bed and clasped her hands. "Why is Maman so agitated?"

"I don't know. I've never seen her in such a state. She and Papa never fight. Come on, lie down and go to sleep. We can't do anything about it."

"I still don't like it." Claire flopped back onto her pillow.

The muffled voices continued to drift up the stairs, both growing louder. After a few moments they heard André slam his palm on the table. "Sacré bleu, Elsie, I invited him!"

"Yes, you did, now, didn't you?"

The girls gave up trying to sleep. Claire tiptoed over to open their bedroom door and they both sat on the bed to listen.

André's voice was still loud. "Well, I don't think as poorly of him as you seem to. I think he's a fine young man. Anyway, you don't know he's a Nazi."

"I don't have to prove he's a Nazi. He wears a German uniform, doesn't he? What more is there? You know what the Germans think."

"He was a mere child when I wrote to Konrad, he can't possibly know."

"Know about what?" Claire whispered. "Think about what, Aimée? What are they talking about?"

"Ssssh. I'm thinking. I wish I knew." Aimée fiddled with the edge of the coverlet. "I have no idea what Maman's talking about, I wish I knew."

A cool and gentle breeze stirred the curtains. Aimée got up from the bed, tiptoed to the window, and sat on the floor. The sound of crickets drifted up from the fields. Light from the quarter-moon illuminated the same lane Hans had walked a few hours before. With a faint sigh, she laid both arms on the windowsill to rest her chin on them and gaze out into the night.

"You still awake?" Claire propped up on one elbow. "What are you doing by the window?"

"Don't worry yourself," Aimée said, her voice low.

"It's Hans, isn't it? You're mooning over Hans."

"Tais-toi." Be quiet. "Go back to sleep. It's none of your business."

"You're afraid he won't come, aren't you?"

So annoying, the way Claire could read her mind. But it was true, Hans was all Aimée could think about. He was just as she had envisioned from the many photos her father had shown them, yet in person he took her breath away. She knew she would never forget the perfect proportions of his face, its distinct features. His whole presence spoke of a gentleness that offset any anxiety his German uniform might stir. Her mother could despise the uniform, but for Aimée his hazel eyes dispelled any such notions.

She'd been touched by Hans' loss of composure when he tried to introduce himself to her. If other men had displayed such manners, she hadn't taken notice. Why doesn't Maman like him? She did her utmost to transmit her thoughts into the bedroom down the hall. Please, Papa, talk to Maman. Make her see.

"He'll come," she said, smiling. "I can just feel it, I know he'll come."

The only response from Claire was slow, deep, regular breathing.

CHAPTER 10

For the second time Hans walked the lane leading to André Ferrand's farm, a bottle of wine in one hand, a bunch of irises wrapped in green paper in the other. The late summer afternoon struck him with intensity, every sensation stronger than normal. Colors seemed brighter, country fragrances more potent, every sound distinct. Leaves floated on the waft of a breeze that was seen but not heard. Bird songs painted the very air.

Sheltered for the moment from the war, his thoughts drifted. Why had the townspeople stared so? You'd think they'd never seen a soldier. And that old woman in the café, she looked so sad. I'll bet she'd lost a son.

A few feet short of the Ferrand's front door Hans stopped for a moment, shifted both burdens to his left arm, smoothed his hair, and inspected his uniform. Satisfied, he stepped onto the porch and looked at his watch one last time. Perfect, six o'clock. Claire startled him by opening on the first rap and ushered him into the sitting room.

"Alors, Hans, c'est vous? Maman? Hans is here."

Madame Ferrand came from the kitchen, drying her hands on her apron. When Hans presented the bottle of wine she inspected the label. "Oh, my, a Pouilly-Fuissé. Why, thank you, Hans. This is quite a fine selection. I'm surprised you didn't bring us a German wine."

"I'm glad you like it. The clerk at the shop did suggest a German wine, but I insisted on a French one."

Relieved the effort and money he'd spent on selecting it weren't wasted, he held out the flowers. "My mother always insisted on fresh flowers whenever we had company, and irises are her favorite. I hope you like them."

Claire, her voice high and breathless, said, "Oh, I love purple irises! They're wonderful!"

"So do I." Aimée nodded. "Aren't you pleased, Maman? So thoughtful of Hans."

"Yes, they're lovely." Elsie laid the flowers on a table and turned to go back to the kitchen. "Now go get your Papa. It's almost time to eat."

Aimée shook her head. "This won't do." She picked up the flowers. "Thank you, Hans, for such a pretty gift. Claire, you go call Papa, I'll put them in water."

Ignoring her command, Claire settled down to chat with Hans, "What does your brother wish to study?"

In a moment Aimée was back with the irises in a green pottery jug that set off their color like a painting.

Hans was answering Claire's question. "Like me, Peter was interested in engineering. But he was called up for military service before he could complete his studies."

"Perhaps he would also come to see us."

Aimée glared at Claire. "You're supposed to call Papa."

Claire wobbled her head as if to say, Bossy-Boots. "Excuse me, Hans, please, I must call Papa to supper."

"Yes. Go." Aimée took Claire's place near Hans. "I apologize for all this running around. Please tell me the rest about Peter."

"Er, yes." Distracted by her beauty, Hans was having trouble formulating an answer. When he collected his thoughts he said, "You see, he was assigned to the Kriegsmarine and has just finished his basic training. He's home, back in Berlin for two weeks, then he reports for U-boat duty."

"U-boats, oh, my. Don't you worry about him?"

"I trust his officers do as they are trained and keep him safe. But, yes, I do worry about him."

André, having come in and washed his hands, entered the room with a smile. "Hans, my boy, how was your day in our fair town?"

"Quiet, I'd say. I posted a letter to my parents and walked around town a bit. An agreeable little place."

"Meet any of our townspeople?"

"In fact, Monsieur, I did, in the café. Pleasant people, you French."

"Eh bien, but now you must come into the dining room. My good wife has a meal ready for us."

Once everyone was seated at the table, Elsie served Hans the soup before serving her family. Aimée took this courtesy for a positive sign, her mother must be softening. She breathed a silent prayer: Thank you, Papa.

André, at the head of the table, was served next. Elsie had directed Hans to a seat on André's left next to her own place, while Aimée and Claire were side by side across the table.

"My word," Hans said, after his first spoonful, "this soup is superb."

André nodded with satisfaction. "I'll wager you don't get such good soup in the army. We never did."

Aimée saw her mother shoot André a look that said he was not to go off on a tangent about war, any war. She and Claire swapped discreet smiles and devoted their attention to the soup.

André had received his wife's message. "Claire, did you help with the committee work this morning for Bastille Day?"

"Of course, Papa. Everything's in order. It should be quite a big celebration."

"Will you have wine, Hans?" André was examining the label before he poured. "Elsie, my dear, where did we get this bottle?"

She didn't look up from her dish. "Hans brought it."

Claire's knee gave Aimée's a nudge under the table.

"Did he indeed? Then we must thank you, Hans. An excellent bottle." After he poured a glass for himself he lifted it to his nose and inhaled. "Ah, marvelous."

When the soup was finished Elsie got up. "Aimée, Claire, please clear away the soup dishes."

André poured more wine for Hans and himself then leaned back in his chair. "Tell me, my boy, what news of your brother, Peter? Does he continue his studies?"

Hans shook his head. "I'm sorry to say, Monsieur, he does not. As I was telling Aimée earlier, he's in the Kriegsmarine, called up before he could finish school."

Claire came from the kitchen with more bread, while Aimée brought plates and set them before André. Elsie followed with le plat principal, the main course. It was rare roast beef, saignant, which André carved, complemented by a savory sauce. After everyone was given an ample serving Hans commented again on the delicious meal, a remark Elsie acknowledged with a nod but nothing more.

Aimée gathered her courage for a small joke. "You may not know it, Hans, but we're glad to have company. If Papa were a beef farmer, we'd probably be serving you chicken!"

When everyone laughed, it lightened the atmosphere. But Hans' laugh was subdued, it lacked the enthusiasm she anticipated. Sensing a change in him, she sought out his gaze and smiled. The effect was better than she'd hoped, like the golden sun emerging from behind a cloud.

Claire, oblivious to what was taking place no more than a meter away, asked, "Hans, what do you do in the army?"

"Without boring you too much, I'm an officer, a hauptmann in the infantry. In your military that would be un capitaine. Nothing glamorous, I just try to be a good soldier."

He looked about the table. André was enjoying the meal. Aimée and Claire seemed to hang on his every word, while Mme. Ferrand, head down, picked at the food on her plate. "Before that, in September, I was an oberleutnant in a light armored reconnaissance company."

Claire shook her head. "I'm so stupid about military things, it would take me years to understand."

André picked up the wine bottle and saw it was empty. "Can you believe it? We've inhaled all that delightful wine." He got up to get another bottle from his own stock. "It saddens me to say, this next one won't be so fine." A twinkle appeared in his eye. "Not being Jesus Christ, you see, I haven't saved the best wine for last."

Hans laughed—the miracle at Canaan, he got it—until he saw Claire's and Aimée's faces suggesting they were mortified by their father. When no one else laughed at André's joke, the host shrugged and poured from the new bottle anyway. While Elsie gathered the plates and brought in the salad, Hans studied Aimée trying not to be too obvious. He found her every bit as captivating as the day before, mesmerized by her gray eyes, their stunning complement to her black hair.

"Were you promoted?" Claire asked.

He hated to tear his gaze from Aimée, but courtesy required it. "Yes, after I was awarded the Black Wound Badge and a couple of other decorations."

"Wounded? Oh, my! Were you hurt?"

"No, not as bad as you might think." He produced a half-smile. "But it did get me promoted."

"I see," Aimée said. "So now that you have a higher rank, will you be safer?"

"That's what I tell my mother in my letters. She worries about me, you know, as mothers do. I write often, but I don't know whether it helps or makes her worry more. After my last furlough in July, before the Polish campaign, mother told me she'd never thought anything could be worse than father being on the front in the last war, until she had to let me go to this one. And now with Peter on U-boat assignment I know she'll worry even more. Father will be fine, stoic, you know, the way men are, but I'm concerned for her."

"Heroic," André put in. "Stoic *and* heroic, we men."

Hans laughed. "Quite true, Monsieur. You'll get no argument there from me."

Aimée rose to collect the salad plates, and after helping her mother arrange the cheese platter, brought it to the table.

Hans helped himself, then said, "Tell me, Aimée, what do you like to do? What are your plans?"

"I like to read, and I like to write letters." She hoped he got the hint, but perhaps she was rushing things. Too soon to know. "And before the war, I wanted to go and live in Paris."

Elsie couldn't let that pass. "Now, Aimée, you know how your Papa and I feel about that."

"Oh, yes, Maman, I know, but—"

André stood up. "Hans, my boy, before it gets dark, would you like to see our farm?"

"Bien sûr. Father will want to know all about it."

"Then let's go. Come, this way, through the back door."

The two of them left, and when Aimée glanced at her mother, she realized Elsie had never abandoned her cool reserve. Was this related to last night's argument? It had to be.

"Here we are, this is our cage de poulet." When André opened the door of the henhouse and ushered him inside, Hans whistled in astonishment. "I've never seen so many chickens at one time. What do you do with them all?"

"It's a simple process. Chickens are the perfect food, you see. When we get baby chicks hatched from fertile eggs, we feed them for four or five months until they begin laying. A good hen can produce two hundred or more eggs a year, and we sell those. When the time comes they're no longer productive layers, then we butcher them for the pot. I'm sure you know how tasty a fat juicy hen can be. As for the cocks, well" —he gave Hans a knowing wink—"without them we would have no chickens, eh?"

"True enough. How many chickens have you?"

"Usually between three hundred and five hundred. That way we can sell about a hundred and fifty eggs a day, then every two weeks we harvest the oldest ones for market."

"I had no idea. What about nighttime predators? Don't you worry about foxes?"

"Foxes, weasels, even an occasional human being. The other predators we worry about are hawks. At night the chickens go indoors to roost, and I shut them inside for protection. But during the day they range free. That's why I keep a rifle handy, and a good watchdog."

"I see this enterprise involves a great deal of work. Father will be most interested to hear about it all."

André dusted off his hands and indicated he was ready to go back outdoors. "You may not be aware of it, Hans, but your father encouraged me to go into this business after the war. So in some measure, I have him to thank for my success."

"Most enlightening. You can never go on holiday, though, can you? No one to care for the chickens."

"That's true for all farmers, we must stay close to home."

They were making their way to the house when Hans swallowed hard. "Monsieur Ferrand, may I have your permission to take a stroll with Aimée? Provided, of course, she would like to come."

"Not up to me." André chuckled. "You must obtain that permission from her mother, mon général."

Hans felt as apprehensive as he'd felt on the eve of the Bzura battle, vulnerable, at risk, with no idea of the enemy response. If his luck held, he might be the victor in this campaign, provided he didn't garner another unwanted Wound Badge.

At the back door André indicated the iron foot scraper for Hans to use before entering the house, and once they were in the kitchen, went into the other room and called out for Claire. What a considerate man. Thank you, André. So kind.

Alone with Elsie, Hans said, "Madame Ferrand"—he had to clear his throat when his voice came out like a croak—"may I have your permission to take Aimée for a little walk?"

At first Elsie wouldn't meet his gaze, craning her neck to look out the window. But then her black eyes bored into him with a force that could melt iron. "Ask her, if you like. A short walk only. I expect Aimée back before dark."

"Oui, Madame, you have my word."

When he went to the sitting room to look for Aimée it was obvious she had heard the kitchen conversation, for she stood by the door holding a light wrap.

Hans, eager to change the rapport between them, addressed her for the first time with the more familiar tu. "You are in agreement about this little stroll out of doors?"

She held out her palms, dimpling with pleasure. "As you see." Ah, progress. She'd responded with her own tu.

He offered her his arm, and they set out through the front door to circle the house. On the path toward the henhouse, he reconnoitered the farmhouse and outbuildings. Twenty meters to the henhouse, the building's about thirty meters in length. Beyond it a country lane meandered southward, parallel to the henhouse. Hans led Aimée toward the lane, aware that Mme. Ferrand was cognizant of every blade of grass on the battlefield. He exercised caution as he walked, careful to keep a respectful distance from Aimée. The farm dog had heard them and came to trot along at their heels.

"Hello there, old fellow," Hans said. "What's your dog's name?"

"Make a guess."

"I've no idea. What are French dogs named? Bruno? Hector? Astyanax?"

She laughed. "His name is Tapis."

At that Hans threw his head back in a guffaw. "Carpet? Your dog is named Carpet?"

"Silly, isn't it? Papa named him that because he was forever lying around. Poor Tapis would adore to be an indoor dog, but he's needed on the farm."

"Aimée, it pleases me that you agreed to go for a walk." With a smile he said, "Even if you brought your watchdog."

"I was hoping you'd ask."

"If I write to you, I mean, if I get the chance, whenever I can, will you write back?" He felt annoyed with himself, struggling so to voice his request. "You did say you enjoy writing letters."

Aimée considered her answer. Moments passed. Her voice was soft and sincere when she looked at Hans and said, "Yes."

They had come to the lane, and as soon as they walked to where the henhouse blocked their view of the house, he reached for her hand. He felt her light yet responsive squeeze. He brought her hand to his lips and kissed it, and the next moment he was surprised to feel Tapis licking his other hand. The dog pranced at his side, wagging its tail. Well, well. Approval from the canine department at least.

A few meters further along when the house came back into view, Hans let go of her hand, and as they ambled along, he bent over and picked up a few small stones, tossing one into a pile at the end of a plowed field.

He felt Aimée's gaze on him, and when he turned, her gray eyes were full of concern. "Hans, does the fighting scare you?"

"It's not the fighting that scares me, it's the unknown." He tossed another of the stones into the air and caught it in his palm. "It's a curious thing how as soon as a battle's engaged, one feels little fear. There's a job to be done. My comrades count on me to do my job, and I count on them to do theirs."

"Look," she said, "the sun's just starting to go down. Don't you love this time of day? I know I do."

He tossed the other stones away, into the ditch. "Thank you, Ma'm'selle, for awakening me! I've had little time to appreciate sunsets or anything else in nature. I can't tell you how glad I am to be here, this feels like the real world. Those clouds, all the varied colors, it's glorious." He wanted to take her hand again, even to kiss her, but until he could win Elsie over he'd have to tread with caution.

The fresh smells of summer, the curing hay, the dog's rough coat, even the sharp tang of the roadside weeds brought him a new euphoria. The sun was halfway into its cradle when he said, "Aimée, I regret to say I believe we'd be wise to go back. I have the impression your mother knows exactly where we are and what we're doing, and she's already made it clear how soon she expects us."

"Ah ha! You understand Maman very well. I can see why you won those medals."

As they came alongside the henhouse again, out of Elsie's view, Hans stopped and took both Aimée's hands in his to draw her close. When he looked down into her eyes, they darted to the side and her head followed, but he lifted her chin and brought her face around so he could kiss her lips. It was a quick kiss, but in that moment he knew his fate was sealed. For the rest of his life, he would want no other kisses than hers. When it ended he swept her arm up in his and broke into a light run, pulling her along. Aimée ran with him, sharing his exuberance, until just as they reached the end of the henhouse he slowed to a walk and opened the distance between them.

"Your mother was expecting us to clear the end of the henhouse, just … about… NOW."

"Oh yes, a good soldier and a good scout. A good spy, too, if one were needed." When she looked up to flash him a teasing grin Hans thought he might burst with pure joy.

CHAPTER 11

Canal du Centre
Monday
15 July 1940

My dear Aimée,

I write to you while still on leave. I am visiting Canal du Centre and inspecting the locks we studied at the university. They are just as amazing as I had thought they'd be, yet far more impressive up close than in a book. I welcome the distraction this provides. Yesterday there was much celebrating of Bastille Day, but life seems to be back to normal today.

I returned to Digoin-Chalons with Jacob and the two officers who brought me to Sermaize-les-Bains. After I rejoined them at the Arc de Triomphe on the 10th, we enjoyed a good meal at a nearby bistro and visited le Tour Eiffel before returning to Digoin. It was a long drive with many stops and I had much to contemplate along the way. I must admit that I envisioned you in every town and village we drove through, particularly in the open country once we were south of Briare along the river Loire.

The summer evening reminded me of our wonderful stroll, especially as the sun was settling low in the west and we had to slow down for a disabled vehicle. Without the wind in my face I was able to take in the open air, and the warm country fragrances brought me back to a certain farm near Sermaize-les-Bains. Isn't it amazing how smells can do that, transport one in an instant to another location, another time?

As we crept along I found myself wanting to get out and

walk. My three companions would have thought me mad, if I had stopped a moment to kiss the back of a hand they couldn't see.

I hope you won't think less of me for that kiss. Was I too presumptuous? It would have been impossible for me to resist, for never had I been in the company of such a beautiful woman. Just to think now that I held her hand and touched that hand with my lips! And once I kissed your hand, I could never have resisted kissing your lips. Every time I think of it, which is at least a thousand times a day, it brings a smile! As I look out the window and gaze on all the beauty around me, I relive our short time together. Please believe me when I say every time I see such beauty, I see you.

I could go on for hours, but if I did so, I would miss my chance to post this letter and dispatch my feelings to you. I must tell you, before I forget, that if I send my letters to you from headquarters, they will be censored. To avoid this, whenever possible I will post them in a town. My rank gives me the freedom to do so. If I'm unable to post them in some town, my letters will contain no mention of my location or activities. Censoring is necessary, and as an officer, I must perform this task for my own company. I don't relish it, but it is one of the many tasks I must do. You would not believe some of the things the enlisted men write!

I hope you are well. Please pass along my regards to your parents and Claire, too.

Before closing, there is something I must ask. Is there someone special in your life? I don't wish to cause you turmoil, yet I want you to know my kiss was sincere. Forgive me if you were offended.

With my tender regards, yours
Hans Krüger

Sermaize-les-Bains
Thursday
18 July 1940

My dear Hans,

How could I possibly be offended? Put your mind at ease; there is no one special in my life, at least there wasn't until you kissed me. I let you kiss me, Hans, because I wanted you to kiss me. Now, let me get on with my letter.

Your letter arrived in yesterday's post. It was on the kitchen table when I returned from work. I can't even predict how many times it was picked up by Maman and Claire and inspected to search for hints of its content. Your handwriting is just as I thought it would be—expressive, yet precise and very neat. Maman was lingering in the kitchen when, careful not to tear any of the pages, I opened it. Once I began reading your wonderful words, I forgot she was watching. She must have guessed what you wrote, for after I finished reading I folded your letter, I kissed it before putting it in my pocket, and began to twirl about the kitchen with my eyes closed. I didn't realize how my performance must have seemed until I opened them and saw Maman staring at me. It was silly of me I know, but that was the effect of your letter.

I, too, have found myself thinking about our stroll. My heart was pounding so as you held my hand, I'm surprised you didn't stop me to say, "Wait, do you hear that noise? What is it?"

Friday evening, after our meal and once our chores were finished, I went for a walk again, just to take in the beauty of the outdoors. I regret I had never noticed such beauty before in all the simple things that surround us. There was a peacock butterfly about the flowers, and while watching it I realized I had never noticed the brilliant colors of the rainbow displayed in it wings. Did you know when butterflies land they always fold their wings up in a certain way as if in slow motion, and if you approach them with caution, you can observe them resting for quite some time before they flutter off in the breeze? I never had. Is it that they weren't there before? They must have been, but now I shall see them forever.

Papa has been so lighthearted since your visit, he talks of little else. He was so pleased to learn of your family. He and Maman talk more of the war now and listen to the BBC. That night after you left, as Claire and I lay in bed she asked if you held my hand or kissed me while we were out. I told her (please forgive me!) there wasn't any time for such foolish things, and besides, Maman was watching. Claire giggled and said, "No, we were *all* watching." Then she went on to tell me Maman said, "If they don't come out from behind the henhouse in two seconds I'm going out there myself." And after we appeared on schedule (thanks to you, for if it were up to me, we might still be there) Papa said, "See, Elsie, I told you they were just out for a stroll."

But since then Maman has been moody, and I don't know why. She and I argued again today. I hate not getting along with her, but she refuses to be anything but harsh with me. I long for the day I can move to Paris.

Before you came to see us I had little to worry about, but now that we've met—perhaps more than just met—I think I shall worry about Hauptmann Krüger, that is provided I have your permission to do so. When your furlough is over, what will your duties be? Bore me with all the details. For now, I must go. I have another letter to write, but I wanted to respond to you first.

Please tell me you will be careful and know that I am forever thinking of you.

With my sincere good wishes,

Marie-Aimée Ferrand

▪ ▪ ▪ ▪ ▪

Sermaize-les-Bains
Thursday
18 July 1940

Dear Louise,

Such news! I met the most marvelous man. He is 26 and the son of a dear friend of my Papa. His name is Hans and he's a captain in the German army. Do not be alarmed, it's not what you think. His father and Papa have been friends for 30 years, so calm yourself, no, I am not a collaborator.

You would not believe how kind and considerate he is, or how handsome. While he was here he took me out for a wonderful stroll. I tell you, anyone that kisses as he does cannot be a Nazi!

Maman continues to be just impossible. She seems to dislike Hans, and she and Papa argued about him after he first came, before the next night when he came to supper. Oh, how I wish I could join you in Paris to live in your apartment! I so much regret not having gone with you when you moved. Maman says I must stay here now that the Nazis have occupied Paris. I told her there were telephone exchanges in Paris and that I could easily find a job. I shall never forgive her if I don't get off this farm! I love my Papa, but Maman almost seems to enjoy being difficult.

And how is Pierre? Have you heard from him lately? I will continue to keep him in my prayers.

Claire is now 16 and seems much older than one year ago. I enjoy her company far more than I ever used to now that Maman is such a trial.

Thank you for your letters. They provide a welcome distraction.

Take care of yourself. With all my heart, I wish I could accept your invitation to come for a visit. Papa would let me go, but I'm quite sure Maman would not. So for now I won't even ask.

Your dear friend,
Aimée

▪▪▪▪▪

Digoin
Wednesday
24 July 1940

Dear Aimée,

I was so happy to receive and read your letter, but you need not sign your letters with such formality. I didn't even know Marie-Aimée was your full name. May we just be Hans and Aimée to each other?

As I go about my duties I think of you and try to envision what you are doing at that very moment, and each evening when the sun goes down, I pause to remember and hope you are doing the same.

Jacob keeps pestering me to learn more of you. He doesn't believe me when I tell him I was going to Sermaize-les-Bains to meet your family and that I had no idea what a treasure I would find. I'm reluctant to tell him much, he's not known for discretion in any situation. Suffice it to say he knows I returned from my leave different in some way than when I left.

You asked me to tell you what it is I do. As soldiers we worry. We worry about where we are headed and what our assignment will be. That is what we do. We never worry about where we have been, but we hope to have learned from those experiences. No, what we worry about is the next battle. Are we headed to Italy or North Africa, north or south, east or west? The Italians are fighting in North Africa now, and I'm afraid Mussolini may ask for our assistance. If that's the case, then off we must go.

But for the present I believe we will stay put, until it becomes clear what's to happen in regard to England. If England realizes that continuing her struggle is useless, then the war will be over and life will get back to normal. For the moment, though, I seem to be stuck in the middle between Italy and England, away from you.

I reread your letter many times during the day, whenever I find a spare moment. When I was with your family for supper that night, I asked you what you liked to do, and you said you like to write letters. I had no idea you do it so well!

You asked if it was permissible for you to worry about me. By all means, please do. Pray for me as well, if you will. Maybe your prayers will help my guardian angel keep me safe.

Thank you for your letters and expressions of affection. They mean everything to me.

Yours affectionately,
Hans

Sermaize-les-Bains
Tuesday
6 August 1940

My dear Hans,

What a special treat. You are so sweet! I was beginning to agonize for I had not received a letter in several days. I was sick with fear not knowing what it meant. I find myself sitting by the wireless, listening to the BBC trying to discover what might have happened to you. And then today I received a small package containing ten letters for me. Ten! It took me hours to read them all. Forgive me for the thoughts I had!

My parents are well and Papa sends his regards. I am so happy to learn of your parents' surprise and even happier to learn of their joy in our exchange of letters. Thank you for the photograph. I shall treasure it always. Jacob seems harmless enough. Perhaps you misjudge him. In any event he does know how to use a camera and take a good photograph!

Why do you say you think Maman is not in favor of our corresponding? She has been difficult, but she has not forbidden me to write. Yes, she has always been nervous about Germans, especially Nazis. Forgive me for saying this, but I don't consider you one of them. Papa says she is just worried about her daughters and the stories she heard about the last war. So, until she absolutely forbids it, I shall continue to write.

While I'm sorry things are boring for you at times, I'm glad, on the other hand, that they are, for that means you are still in Digoin and not in a battle. I don't like the fact I may not always be told where you are. The first thing I do when I open your letter is to look at the top of the first page to see where you were when you wrote. I find it comforting, knowing you're still in France. The second thing I do is look at how you signed your letter. Yes, we must be Hans and Aimée to each other, nothing else will do.

I'm also in accord with you that my thoughts and feelings, like yours for me, are growing stronger. I never thought I would find myself in such a position, and I must admit while it's not a situation I would have chosen, in life we must accept what we are given and trust that the best will come of it.

At least that's what I tell myself when my co-workers at the telephone exchange talk about such things. I don't know whether they know of my feelings for you, but they know you were in Sermaize-les-Bains and that you came to supper. One of the girls at the exchange, Yvonne, has received news of the death of her brother in the fighting around Dunkerque, and she fears for the loss of her fiancé as well. When news like that comes it's very sad and quiet at the exchange. Even Cècile couldn't make us laugh. At such times, I'm afraid, the others look at me as if they think you were responsible for it.

But I must stop, as it's not good for me to dwell on such things when I have no control over them. It's late and I must crawl into bed. Claire will want to talk.

Thank you again, dear one, for such a pleasant surprise. I'm accumulating quite a collection of letters to hide.

Yours with every affectionate thought,

Aimée

▪ ▪ ▪ ▪ ▪

Digoin
Friday
16 August 1940

Dear Aimée,

It pleases me to learn you enjoyed your packet of letters. I can't say what possessed me to torture you so, but I knew you would forgive me when you saw a week's worth in your hand. I found the ribbon at a shop in Digoin where the shopkeeper was kind enough to let me have just a bit. And as you can see, we remain in Digoin for now, but more about that later.

I regret your friend Yvonne must suffer because of the war. It's not of my making, but I must do as I am told. Rest assured, our division was not near Dunkerque in May. We came across through Luxembourg and Belgium and stayed south from there, never making it west of Reims. Other elements of the German army were responsible. Even so, however, I must accept that I am a part of the German army she now despises. But I'm sure Yvonne doesn't see it as a soldier does.

I have witnessed a great many things that cost me sleep at night, things that do not make me proud, things that happened in Poland. At first I thought the way I felt was because I'd never been in combat before. But then I came to see that the men responsible for these dreadful acts weren't restrained by their superior officers, officers who should know better but have no doubt witnessed even worse. These men were simply following orders.

My fear, Aimée, is that more and more often the necessary restraint will be missing, and the line between civilized and uncivilized behavior will be crossed. And once that line is crossed, it cannot be undone. But I write of things that will alarm you, which I mustn't do.

The boredom and monotony have been less here, as we have been assigned to security details, but the further we get into the summer, the fewer problems we encounter. Each day I must lead a group of men to a different town or village and carry out an inventory of all that pertains to the local government, all the employees, the elected officials. It won't surprise me if some day we're required to make an inventory of the inhabitants of the cemetery! And then come the reports. When I return to quarters I must type up my report and file 15 copies! At least no one is shooting at us.

I hear interesting rumors, each one associated with its own expert—someone who knows someone, who knows someone at headquarters. If the army had no rumors, it would have nothing. One week's rumor has it we're staying put and will be assigned to build schools, the next week's rumor has it we're off to Paris. Others have us returning to Germany, with the English about to surrender. Those who don't believe that have us heading to Calais to invade England.

My favorite rumor at the moment is that we shall head north and invade Sermaize-les-Bains, forced to remain encamped there for the duration to provide aid and comfort to the "helpless" inhabitants. But an even more wonderful rumor—possibly not a rumor at all—is that I may get a week-long furlough in September!

I hope your father is right about your mother. Perhaps it's best you not ask her what she thinks about our writing to each other. I'm sure I say this because I want so much for your mother to like me. It is natural for a mother to protect her young, and no mother can be blamed for that. My mother would do no different. After all, you're no longer a child, despite how she may see you.

But enough of that. Remember I think of you often and I hope the rumor about a week's furlough is true. You do want me to come if I can, don't you? If it's true, I shall travel by train. As dearly as I have ever clung to anything in my life, I cling to the memory of our stroll and stolen kiss. As each day flows into the next, I know that brings me one day closer to seeing you again.

I remain tenderly yours,

Hans

▪▪▪▪▪

Sermaize-les-Bains
Thursday
22 August 1940

Dearest Hans,

Your letters arrived finding me in good spirits. You write of things that are distressing, but not knowing what is to happen to you is distressing enough, so do not change a thing and keep writing whatever you wish to write.

Yes, I want you to come when you have a furlough. How could you think I might not?

I'm relieved to learn you had nothing to do with the fighting at Dunkerque. I won't bring it up, but if someone does mention it I will be sure to set them straight. You must understand that many French people harbor strong feelings about the Germans, but I can't help that. I for one am developing strong feelings for one German in particular! Also, I favor the rumor about Sermaize-les-Bains, but is it too much to hope for?

Very well, I will take your advice and not ask Maman if she approves of our writing. I know Papa will be on my side even if she doesn't like it. At night I hear their discussions, arguments really, that hint at serious conflict, but I can never comprehend what they say. It may have to do with the increased demands on Papa for our chickens and eggs.

In one of your letters you mentioned you had heard from your parents. Have you any news of Peter? One day I hope to meet him and learn how they live on a U-boat. And Hans, you must promise me that you write no less to them just because you write to me.

During the day on my walk to and from work, I sometimes see many airplanes fly overhead. I have no idea how high they are, but they seem so determined to reach their destination. From the BBC broadcasts, I cannot tell if they are German, or perhaps British. Papa also does not know. They appear so distant, it's hard to remember there are people inside directing their course and actions. At night, lying in bed with the window open, I can sometimes hear the steady hum of planes overhead although I can't see them. At times it sounds as if the sky teems with them, but I don't know. I wonder if they are safer than the soldier on the ground, but then I remind myself they're headed into battle, while you're safe in Digoin, so then I quit worrying.

Claire keeps asking about you and what it is you write. She may be asking to make me believe she hasn't found your letters and read them all, or she may ask truly from curiosity. I hope I have them well hidden, but with just so many places to conceal them, how can one know for sure? Whatever the case, don't even think of not writing or not telling me your every thought.

As for Maman, things have been quieter between us, for which I believe I have Papa to thank.

Please let me know as soon as you discover which rumor is true!

Yours with my heartfelt affections,

Aimée

▪▪▪▪▪

Digoin (still)
Monday
9 September 1940

My dearest Aimée,

The rumor is true. A week's furlough—28 September to 6 October! I will travel by train, but I don't yet know the best route. I should arrive in Sermaize-les-Bains on the 28th, probably late in the day. Again, I shall take a room at the hotel so as not to inconvenience your family.

Whenever we have confirmation of one rumor, another is spawned. It seems the security assignments in this region have been completed so the 3.Infanterie-Division may be reassigned. Speculation is rampant about where we'll be sent. It's too much to hope that it will be in the northern sector. Wherever it is, I'll probably know of it by the time I leave 15 days from now.

How I enjoy your letters. Thank you for every one. Jacob is mad with jealousy. He fancies himself such a Casanova, yet he never gets a letter to brag of. And then there is quiet Hans who goes away on furlough, in the country no less, and since his return has been blessed with at least three letters a week. Poor Jacob, he can't stand it!

I'm grateful I can write to you of things I can't share or discuss with Jacob. While he is my best friend, there are things that, as a soldier, I'm unable to mention. Please don't think for a moment I don't trust Jacob, but if he were to repeat some of the things I might say, there could be repercussions. As you read this you must be asking yourself, What is it Hans wants to say? There's a great deal I will tell you one day, but this isn't the time for it yet. Ever since the Polish campaign and our push through Belgium and Luxembourg, I've been feeling unsettled about things I witnessed and reports I heard, and yes, even things that I, as a soldier, have been ordered to do.

After our initial campaign near Kutno, our company was mobilized and on the road. It was a passable road, but at times we encountered curves that slowed our progress. When we moved through one such area, we came upon a farmer grappling with his team of horses and a broken wheel on an empty wagon. As he struggled to unharness his team, more and more vehicles arrived to block the road, and his horses spooked. A squad of our men surrounded the wagon, lifted it off the road, and dumped it in the ditch.

The farmer protested to the nearest officer, an oberleutnant. The oberleutnant went over to the farmer, took out his Luger pistol, pointed it first at the farmer's chest, then whipped around and shot the horses. Both horses, dead. He flicked a spot of mud off his uniform after he holstered his pistol, got back into the troop transport, and ordered the convoy to proceed. To this day I'm surprised that farmer is still alive—if he is—and have often wondered why. Could it be because there were witnesses? Perhaps. Why do such things happen? I feel a coward for failing to act. The poor farmer did nothing more than happen to be in the wrong place at the wrong time.

While we were in Paris, Jacob encountered an old friend of his, I think from the 225.Infanterie-Division. When that division was crossing the Schipdonk Canal in May, the road over the canal was packed with refugees, the bridge being defended by the Belgians. The division was under orders to continue its drive west into Belgium in pursuit of the British, and in the confusion, dozens of civilians were shot. Jacob said that several were herded into a church, then someone tossed a grenade amongst them, killing many. Why? This is senseless and accomplishes nothing for "the Glory of the Fatherland."

How can such things be? What did these people do to deserve such treatment? I'm proud to be a German, but not so proud, at times, to be a German soldier. Knowing of the growing trust between the two of us, I feel confident one day you will help me understand it all. The thing I fear most is that you should ever think ill of me.

I wish I had the courage to say more, but enough for now. Let me tell you, instead, how I long for the end of the month. Is it too much to ask that we find many more opportunities for time alone together, for long walks, conversation, kisses? This may be my last furlough for several months, given the stubbornness of that chubby little Churchill.

I can't wait to see you on the 28th. Until then, I remain

Yours with my devotion,

Hans

CHAPTER 12

"Good afternoon, Hauptmann Krüger." The clerk at the hotel remembered Hans from his visit in July. "Here to see the Ferrands again?"

"Yes, for a few days." When it came to rumors Hans found the similarities between the army and the civilian world amusing. How long would it take for the town's citizenry to learn he was back? One day, two at the most? He decided to satisfy neither the clerk's nor the town's curiosity.

"Henri, your name's Henri, is it not?"

"Oui. Is there something else I can assist you with?"

"Yes, would it be possible to have the same room I had last time? I enjoyed being able to look out onto the main street."

The clerk pushed the register toward him again, along with the desk pen. "My pleasure. Would there be anything else?" He handed over the room key.

"No. No, thank you." Hans took the narrow stairs two at a time. No need to help me, just go ahead and tell everyone you know I'm in town again.

Hans contemplated stopping to buy flowers, then thought better of it. He realized it would be more polite to telephone first, but he couldn't resist the possibility of surprising Aimée. If she weren't at home, it could be a good opportunity to spend more time with her parents, especially Mme. Ferrand. That was one ally he very much needed but hadn't yet secured.

He had the route to the Ferrand's committed to memory now, and he had even discovered a shortcut. As the farmhouse came into view, he noticed movement at one of the windows. The curtain hadn't stopped trembling when Aimée burst from the front door at a run. Then, just before she reached him, she stopped short. Why? He didn't know, but not caring who was watching, he took both her hands in his and drew her close.

"You know I want to kiss you, Aimée, don't you? It's all I think about."

The color had risen to her cheeks. "Please, wait for a better time. Oh, I'm so glad to see you!"

They drew apart so they could take in the happy sight of each others' face, then Aimée locked elbows with him to escort him into the house.

"Maman! Papa! Hans is here!"

Claire came running first, and stood in front of him, not sure what to say or do. She rested on one foot, then the other.

Hans made a small bow and took her hand. "Claire, how nice to see you again. And don't you look pretty today."

Claire ducked her head, examining her dress. "This old thing? It's just one I wear when I help Papa gather eggs. I'd have changed if I'd known—"

At that moment Elsie Ferrand appeared. Hans stood up straight and offered his hand. "Bonjour, Madame. It's a pleasure to see you again. I hope you are well?" He wished he could have thought of something more engaging, anything.

She seemed not to have noticed his outstretched hand. "Thank you, it's good of you to stop by."

Damnation. She's discouraging me, speaking as if I'm just passing through.

A sudden current of cool air flowed from the kitchen as André came in the back door.

"Hans, my boy, how are you?" he called from the sink, where he was washing his hands. "I hope you had a good journey. How long will you be staying in Sermaize-les-Bains?"

At the same instant Elsie called out, "André!" and Aimée chided him. "Papa!"

André ignored the reprimand and carried the towel he'd wiped his hands on with him into the front room. "Hans, please forgive my lack of manners. It is nice to see you. Now then, tell us what you've been up to."

Both Aimée and her mother shot looks at him as if warning him not to monopolize the conversation. "You see," he said, unfazed, "I couldn't help but notice when the mailman leaves our mail, there's often a letter for Aimée. She won't let me read them, nor will she read them to me. So you must tell me what you've been up to, or else you'll have to write *me* a letter."

Aimée got up and went to her father, slipping her arm around his waist and planting a kiss on his cheek. "Papa, you're such a tease."

Claire was all but dancing with excitement. "Maman, please, may Hans stay for supper?"

Elsie pursed her lips, then said, "I suppose we have enough to go around."

Hans was beginning to fear he'd never win this battle when Aimée edged close to take his hand. "We'll see everyone later, because Hans and I are going for a walk. Maman, don't worry, we'll be back soon."

Hans held the door open then followed Aimée out and closed it behind them. "Let's go this way for a change." He indicated a different direction from the walk they'd taken before.

Aimée slipped her hand through the crook of his elbow. "Oh, Hans, I can't tell you how happy I am to see you. I thought today would never come."

He didn't answer right away, just nestled her hand close to his side as they walked. At the end of the field, when they came to a low stone wall, he stepped across first then helped her over, giving her hand an extra squeeze.

"Well?" she said.

He exhaled, letting his shoulders drop. "I feel just the same. I was hungry for the sight of you. I must say, though"—he made a rueful face—"your mother doesn't seem to have been pining for the sight of me."

Aimée shook her head. "She'll come around, you'll see. No one could help growing fond of someone as dear as you."

As they joined the road Hans noticed a wild rosebush in the ditch. He stopped, got out his pocketknife and cut a blossom, stripped off its thorns and presented it to Aimée. "Beauty pays tribute to beauty."

She held the rosebud as she searched his eyes. "I hardly know what to say. I am just an ordinary girl, you know."

"Not to me. Nothing ordinary about you. Chérie, you're the most extraordinary girl I've ever known." He glanced back toward the house. "Come, though, let's walk a bit faster, around this next bend in the road."

Happy to oblige, she picked up her pace and walked on with him in silence for several minutes until the house was no longer in sight. They had to step to the side of the road to let a man driving a farm cart pass.

"Bonjour, Monsieur Pelletier," Aimée called out. Without so much as a glance, he replied, "Bonjour, Aimée."

"That was our neighbor, the one who lives over there." When she finished pointing she said, "You wrote you would know of your orders by now. Have they come?"

He stared off into the distance. "They have, though I assure you they're not of my choosing." He brought her hand to his lips, turned it over for a kiss, and as he let the tip of his tongue touch her palm for an instant, he heard her quick intake of breath.

"It's not good, is it?" She pressed the kissed hand to her chest.

"I doubt you'll think so. We're being mobilized, most likely returning to Germany."

"Mon Dieu. When?"

"After I get back to Digoin, but I don't know when." He drew her to him and held her close, inhaling the fragrance of her. "You mustn't worry, chérie. I'm sure it's just a staging operation, to let us take on replacements and continue drilling."

He didn't tell her it was also to compensate for losses suffered in the Polish and French campaigns. "Nobody knows the specific date or destination, but it's reasonable to assume we'll be pulling out of France."

He turned his head, pressing hers to his chest, and spoke into her hair. "Oh God, Aimée, this war. Why do such things have to be?"

He could feel her body respond to him. The air around them seemed electrified, demanding more than a careless embrace.

"It's awful, I know." She gazed up at him. "But let's not spoil what we have in this moment. You're here with me, we care for each other, and that one thing seems like a miracle to me. I have to believe there will be better days."

"Stupid me, I've made you worry enough for one day." He released her and tried to smile but couldn't quite manage it. "Look, if we don't return soon, you know that a certain lady will be sending out search parties. Time to turn back, yes?"

Aimée stood motionless, then stretched on tiptoe to take his face between her hands. When Hans bent to kiss her it was a long kiss, a deep kiss, a pledge sealed with no need for words. They held each other as if they could never bear to let go. Their world would never be the same again, that much they knew. When they drew apart they embraced again before retracing their steps toward the farm.

"Aimée, these are feeble words for what I want to tell you, but I thank you for your letters and for what you've given me. I've never known such joy." He skipped ahead a step, then turned around and smiled. "Do you know, I can tell you to the very last detail what you were wearing when we first met?"

"Hans Krüger, do you expect me to believe that?"

"It's true. I've had eighty-four days to relive it again and again in my mind."

"Very well, then, what color was my blouse?"

"White with a small blue print pattern, whatever you call it." He kept walking backward, facing her. "You were beautiful. Your hair was pulled back and tied with a blue ribbon. The ends of your hair reached to the middle of your shoulder blades, and you held your body as straight as one of those irises I brought your mother."

"Didn't you notice anything else, eighty-four days ago?"

"Oh yes, Claire had two arms and two legs." He grinned, having fun. "So did your mother and so did your father. Quite amazing."

"I'm astonished. You are the clever one!"

They were back at the stone wall, and as Hans helped her over it again, she let go of his hand and blew him a kiss.

The hotel clerk no longer asked Hans questions. Like most in Sermaize-les-Bains, his presence was accepted as a necessary evil. Every day Hans found some opportunity to walk to the Ferrand's farm, often helping André with chores until Aimée came home from her job. At other times he remained in his hotel room to write his parents in Berlin, or stopped in the café for an apéritif or a coffee and a pastry. He visited the church and took time to say a prayer and light a candle for his brother, and when he discovered a bookshop, he browsed its shelves and bought a book about the various regions of France.

While it seemed far too short to him, his furlough at least afforded enough visits, shared meals, and country walks to cement his and Aimée's relationship. As he came to know the family better, feeling almost as if they were his family too, Hans began to worry about them. He kept harking back to his father's letter from André, the one written twenty years before that he'd read in his father's study, telling of Elsie's birth and adoption.

In Germany, he knew, anti-Semitism was on the rise. When Hans had read, in 1938, the "Law for the Protection of German Blood and German Honor," he gave it little thought, knowing it was required reading for all officers of the Wehrmacht. At the time, he thought it made perfect sense, since it was what the Führer decreed. His fellow officers never discussed the ban on marriage between Jews and other Germans, most likely because the Reich Minister of the Interior enforced harsh sanctions for violations of the ban. But now things were different.

What if someone discovers I'm involved with a woman of Jewish blood? And why did we need fifteen copies of the security files? Gestapo, no doubt. When he considered that, Hans realized how devious it was of the Führer to separate the Wehrmacht from the Gestapo. Suspicions had been raised about the Gestapo, but because no one ever knew for sure exactly what its role was, separating the two was brilliant. What better way to undermine the conscience of the good soldiers of the Wehrmacht?

While he was with Aimée on the last day of his leave she commented that his silences were longer than usual. "Hans, what are you thinking?"

"Nothing, nothing at all. Just wondering when I'll see you again."

She crossed her arms on her chest. "Hmph! I don't call that nothing. So, when *will* we see each other again?"

He looked into her eyes to see that they gleamed with tears. He reached for his handkerchief to dab them away, then held her face between his hands and kissed first the tip of her nose, then her lips. When she melted into his arms he felt an ache as sharp as a knife between his ribs.

"I don't know, chérie. I wish I did, but I don't."

"Will you write to me every day?"

"I will write every single day to tell you how much I love you." The words she had waited for were out, springing from him unbidden. It was true, and he was ready to claim it in all its fullness. "My God, Aimée, you have no idea how powerful my love for you is. I love you more than I've ever loved anything or anyone in my life. Can you say the same?"

She nodded, her heart too full to speak.

Knowing he must get back to catch the evening train, several times he tried to leave but found doing so too painful. Each time he gathered Aimée into his arms and kissed her again and again, afire with longing, until at last she managed to pull away.

"You must go, Hans. You can't be late getting back to your camp."

"I know." He was on the verge of tears himself. "Aimée, believe me when I tell you, I will come back to you. I promise."

"I believe you, Hans. I do. Oh, my love, please be safe! I fear for you so much!"

Hans kept her in sight as he walked, waving all the while. When he reached the main road and Aimée was out of sight, he turned to plod on toward the town, retrieved his handkerchief, and added his own tears to hers.

CHAPTER 13

"Goddamn it, Oberleutnant!" Hans shouted, "Get that machine gun in position and hold it. Hold it now, or I will shoot you myself!"

Things had changed on the eastern front. The initial Russian response to the German attack and declaration of war had been weak. On 22 June 1941, the German army, comprising 3,000,000 soldiers divided into three groups, had invaded Russia. This concentrated surprise attack had been in the planning stages for more than six months, and at first the Germans gained the upper hand, routing the Soviets in Bialystok, Minsk, Raseiniai, Brody, Smolensk, Uman, and Kiev. In the course of these battles the Russian army lost more than half a million soldiers, leading the Germans to expect continued success.

But now the hated invaders were threatening the country's capital—Moscow—to meet a Slavic tenacity fueled by fierce love for Mother Russia. Moreover, the Soviet troops were made bold by the prospect of fighting with their favorite ally—winter.

Their original firing line should have given Hauptmann Krüger's company a significant advantage against the Russians, yet despite their numerical superiority over the Red army and a new firing position, three German assaults had been repelled. Stalled just thirty kilometers beyond the outskirts of Moscow, with German casualties mounting faster than at any time since the third week of June, Hans began to doubt the German soldiers' resolve.

He retreated to the command post to clarify his orders with a question for his superior officer. "Major, where is the Luftwaffe we were assured would lead us to victory?" Unable to make sense of the confusion, he slammed his fist down on the table. "These goddamn Russians are decimating my men!"

"Hauptmann Krüger, are you questioning your orders?"

"No Major, I'm not. We're supposed to be a mobilized division, yet at the moment there's nothing mobile about us." This was a battle of nerves he could never win, but having already lost a third of his command, he considered his questions justified.

The major glared. "Hauptmann Krüger, I don't have to remind you, German field tactics do not call for our tanks to make a frontal assault on known tank defenses. Once again, I'm telling you to advance your troops and be prepared to deploy your anti-tank personnel."

"Major, my men need to know they're being supported. Where's the Luftwaffe, where's the artillery we were promised?"

He got no response from the Major, who'd returned to an intense study of his charts.

"Major, I must protest—"

"Do not try my patience further, Hauptmann Krüger. DISMISSED!"

Was the man a coward or just an idiot? Probably both. Close to despair but seeing no other option, Hans saluted and returned to his command.

Hans removed his field glasses from their leather case to survey the battlefield. He could make out three well-entrenched machine-gun emplacements, two on his left and one to his right. Several bodies in front of each position attested to the bravery of the German soldiers. Most lay still, though a few were moving, and in between the bursts of machine-gun fire the agonizing screams and moans of a dying company reached his ears.

A medic had struggled to aid the first group of wounded, but now he too lay prone, dead, over the body of a grenadier. A pool of blood had oozed from his lifeless, bullet-riddled corpse. It was clear this well-entrenched line of Russians was hell-bent on defending their capital and their homeland, with the advantage of having dug in their defenses before the freeze. And now cruel Father Frost had caught the Germans by surprise.

Hans handed his binoculars to a NCO. "Unteroffizier, do you see that elongated area perpendicular to our lines that's free of bullet craters?"

"I'm not sure, Hauptmann Krüger."

Hands on hips, Hans considered his alternatives. "Keep looking. I think we might be able to make a crawling advance on those machine-gun nests."

"Yes, Hauptmann."

When the NCO saluted him Hans had to struggle with himself not to shout. "Unteroffizier." He took a deep breath. "Unless you want to get us both shot, never, I mean *never* salute me in the field. Snipers love to have someone point out their targets for them. Got it?"

"Yes, Hauptmann. I'm sorry, sir." The man's hand seemed to want to fly outward again, though he restrained it.

"Now look again, see if you can make out what I'm talking about."

"Yes, sir. I'm sorry, sir." The unteroffizier studied the field then handed the glasses back to Hans. "Sir, I think we can get to within a few meters. One or two stick grenades and we might break through."

"Ja, with a little luck, we just might." Hans stamped his feet, so cold he couldn't feel them. They'd need not just a little luck, but a very great deal of it. He looked around. "Where's the oberleutnant?" As he asked the question he spotted the man, dead, lying amid the other soldiers' corpses.

"Unteroffizier," Hans said, "come with me." The few men left in his squad were waiting to hear his orders. "Mueller and I are going to crawl up that slight depression. When you see us give the signal, start laying down covering fire and don't let up."

"Yes Hauptmann!" one of the grenadiers said.

"And for God's sake, try not to shoot us."

With hand signals to the squad on the right, Hans indicated his plan of attack between the two squads. Choosing the lowest spot to begin their advance, he and the unteroffizier crept beneath a withering canopy of machine-gun and rifle fire. If I survive this, he told himself, I vow to find that major and shoot him. Hans knew he'd lied to Aimée about having no fear in battle. Now, as round after round whizzed less than half a meter above their heads at nearly 800 meters per second, he was as terrified as he'd ever been in his life. And yet he kept crawling forward.

When they were within ten meters of the two Russian machine-gun nests on the left, Hans halted his advance to check on the unteroffizier.

"Mueller," he whispered, "wie geht's?"

A hoarse whisper came back. "Still here, Hauptmann. Just scared shitless."

"Jawohl, aren't we all." Hans managed to catch his eye. "Keep your wits about you and your head down. I'll activate this stick grenade, then on the count of three we'll charge the first machine gun. Got it?"

"Ja, Hauptmann." Mueller's voice shook.

Hans checked his rifle and laid the grenade alongside his right shoulder. Then, taking a deep breath, he activated the grenade, counted to three, and tossed it into the machine-gun nest. His missile launched, the instant the grenade erupted he sprang up like a cat on a field mouse and began firing into the machine-gun nest. One Russian was slumped over his weapon, motionless as if napping. Another was stunned, bleeding from a neck wound. A third Russian was just raising his rifle when a bullet from Hans' Karabiner 98k tore into his chest, knocking him backward so hard it flung his hands out and up. Not waiting to see if he was dead, Hans crouched down to advance on the other machine-gun nest from behind.

Alerted to the action on their flank, the Soviets in the second nest were trying to reposition their machine gun when Mueller appeared, killing all three with the same number of shots. First to die was the Russian who'd attempted to fire the machine gun, a single bullet placed in the forehead beneath his helmet's rim. His other two shots found their targets in two Russian hearts.

It seemed to Hans he was sweating chunks of ice. "So far so good, Mueller. Next move, we slip behind this knoll and take out the machine gun on the right. GO!"

At Hans' signal, as he and Mueller attacked, both German squads stormed the Russian line of defense. Quick to react, the Russians poured reinforcements in from both sides of the breach to repel what was about to become a German foothold in their line. At the same moment a Red soldier popped up behind a mound of dirt firing his rifle, Hans and Mueller let loose a hail of gunfire. The sniper was thrown back two meters, dead.

But when Hans tried to stand, he staggered. A sudden escape of air from his lungs made it hurt to breathe, impossible to get air into his chest. The hand he touched to his chest came away wet, an unfamiliar kind of wetness, neither hot nor cold. My God, he thought, I'm bleeding. His vision blurred. He'd been cold before and was used to it, but now he felt as if someone had buried him in snow. His breathing became so shallow he couldn't draw a breath without feeling like he was suffocating. His heart raced. Everything around him was turning gray, sounds were fading. Before he lost consciousness he was thinking this must have been how Napoleon and his army felt in the winter of 1812 when they knew their siege outside Moscow had failed.

A faint cry of "Medic!" was the last thing he heard.

CHAPTER 14

Her chin propped on one hand, Aimée sat at the kitchen table watching the food congeal on her plate. Elsie felt helpless, unable to find words that would comfort her child. Seeing her daughter consumed by such grief tore at her own heart. Without a doubt, for Aimée uncertainty was harder to live with than bad news. As she had done every day for weeks, Elsie pulled a chair next to Aimée's and massaged her shoulders, finding no resistance. The girl's body yielded as if she didn't care which way they moved. Her face was a mask of resignation. The anxiety, then the despair that had once been present was long gone, replaced by a blank and lifeless stare. The gray eyes that once had sparkled were as cloudy as a February day, and she seemed chilled, as if no amount of clothing could bring her warmth.

"Ma fille, don't you think the fact you've heard nothing is a good thing?"

Elsie had said this so often she found herself beginning to believe it. She hadn't believed it when she said it first in December, but a month later she didn't know what else to say. After all, it was possible hearing nothing meant Hans was alive. If he'd been killed, wouldn't his parents have got word to the Ferrands somehow? But no word had come.

Aimée sighed. "Maman, how can you say that?" She was again toying with a stray strand of hair, a gesture that was now habitual. "It's been over a year since I've seen him and his last letter was weeks and weeks ago." The despair in her voice hung in the room like a thick fog.

Elsie searched her mind and came up with something new. "Eh bien, Aimée, as much as I hate to say this"—she got up to busy herself putting dishes away—"perhaps the silence means he's a prisoner of war."

Her daughter's voice became a wail. "Oh, Maman, I beg you, even if you think such things, please don't say them." She picked up the table napkin to blot her puffy eyes.

"But in many ways, that would be better."

"A prisoner of war of the Russians! Tell me, just how could that be better?"

"If he were taken prisoner, he'd no longer be fighting. No one would be shooting at him." Elsie turned from the cupboard and hesitated a long moment before she said, "Don't you think if he were a prisoner, they'd be feeding him, taking care of him?" She avoided saying what kind of feeding and care it could be in Russian hands.

When Aimée lifted her head and turned to her mother's embrace, for the first time Elsie detected a glimmer of hope in her eyes. "Oh, Maman," she sobbed, "I do love him so."

Elsie caressed her daughter's locks and rested her cheek against Aimée's dark hair. "I know you do, ma fille. I know." She tried to absorb at least some of Aimée's pain, having long since suppressed her reservations about Hans. Her daughter's happiness was her greatest concern, her own safety insignificant by comparison.

She contemplated telling her daughter her secret, just as she had a thousand times in the past, yet once again decided there was no point in sharing that knowledge. Day after day she felt as if she was walking around inside a veil of guilt. Would things be easier if Hans were truly dead? Is he a Nazi or not? If he knew we were Jewish, would he turn us over to the Gestapo? And how could he know? More and more of the time now her helpless feelings threatened her, making her distant and silent when her family needed her support. May the good Lord forgive me, but sometimes I do wish he were dead. Yet that wasn't the answer either, for there were thousands of Nazis, Gestapo, thousands of unknown others who might discover the fatal secret at any time.

"Major Krüger." Hans was aware of someone speaking his name and touching his arm. He thought the voice had said Major, but he wasn't hearing very well. Krüger, though, he knew he'd heard that. When he attempted to move, an intense pain in his chest made him draw his right arm back to where it had been. He grimaced when he opened his eyes and tried to focus on the light.

"Major Krüger, can you hear me?" There it was again, that voice calling him Major.

Hans moaned, then said, "Ja. Ja, I can hear you. Where am I?"

"In a hospital."

"Where?"

"Berlin, the Stubenrauch-Krankhaus. I'm the surgeon who operated on you."

Hans could make no sense of it. "The SS hospital?"

The man at his beside replied. "That's correct. An exception was made for you as a consequence of your military record and your service to the Führer."

The surgeon reached for Hans' wrist and laid a finger over the pulse point. "Good, good, your heart rate has come down." A nurse handed him a clipboard, and after studying it he added, "Your fever has broken as well. This is very good."

Hans winced, feeling something being pulled away from the skin of his chest. At first he couldn't see what it was, but then the surgeon handed the nurse some bloodstained gauze after sniffing it.

"Do you remember being shot?"

"Ja, I think I do. I remember the Russian standing in front of me, raising his rifle, then falling back. I couldn't breathe. I had a crushing pain in my chest."

The surgeon worked to remove the whole dressing. All at once a particular touch of those probing fingers made Hans gasp.

"This is coming along, not healed altogether, but better. The medic stabilized you first, then got you to the field hospital, the Kriegslazarett, where you underwent an emergency operation. The first operation—"

"First operation?"

"Yes, the first one was to control the bleeding and pack your wound. You were shot in the chest and had to be sedated to the point you probably don't remember anything. A second operation was done a week later to remove the shattered rib, the packing, and to control additional bleeding. Since then you've been quite delirious with fever."

Hearing soft footsteps near the bed, Hans turned his head to see a nurse. "Might I have a sip of water, please?"

"Of course." She had it there in seconds, with a glass straw for him to sip through.

He laid his head back on the pillow. "Is that all that happened to me?"

"No, there's more," the surgeon told him. "You were transferred here and we had to operate a third time because an abscess had formed close to your heart. We had to irrigate your chest cavity as well as remove a portion of your right lung. Do you understand what I'm saying?"

Hans nodded.

"You're very lucky. In most men, that much infection would be fatal."

"How long have I been here?"

"Three weeks."

"Three weeks? God in heaven, what day is it?"

The surgeon glanced at the nurse. "5 February 1942. Thursday."

"1942! That can't be. Do my parents know I'm here?"

"Yes," the nurse said. "They've been here many times to see you. We have instructions to phone them with any news about you. I will call them this instant, Major Krüger, to let them know you're awake."

"No. Hauptmann," Hans said. "Hauptmann Krüger."

The surgeon corrected him. "She's right, it's now Major Krüger. Along with your awards of a Silver Wound Badge and a Knight's Cross, you've been promoted to the rank of major. Something you can be quite proud of. Your decorations and rank insignia are to be presented to you while you're here."

Hans was taking this astonishing information in when the surgeon said, "Tell me, Major, who is Aimée?"

The question was so direct and unexpected Hans felt perspiration seeping onto his brow. "No one important, only a girl I met in France." Careful, you're in an SS hospital. Be calm, take your time. "Why do you ask?"

"Just curious. You often moaned in pain, usually at night. Whenever it happened we had to increase your sedation, not wanting you to become agitated. You sometimes seemed to be speaking in your sleep to an Aimée, now and then to someone's mother."

Hans forced a smile. “Our minds can play strange tricks under the influence of drugs.” He prayed he sounded calm. “I often saw it on the battlefield when a wounded man was given morphine. Have I been given morphine?”

“Quite a bit,” the surgeon said. “It probably was just the morphine.”

Within an hour the nurse was stroking Hans’ arm in an attempt to awaken him. “Major Krüger, you have visitors.” She directed a stern look at Konrad and Greta Krüger. “A short while only. He needs his rest.”

Hans’ mother stood motionless over his bed and began to weep. He looked up, took her hand, and said in a hoarse whisper, “Mother.”

Konrad Krüger stood beside his wife and reached to touch his son’s leg. “Son, this is a great relief. Your mother and I, we were beside ourselves with worry. We’d heard nothing for weeks.”

For their sakes Hans did his best to gather his strength. “Everything’s fine.” He straightened his body, trying hard not to wince. “I’ve been given excellent care. I hope you won’t worry further, because they tell me my recovery should be complete.”

He motioned for his father to shut the door, then said in a confidential tone, “Father, have you written to Aimée?”

The response was a shake of the head. Konrad found a chair and moved it so he could sit close to the side of the bed. “I didn’t write, son, for a very good reason.” He glanced at the door to ensure it was closed before going on with his muted explanation.

"At the end of 1938 I had planned a business trip to Paris. I intended to travel to Sermaize-les-Bains to call on André and his family. You probably won't recall, but it was the week after Ernst vom Rath was murdered in Paris. The Gestapo had already questioned me about some Jewish writers who'd submitted manuscripts to our press, then one of our editors, also a Jew, disappeared.

"I went to his apartment to check on him and was questioned again. On the morning I was to leave for France, I first went to the office to collect what I would need for the business meeting, and on the way home to pick up my suitcase I became aware of being followed, I believe by the Gestapo."

Before continuing, he lowered his voice further. "I canceled my trip, certain I'd have been followed all the way to Paris. I came home that day and wrote one final letter to André, explaining I could no longer write and telling him I was afraid for him and his family. The truth is I was afraid for our family, too."

Hans could tell how painful this admission was for his father. The fear he detected in his father's eyes was a surprise. "Hans, I burned all the letters, I had to."

"I know."

Konrad's eyes widened. "You know what?"

"I know you stopped writing. Monsieur Ferrand told me he hadn't heard from you since 1938." He gathered his breath to steel his nerve. "One day before I left for the army, you and I were in your study discussing my plans when you pulled open the drawer where the letters had always been." Hans paused again before he said, "I could see they were gone."

His father took a moment to grasp the significance of what Hans had just told him. "You read them, then?"

"I did, Father, I read them many times, when you were out."

"All of them?"

Hans blinked. "Yes, all. I understand your fear, and I must tell you I believe it's justified."

"Do the Ferrands know that you know? Does Aimée?"

"No, I'm certain they do not. You may be sure I've never spoken of it."

"Good. The day may come, though, when—"

Konrad jumped when the surgeon burst through the door. He stood to offer his hand. "Konrad Krüger," he said. "This is my son."

The surgeon shook his hand. "A pleasure to meet you, sir. And this is your wife?"

Greta, who had stood back from the bedside, smiled. "Doctor, we are most grateful for your care. Thank you for giving our son back to us."

All business, the surgeon didn't return her smile. "You may be very proud of your son. He has served his Führer with distinction, but now"— he checked his watch—"I must be off and Major Krüger must have his rest. Good day to you." And the door closed behind him.

Before his parents left, Hans touched his fingers to his lips then held his hand toward them as if to pass a kiss. Konrad took his hand and held it. "I will take care of that matter for you. If you need anything, any writing paper, anything, let me know. You've made us very proud, Hans, I trust you know that."

Greta bent over the bed to kiss her son's forehead. "God keep you, Hans. I shall continue to pray for you night and day." When she patted his shoulder her voice broke. "It's terrible you were wounded so. But you're no longer on the front lines now, and for that I shall always be thankful."

Despite his gratitude for their abiding love, Hans found no words to say.

Once his parents were gone the nurse re-entered the room with a syringe. "Time for your pain medicine." Again, the morphine was driven into his muscle, and Hans faded, his mind drifting back into the fog.

"Shoot her, Oberleutnant! Shoot her, I said!"

The oberleutnant stood paralyzed. The look on his face showed he could hear the hauptmann, but he was physically incapable of following the order. They had just burst through the door, the oberleutnant with his rifle raised, the hauptmann behind him, and with one squeeze of a finger the oberleutnant had shot the Polish soldier dead. But now a woman cowered in the corner, against the wall.

The dead man was the very sniper who'd been killing their comrades. The platoon had been making a sweep of the street, concentrating their fire on the window the Pole had been shooting from with such disastrous effect. When they failed to stop him, the hauptmann knew what had to be done, so under covering fire from the platoon he and the oberleutnant made it into the building, up the stairs, and into the front room. The startled Pole had spun around intending to shoot the intruders, but a single round from the oberleutnant's rifle found its mark.

He was about to pull the trigger a second time when he saw that the person in the corner was a woman. She had no weapon, posed no obvious threat. Why she was there at all they didn't know, but the hauptmann was yelling, ordering him to shoot her.

He froze.

The woman's eyes darted around as if searching for an exit. In those last seconds she had just two choices: jump out the window or dash for the door. When her terrified gaze settled on the door, the oberleutnant aimed his rifle in that direction, cutting off her escape. The look on her face changed to absolute fear in an instant, her eyes black holes. She stood still, seeming to know her fate, when the hauptmann first shouted his order.

"Shoot her, Oberleutnant! Shoot her, I said!"

When the oberleutnant didn't move, the woman stretched out her hands, palms forward, pleading in Polish for her life.

Again, the hauptmann barked out his order. "I command you to shoot her!"

Oberleutnant Hans Krüger fired, and the woman crumpled. The life draining from her body seemed to be transferred to Hans. Before running from the room and downstairs into the street, he gave the soldier a violent kick to confirm he was dead and was about to do the same to the dying woman, when he staggered.

The coat about the dying woman's waist fell open exposing a belly that rolled with the obvious movement of her doomed, unborn child.

Berlin
Friday
6 February 1942

My dearest love,

I can't tell you how sorry I am you've had no word from me in all these months. Please forgive me. It seems forever since I held you in my arms. Oh, Aimée, I miss you so, it's as if I'm missing a piece of my heart.

First of all, I'm fine, at least I am now. I was wounded in the fighting outside Moscow and had to undergo three different operations. The last one was to clear an infection and remove part of my lung. I confess at times the pain has been intense, but morphine relieves it. I wish it would relieve the bad dreams and flashbacks, but those also seem to be improving, at least for the moment. I have some fears I may become too dependent on the morphine, but do not worry yourself. The surgeon dismisses these concerns with a wave of his hand.

My writing may be a little shaky, not surprising in view of my wound and the dressings. You'll be relieved to know that I still have the use of all of my limbs. My wound is in the chest, but with time I should recover, good as new. My doctor says it could be several months before I'm able to return to duty, so my challenge for the present is to regain my strength. I'm told I lost a lot of blood, which explains why I'm still somewhat weak.

After being treated at the front I was transferred to the Stubenrauch-Krankhaus, an SS hospital here in Berlin where I am now. I don't know yet how long I will remain here, but I hope after I've improved enough I can be discharged from the hospital to go to my parents' apartment. If you're wondering why I'm at an SS hospital, an exception was made for me on account of my wound and what they say was my bravery in battle. I know a lot about the first, but I don't believe I'm quite as brave as others say.

There isn't a waking hour I don't think of you and I can't wait until I'm able to hold you again. These fifteen months have seemed like fifteen years—far too long. I hope you and your family all are well. Know that I miss you and long to see you with every breath I take.

Do not write to me here at the Stubenrauch-Krankhaus, as I feel sure my mail will be intercepted and I want to be the one to read your loving words, no one else.

For now, I will assume you received my letter and that your feelings for me haven't changed.

Yours till the end of time,

Hans

Hans prayed Aimée would understand and not be alarmed by his request. How ironic, to be here in an SS hospital, not an SS man at all, just one among many millions of soldiers of the Wehrmacht, and the SS knows nothing of my actions in the Polish campaign or of the Ferrands.

He squeezed his eyes shut, longing to erase the loathsome memory forever and push it so deep into the recesses of his mind it could never surface again. Yet somehow he knew he was longing for what could never be.

Konrad was back for his daily visit and had closed the door to the corridor. "Hans, my tiger, anything you'd like me to do for you today?"

"Ja, I have a letter to Aimée. I've told her of my injury, nothing more. I asked that she not write to me here."

"Very wise given that you're in an SS hospital."

"What can you tell me about the progress of the war?"

His father studied his face. "Quite sure you want to know?"

"Oh, yes. I want to know how soon it will all be over."

"Very well, then. The German advance on Moscow was thrown back about two hundred kilometers. Both armies suffered staggering numbers of casualties. The German offensive appears to be stalled. General von Brauchitsch was relieved of his command in December. But here's the biggest news. On 7 December the Japanese attacked the American fleet at Pearl Harbor, in Hawaii."

Hans raised himself higher in the bed. "You don't say! Churchill must have been beside himself with glee to see the Americans goaded into war. But if they're fighting the Japanese, what about Europe?"

"After Pearl Harbor, the Führer declared war on America, so now the Americans are fighting the Japanese in the Pacific and soon, the Germans in Europe, alongside the British and the Russians." He shook his head. "God knows the Führer didn't have to do such a thing, but he did it nevertheless. For the time being the Americans seem more involved in the Far East, as the Japanese have been victorious in all of their campaigns. I think this next year will be crucial."

Footsteps in the corridor moved Hans to pass Aimée's letter to his father. "You will post this for me?"

Konrad tucked the envelope inside his overcoat and stood to leave. "Worry no more, I shall see to it." He laid a hand on his son's shoulder. "We're very thankful you're making such good progress, son. Mother will be so pleased when she can have you back at home."

"I look forward to that myself. Take care, Father. Make sure no one follows you to the post office."

His father nodded and went out.

CHAPTER 15

Sermaize-les-Bains
Wednesday
18 February 1942

Honored Monsieur Krüger,

I am in receipt of your recent remittance and wish to thank you for this payment of the outstanding balance. With sincere hopes that I may serve you in your future business,

Respectfully,
A. Ferrand

CHAPTER 16

While the crisp white sheets on his bed reminded Hans of the mantle of arctic-blown snow that fell the week before the battle for Moscow, he needed more than clean sheets to refresh him. These weeks in his parents' apartment seemed to drag, each day many hours longer than normal.

As Trudy, the nurse charged with overseeing his convalescence, busied herself about his room, Hans watched her every move. Her plain round face bore a degree of sadness, although it seemed unaccustomed to frowns, it was a face that had seen happier times. Calling her stout would be too harsh, plump too generous a word, she looked healthy, strong. If her demeanor weren't subdued he'd have said she was robust. He'd seen little change in her from the moment she began caring for him in March, after his parents brought him from the Stubenrauch-Krankhaus.

The hole in his chest wall was slow to heal, but it did so without further drainage or fevers. For that reason alone he'd been allowed to move to his parents' apartment. His recovery was expected to be complete, so he'd not been discharged from the Wehrmacht, and as soon as his physician deemed him fit he expected to return to active duty. Trudy seemed to believe that making this happen would be her contribution to the Fatherland, and thus far her efforts had been successful. Three months had passed since his discharge, and with spring well on its way toward summer both his strength and color were returning. His spirit would be the last to heal, if it ever did.

He had to say something, though. Couldn't lie there moping all day. With an effort, he said to Trudy, "And how is the Kommandant this morning?"

"Ach, aren't we in a sassy mood! I was beginning to think that hole in your chest let something else escape aside from air."

She went on straightening the articles on the dresser. "I must bring you some fresh water, yet for the life of me I don't know where all this dust comes from. It's shocking!" She swept her hand across the dresser top. "Just look at it!"

"And what do you expect me to do when I get over there to look at it? You must help me dress first."

Her face brightened. "My, it's good to see you getting so frisky. Would this have anything to do with a certain letter you received yesterday?"

"Perhaps."

"And is 'perhaps' a certain fräulein?"

"Yes, if you must know. Her name is Aimée," Hans was surprised at how much he relished the freedom of saying the beloved name aloud. "Now are you happy? You got the information you wanted. I'm sure the Gestapo would be greatly interested in your tactics."

Trudy smiled and paused a moment in her tidying, a hand on her hip. "Who is she, and when did you see her last?"

"Have a seat for a minute and I'll tell you." Hans looked to the chair. "In the autumn of 1940 my division was in France, in the Canal du Centre region. I saw her last just before we were mobilized for the invasion of Russia."

"How did you meet?"

"It's a long story."

"Well, as you know, I'm here all day. I have plenty of time."

Hans considered how much to tell her. Who are you, anyway? I don't even know who you really are. He took a deep breath and began.

"When we were pushing through France we swung south of Reims and past several small towns and villages." He was making part of it up to satisfy her curiosity. "Our convoy was resting along a road beside a farm, and I was standing off to myself. The afternoon was a hot one. At this farm, a man and his two daughters were carrying chickens and putting them into crates, probably to send to market. The older daughter looked to be about twenty years old."

Eager for more, Trudy sat forward in her chair. "Aimée?"

He squirmed, shifting his weight in the bed. "Ja, it was Aimée. Her sister was younger. Anyway, this farmer shouted to me and asked if my men would like some water."

"What did you say to that?"

"I went over to my men, and the first thing I said was they were to get their minds out of the gutter."

Knowing soldiers, Trudy smiled. "But to the farmer, Aimée's father, what did you say to him?"

"I said nothing."

"What do you mean, you said nothing? Did you not accept his offer of water?"

"I did not. I merely thanked him for his offer and sent the men back to their vehicles."

"That can't be all that happened," Trudy said.

Hans was fiddling with his wristwatch, setting the time. "No, not quite. The next thing I did was to ask the oberleutnant to let me see the maps. I studied them, made some notes, and gave the order to move on."

Confident he'd set the hook deep, he waited for her next question before reeling in the line.

"I don't understand. If you said nothing, how did you come to meet her, this Aimée?"

"In July after we settled into our bivouac area some of us were given leave. For me, two weeks. Four of us headed to Paris—by then our troops had occupied the city—and on the way, we stopped off in the town near that farm. Remembering the farmer's kindness, I thought I would walk out to the house, introduce myself, and thank him."

At least part of it was true. He had walked up to the house, and he had introduced himself. "I suppose that family harbors no hostility toward us Germans, because the father invited me for supper. I accepted, and that was when I met Fraülein Aimée. After the meal I invited her to take a stroll with me. It must have been the uniform because afterward she asked if she could write to me. Seeing no harm, I told her she could. I never expected to hear from her, but she surprised me there."

Trudy seemed to be calculating something in her head. "How far was this farm from your camp?"

"Three hundred fifty kilometers or so."

"Three hundred fifty kilometers! You drove that far on the chance of seeing this fräulein again?"

"Well, we were on our way to Paris, after all, and it wasn't much of a detour. Her father had been kind, and as you know, soldiers are always on the lookout for the ladies."

"Ach!" Trudy sighed. "What it is to be young and in love!" She stood up to resume her dusting. "So you found a way to see her again. That was July, and the last time you saw her was in October?"

"Ja, just before we returned to Germany I went back again."

"And went for another stroll?"

"Perhaps."

"Shall you see her again one of these days?"

"Who knows? Before that happens I must be well enough to travel. And if I'm well enough to travel, the Führer may send me to North Africa."

"But this lovely girl, you don't want to see her again?"

"I'm a soldier, and soldiers have a duty to the Fatherland. I may see her again, and if that is to be, fine. But I don't expect it. Now, help me get up and dressed, Frau Kommandant."

Hans looked around the clinic waiting room, wondering about the wounds he saw. Did the sturmbannführer on his right lose his arm from infection, or was it blown off? The man's face was even harsher than most of the Waffen-SS officers one saw. The longer Hans had to keep coming back to the Stubenrauch-Krankhaus for appointments, the more difficult he found it to respect military protocol. The absolute arrogance of these Waffen-SS was unbearable. Even though he and the sturmbannführer were of equivalent rank, it was obvious the man considered himself Hans' superior.

The man examined Hans' uniform with obvious disdain. "Major, did you fight in Russia?" The Waffen-SS officer did not attempt to conceal the contempt in his voice.

Unable to wear his Knight's Cross because the ribbon constricted his throat, Hans realized he had no visible wounds. The man must not have seen his Silver Wound Badge.

"I did for a while," Hans said.

"How long a while?"

"Long enough to get shot in the chest storming a machine-gun nest." Hans turned so the sturmbannführer could see all the decorations on his left breast. "Because the ribbon around my neck makes breathing hard for me, at present I can't wear my Knight's Cross."

The sturmbannführer changed the subject. "While you

were in Russia, did you shoot enough Jews? To kill Russians for the Fatherland is a wonderful thing, but killing filthy Jews is even more glorious."

"Major Krüger?" The receptionist looked at Hans and smiled. "You're next."

Glad to leave this conversation behind, Hans entered the examination room as directed, removed his tunic, and donned the cotton gown to wait for the surgeon. He had no interest in the Nazi reading material strewn about everywhere. Remember to ask him how soon I can travel, he reminded himself, and when can I return to duty?

But that word "duty" triggered horrible and unwelcome thoughts. The unwanted image of the helpless Polish woman flashed into his mind, her terror at knowing he would shoot her, her look of serenity once she had died. He could see her mouth, agape as if to say, "Why are you doing this to me? I did nothing to you." He closed his eyes, counted to ten, held his breath—all strategies that sometimes drove the images away. This time they refused to depart. Why did there have to be movement beneath the coat? Were two lives really taken if only one was breathing the air? That's a stupid question, Hans, you idiot. It's over, it happened, you can't—

"Good morning, Major." The surgeon again. "How are you getting on?"

"Quite well, for the most part."

"Any pain?"

"Some, but only when I move. It almost feels as if something was left behind."

"Yes, this is not uncommon, but your Röntgen film shows no bullets or shrapnel. Have you noticed any drainage from your wound?"

"It's possible. My nurse changes the dressings for me, and

every time she does so her face seems to suggest the wound isn't healing, but she says nothing. Furthermore, she carries the dressings away, so I never see what's there."

"Any foul odor?"

"None."

The surgeon lifted Hans' gown to inspect his wound in silence. He didn't touch it, but instead brought one hand to his chin while staring at the place as if he had magical powers to heal it. Hans could hear the man's fingers rasp against the stubble left from too hurried a shave. When the surgeon dropped the gown he sat down to look Hans in the eye.

"I regret to tell you, Major, I'm not at all happy with your wound. It has failed to close and I can't possibly send you back to your company until it does."

He picked up Hans' chart and flipped through a few pages. "I believe we must perform one more operation to excise the area that refuses to heal. If we proceed with this, you should do well. If we don't, your risk of infection is too great. A wound that breaks down in this location is not good. Neglecting it would be very serious for you."

"Is it infected?"

"There is no infection, but it's not healed, and it should have done so by now."

Hans considered his options. "Tell me, doctor, how confident are you this will work?"

"Very."

Why did I even ask? He's a surgeon. He exudes confidence. "Then go ahead and set a date. The sooner it's done, the sooner I get back to living again."

CHAPTER 17

Hans' recovery from what he hoped would be his last surgery was smoother than anticipated. Even though he wasn't ready for active duty, he persuaded his surgeon to allow him to travel. The change of scenery heightened his enjoyment of the season, such a beautiful, cloudless, fall day that it made him disregard the annoying air raid of the night before. Well after midnight the air raid sirens had signaled the approach of RAF bombers from Britain. Thus far in the war these raids had been infrequent, little more than a nuisance. Whatever their effect, there was little doubt Churchill relished it.

Just outside the main rail hub west of Berlin a British bomb had landed on a critical portion of track. Repair crews were working nonstop to repair the damage while delayed traffic was rerouted. After what seemed hours, the train Hans had taken began to lumber along the steel ribbons that stretched to Frankfurt. He looked at his watch for the fifth time in an hour and tried to forget about the war. At this rate I'll never get there.

As the train swayed back and forth its rhythmic motion seduced him to sleep. Forty minutes west of Berlin they hit a patched section of track and his head snapped forward, jarring him awake. At once he looked up to see he was no longer alone. Had he drooled on his uniform as he napped? He ran a hand across his chin and glanced down, observing no damp spots. Reassured, he turned his attention to the man in the opposite seat who was staring at him like a wolf stalking its prey.

The stranger brushed at his lapel. "I hope you have no objection, I closed the window. The soot began blowing in after we rounded a turn."

"No, no objection."

The man went on staring. "Paris?"

"I beg your pardon?"

"Are you traveling to Paris?"

Hans found the man's tone disagreeable and intrusive. The train was going to Frankfurt, why ask about Paris?

"Yes, as a matter of fact."

"Have you been to Paris before?"

Hans began to believe he should find another seat. His upbringing had taught him to dislike and even spurn strangers who asked personal questions. Who was the man, anyhow? Had he been in the Berlin station? He must have boarded the train after it left Berlin or else moved to this compartment after they were under way. Hans glanced around. No other suitcase than his own.

Dressed like a businessman, the man didn't act like one. Businessmen weren't intent on studying everything in front of them. Most read a newspaper or kept to themselves, content to watch the scenery pass. A fellow such as a salesman might want to chat; engaging and approachable was how salesmen were. But this man carried no sample case, no brochures.

With stolen glances, Hans continued to study him, noting that he wore a gold chain around one wrist. His dark hair was cropped close, he was clean-shaven. Like his suit, the hat and coat on the seat beside him were black. Jewelry, and too much black. Without a doubt, something disagreeable about him.

Hans had left the stranger's last question unanswered, for he felt sure the answer was already known, and he didn't like it. Remembering his father's account of being questioned and followed by the Gestapo, when he did reply, he made it deliberate, calm.

"Yes, a few years ago."

The man cocked his head to one side. "Ah. Paris in June is lovely, is it not?"

June, why mention June? This smelled of Gestapo. Better be stingy with information. "I couldn't say. I was there in July."

"Are you planning any other trips on your leave, Major?"

"Sightseeing in Paris. That's all." Hans refused to elaborate. Growing more uncomfortable by the minute, Hans tried to concentrate on the countryside as it sped past but that didn't help. After a few minutes he stood and adjusted the shade on the compartment window.

"I see you are with the 3.Infanterie-Division, Major." The man picked up his newspaper, opened it, refolded it, placed it next to his hat and coat. "You're headed west, while your division is in Stalingrad. So I assume you're traveling to Paris."

When Hans said nothing, the man pressed him further. "I hear they are at the Volga, your regiment."

Hans winced as he shifted his weight, hoping the man would notice his pain. "So I understand. Once my wounds heal I'm sure I shall join them." He watched the trees roll by. Every time a farmhouse came into view, almost by instinct, Hans planned a frontal assault upon the structure. With supporting fire, I'm sure I could make it to the stone wall … twenty meters to the house is critical … sprint to the window, toss a grenade, bolt through the door.

Again the train slowed to a crawl, and the car Hans was riding in heaved as it rolled over a switch point. When he stood up and opened the window to investigate the delay, he saw his train had diverted onto one of two parallel tracks.

Beyond it on the other track, headed in the opposite direction, was another train, motionless. As he watched, the other locomotive began to move, crawling at first, but after three or four cars went by he could hear the couplings collide, one after the other. The halted train was neither a military nor passenger, its locomotive was pulling cattle cars, nothing else, perhaps twenty in all. That's odd. Why were there no cars of other types, freight cars or coaches? And why would there be an SS soldier on top of each car?

When the sharführer at the front of the train stood up and blew a whistle, all the SS soldiers clambered down onto the tracks at the far side of the train. Hans could hear someone barking orders, but when he tried to look under the train to the far side all he could see were the black boots of the SS soldiers.

Hans thought he saw movement in one of the cattle cars. Looking closer, he was surprised to see two sets of fingers emerge through a horizontal crack near the top of the car. Delicate and small, they had to be a woman's, for they were too high up to be those of a child. Yes, a woman for sure. She seemed to be trying to pull herself up to peer through another small hole in the car's side. Hans tried but could make out nothing else, save those grappling fingers.

The man in the dark suit stood up to watch, crowding against Hans at the window.

The sharführer who had blown the whistle stepped over the coupling between two cars and surveyed the length of the train. To Hans' distress, the sharführer happened to see those delicate protruding fingers. Running to the side of that car with arms raised over his head, he slammed his rifle butt against them with such force Hans could see the wooden slats quiver.

When the fingers jerked back into the darkness it took

every ounce of restraint Hans could muster not to roar out in protest, for he knew disclosing his fury to the enemy at his side might cost him his life. So close Hans could smell his sweat, the man in the dark suit continued to stand there scowling. "Dirty Jews!" he said before he sat back down.

A quotation from his English studies—Discretion is the better part of valor—popped into Hans' head. "Ja, dirty Jews." He despised himself for saying it.

The unpleasant voice came again from the other seat. "Tell me, Major, do you think these Jews deserve to be, er, shall we say, relocated?"

Hans, considered his response with caution, closed the window, lowered the blind, and resumed his seat. "Relocation seems reasonable, if that's the best thing for the Fatherland. I'm no politician, though, only a soldier following orders, so it's not a question for me to decide."

At that moment, on the other side of their car another locomotive roared past on the open line Hans' train had been diverted from. He got up and went into the corridor to watch it pass and saw it was loaded with military personnel, tanks, armaments, trucks and the like. The man in the dark suit had followed and again stood at his side. Hans found it difficult to tolerate the mingled odors of sweat and the pomade on the man's hair.

"For the Russian front, no doubt," the man said.

Hans made no reply.

As the last car of the military train roared past, their own car lurched forward, and once it cleared the switch their speed increased until the train settled into its rhythmic clickety-clack. The man in the dark suit gestured with his hand to indicate that Hans should return to the compartment and follow him in.

Seething with rage, Hans could think of nothing but those cattle cars full of Jews. How many must there have been? Where were they headed? He had heard rumors about the relocation of Jews but never credited them. Now he had seen the reality. Hans had little doubt the man in the dark suit knew all about it. And for the love of God, why was he sticking so fast to this compartment, prying into Hans' affairs? Best to say nothing, keep silent, aloof.

When the door slid open the conductor stepped halfway into the compartment, his feet apart as he leaned against the doorframe. He gave little attention to the man in the dark suit and looked at Hans. "Ticket?"

Hans reached into his tunic and produced his ticket.

"You are going to Frankfurt?"

"Yes, then on to Paris." No reason to deny it, Gestapo man already knew.

The conductor examined his ticket, then said, "All is in order. We expect to arrive in Frankfurt four hours from now." After the conductor was gone the man in the dark suit spoke. "Major, may I invite you to join me in the dining car?"

Hans shook his head. "Danke, nein. I would much prefer to rest."

"A pity. I shall rejoin you soon."

Clasping both hands under his right thigh, the man lifted that leg to help him stand, then steadied himself by holding the upper rail and took a step forward with his other leg. After a slight yet perceptible pause, his right leg swung into place. Once upright, his gait as he departed the compartment seemed unremarkable. Hans assumed the stiffness was from sitting too long and thought no more of it.

Relieved to be alone, Hans felt safe. He could think about Aimée without fear. But that's foolishness, he told himself, such foolishness. There's no way the man can read my thoughts, none.

He stared out the window, remembering his last letter from Aimée. How sweet and alive her words had been, as vibrant as her very presence. She wrote such loving letters, and he welcomed the distraction they provided. He understood now why people called French the language of love, for there could be no lovelier sound in the world than "Je t'aime." Well, perhaps "Je t'adore." Hans smiled at that.

He speculated about why it had taken her so long to accept and express her feelings—perhaps her mother's repressive influence, perhaps because he was a German soldier, perhaps it was Aimée's first experience at love, perhaps all of those things. But once she confessed her love for him, he knew it was forever.

He smiled again thinking about one particular letter, its poetic description of four yellow goslings with their pure white mother as they waddled along the shore of the pond. The mother goose had bustled about, raising her wings, corralling them into a group before entering the water, always vigilant to danger. When Aimée wrote that she thought this must be a model for a family's tender care, he knew her sentiments were genuine.

The hypnotic motion of the train sent his head slumping forward again. Giving in to the relaxation, he shifted his body and settled his head into the corner, within minutes he sank into deep slumber.

The man in the dark suit snatched the rifle from the sharführer and smashed its butt against the side of the cattle car. When the board supporting the bent fingers gave way and fell outward, striking the sharführer on the head, he raised the rifle, ready to shoot into the car. The gap in its wall revealed a horrific site—a chaotic mob of disheveled and frightened men, women, and children, raising their arms to block the sunlight's sudden assault.

As if the fallen board signaled a break for freedom, the captives surged forward, pressing the poor soul in front up against the wall. A second board gave way with a loud crack to expose more of the occupants' upper bodies. All were black with dirt and filth, except the one the grappling hands belonged to.

That one wore a radiant white dress.

When a third board gave way, Aimée stepped into the opening. It was she in the white dress, and behind her cowered Claire and Elsie Ferrand. At once Hans recognized the emotion behind Aimée's distraught, helpless face—abject fear.

"Hans, why?" was all she said as the bullet slammed into her chest.

Soaked in sweat, Hans bellowed and reached out. When he oriented himself, he realized the man in the dark suit had returned and seemed to be shoving a pad and pencil into his coat pocket.

"Do you dream often, Major?"

Hans, still shaken from the nightmare, gazed out the window and said, "Ja, ever since Poland I have bad dreams."

CHAPTER 18

The telephone exchange buzzed with activity, its three operators keeping a constant finger on the pulse of Sermaize-les-Bains. When not routing gossip, they exchanged it like stallholders in a street market. Their status in the town was such that no one questioned their veracity.

"So, Aimée." Without interruption, Yvonne rearranged plugs to connect one caller to another. "This Hans you talk about forever, is he not your lover?"

Not busy at the moment, Aimée sighed. "How many times do I have to tell you? I love him, but he is *not* my lover."

"Oh, yes, Aimée, we believe you," Cécile chimed in. "He comes all this way from Berlin because he is your pen-pal. We understand." When a light flashed on her board she handled the next call. "Yes, one moment," she spoke into her mouthpiece. "I will connect you." Click, connection made.

Cécile looked at Aimée to see if she was listening. "So tell us, is his name Hans or Hands?" A wave of earthy laughter surged through the room.

Aimée let the next call ring longer than usual. "Cécile, that's mean. I can't believe you'd actually say such a thing." She deployed her plugs and spoke into her mouthpiece. "Allo, Henri? Has he arrived?" Instantly she beamed. "Thank you, Henri. No, no, I won't say a word."

Yvonne and Cécile exchanged glances and nods. "Go," Cécile ordered. "We can handle things. You run and meet your pen-pal."

Yvonne giggled. "Tell Hands Allo from us."

"But Maman, Hans has done nothing." Aimée was ready to stomp out of the house. "He has done nothing at all to deserve this. I have done nothing. How can you be so unfair?" She flung through the door to stand looking toward the henhouse weeping, arms crossed on her breasts.

Elsie followed her daughter out. "Very well, young lady, just tell me how you know he isn't a Nazi. He wears a German uniform, doesn't he? That's proof enough."

Aimée spun around to face her mother. Tears flowed down both cheeks. "Why are you like this? Why? You know he wears a German uniform, but that doesn't make him a Nazi." She uncrossed her arms and clenched her fists. "I can't believe you're doing this when you know at this very moment he's on his way from the hotel."

Elsie's expression never changed, lips clamped together, eyes hard.

The anxiety from all the anticipation, the endless wait, and months of worry erupted in a flood of tears as Aimée rushed into Hans' arms. He ignored the discomfort in his chest, lifted her off the ground to spin her around and set her back down. "My God, it's good to hold you again."

Their mouths came together then in the long, impassioned kiss Hans had been dreaming of for so many months. He kissed her again and again before Aimée pulled away.

"I can't take this any longer," Aimée blurted out.

He refused to let go, caressing her neck and kissing it. "What can't you take? You know I have no choice in any of this."

She stiffened. "I can't take my mother any longer. She's so irrational, she refuses to understand. Oh, Hans, darling, can't we just run away together?" With her head still on his shoulder, she dried her tears on her sleeve. "All I want is to be with you. It's so unfair."

He took out his handkerchief and dabbed at her cheeks. "Yes, I agree it's unfair. Nothing about it is fair, but nothing we say or do will change things."

"Oh, Hans." Aimée stood silent and stared into the distance. "I don't know what's come over Maman. When we were children, she was always so loving, so kind, so understanding! But ever since this summer, any time your name came up, she would go quiet. If I asked why, she would only say, 'Oh, it's nothing.' And before we got your letter from the hospital, when we didn't know what had happened to you, she said you'd be better off being a Russian prisoner, as if she was glad."

Hans took her hands and began to kiss them. "Chérie, I love you more than anything in this world. No one can ever change that. Don't worry about your mother, she has her reasons I'm sure."

Aimée's sobs softened and with hands linked they began to walk toward the stone wall by the road.

"There's not a waking moment I don't think of you," he said, "or of our moments together. I read your letters over and over." When Aimée's distraught face from the cattle-car dream flashed into his mind he pulled her to him to sit on the stone wall as he continued. "There's little I can say to console you. This war is a hideous strain on everyone. My parents haven't heard from Peter in months." He tightened his grasp on her hand but found no warmth. "I don't know where I'm to be stationed, probably back to the Russian front, and who knows from there. So far I've been lucky, but good luck can't last forever."

He waited, hoping for reassurance from her, the sadness in her eyes almost more than he could stand. "The last thing I want is to be the cause of so much distress in your family, or for you." When long moments passed and she didn't answer, he went on. "Aimée, I-I-I think I should go back to Berlin. I'll soon be ready to return to duty, you know."

"No, Hans," she wailed, and burst into tears.

Hans gathered her in his arms and kissed her forehead. "Listen to me, chérie, it's better this way." He swept her tears aside with his fingers then lifted her chin to kiss her salty lips. Not surprised when she didn't respond with her former passion, he said, "There's no future for us. I don't want it to end, but what choice do we have?"

"Hans, I can't go on without you."

"For now it's best. Can't you see that?"

Aimée's lower lip trembled. "No. No I can't. I don't want to see it."

"If I survive, and if you're still here when the war's over, then maybe we could have a life together. But now—you must see the futility of it."

Aimée hung her head. When he encouraged her to stand up and walked her back to the house in silence, he was fighting his own tears.

In the kitchen André and Elsie ceased speaking the moment Hans and Aimée walked through the back door, their conversation halted in mid-sentence. André stood up, quick to regain his composure.

"Hans, my boy, you haven't told us of your plans."

"No, Monsieur, for I'm unsure of my future at the moment myself." He risked a glance at Aimée to see her chin quiver. "Monsieur Ferrand, please know how grateful I am to you and your family for all your kindness. For the time being, I must go back to Berlin to await orders."

"Then I wish you Godspeed," André said. "I trust you'll convey my sincerest regards to your father."

"I shall be glad to do so," Hans said.

André straightened a dishtowel on its rack and reached to shake Hans' hand. "I shall miss you."

Hans shook it, with the firm feeling that under different circumstances, he would always be welcome in André's home.

"Please keep yourself safe," the older man said. "I do pray, as I know Konrad does, that you survive this war."

Hans turned to Elsie. "Madame Ferrand, I regret to have been the cause of so much discord in your family. I want you to know I understand, truly. I love your daughter, and my only wish is for her safety and well-being."

Unmoved, Elsie Ferrand did not reply.

But Hans persisted. "Before the war began, that summer of 1939, my father extracted a promise from me. He made me swear if I was ever able to be of assistance to your family, I was to do so. It is a promise I intend to keep."

With that, he turned and left the house by the front door. He was halfway down the path when he heard the door slam. He stopped and turned to see Aimée run to him, throw herself into his arms and kiss him with all the fervor he had ached to feel. Finally, she broke free and cried out, "Je t'adore, Hans Krüger! Je t'adore!" before running back to the house with her hands covering her face.

"And what if he is a Nazi? Is that the worst thing in the world?"

"Oh, Aimée, there's so much you don't understand. I'm not trying to hurt you. I'm trying to save you."

"Save me from what? From Hans?"

Elsie Ferrand knew the day she'd always dreaded had arrived. "Aimée, ma chère, come sit down next to me. It's time you knew." She took a slow, measured breath and let it back out. "Aimée, I'm trying to save you, to save all of us, from the Nazis."

Aimée looked puzzled.

"I'm sure you've heard how the Nazis hate Jews. You girls at the telephone exchange hear everything, so I'm sure you heard in July about the Nazis rounding up Jews in Paris and deporting them." She reached out and took Aimée's hands. "Ma p'tite, where do you think they take them?"

Aimée jerked her hands free. "Yes, Maman, I've heard. We all have. What does that have to do with me? We're not Jewish. We're Catholic. We go to Mass every Sunday."

Elsie shook her head. "Aimée, you're not listening."

"Not listening?" The girl stood up, angry, hands on her hips. "Not listening? I listen to you every single day. I listen to you complain about Nazis. I listen to you complain about the rationing. All I do is listen." Her stare became a furious glare. "You're such a witch!"

When Elsie slapped her, the sound echoed off the kitchen wall. Horrified at what she'd done, Elsie snatched back her hand as if it had been burned.

Aimée looked stunned. She'd never been struck in anger.

At once Elsie tried to draw the girl into her embrace. "Please forgive me, Aimée, I'm sorry. I should never have lost my temper." She reached out to touch the fiery mark on Aimée's cheek.

Aimée jerked her head free. "Get away! I hate you!"

André had heard the argument from upstairs, for he ran into the room to stand between the two. "Aimée! Elsie! Stop this at once! This is insane. Ma fille, listen to what your mother is telling you."

"Oh, Papa! Will you betray me too? I can't believe you'd take her side."

"Now, now, Aimée, calmes-toi. Please. What your mother says is true. Where do you suppose the Nazis take those Jews? On holiday? Your mother is trying to tell you something of vital importance. I insist you sit still, listen to what she says."

André arranged the chairs around the table so they all could sit down, then took the one closest to his daughter and laid his arm around her shoulder.

Aimée was still in turmoil. "But what happens to the poor Jews is nothing to do with us. Hans is not evil, I'm sure he doesn't hate Jews, though I've never heard him even mention it. I tell you, this is crazy talk. No one will harm us."

When Elsie didn't respond André spoke for them both. "Aimée, the Nazis *are* evil. These Jews who're being deported, I'm telling you, they're never heard from again, ever. Evil, nothing but pure evil."

Aimée shook her head and crossed her arms in front of her chest. "That may be so, but nothing you can say will convince me we're in danger from Hans or from the Nazis. We're farmers, Catholics even. Who would want to harm us?"

Elsie scooted her chair close to Aimée's other side as André watched in silence. Twice she took a deep breath, then clasped her hands and said in a firm voice, "Aimée. I was adopted."

"*Adopted*?"

"Yes, I was adopted when I was a baby."

Aimée let out her own breath so hard her shoulders sagged. "Well, that's a shock. I never even suspected it."

"No, and why should you?"

Aimée turned to stare at Elsie. "But what does your being adopted have to do with the Nazis? Is this some kind of joke?"

"No, It's no joke. Your grandmother and grandfather Blaisé adopted me."

Puzzled, Aimée studied her mother's face. "But that's impossible. You look just like Grandmère Blaisé."

"Perhaps I do. But, Aimée, my real parents were Jewish. They died in a fire when I was only a few months old. There was no other family, so neighbors took me to the priest in Revigny-sur-Ornain, knowing he sometimes arranged adoptions. When no one in his parish could take me, he got in touch with his friend, Father Feuillerat here in Sermaize-les-Bains. Father Feuillerat had two parishioners, your Grandmère and Grandpère Blaisé, who wanted children but were unable to have them, so when he told them about me, they took me in and raised me."

"Your real parents were Jewish?"

Elsie nodded.

"Papa, did you know this?"

"Yes, ma fille, I knew. Father Feuillerat told me, before we were married."

"Does anyone else know?"

"No one other than Father Feuillerat, and he may very well have forgotten. He's getting old, you know, and he's never mentioned it again. I shall obviously never speak of it to him or to anyone else. While I feel confident he's not a Nazi sympathizer, with this Vichy government one can't be sure."

Aimée covered her mouth with her hand for several moments, taking in this astonishing news. When she spoke again, she was quite calm. "There's no way Hans can know, is there?"

Elsie looked worried. "He has said nothing to you about any of this?"

"Of course not, Maman. He is *not* a Nazi. How many times must I tell you?"

Elsie got up from the table and began to pace. "Perhaps Hans doesn't know, but I'm afraid his father does. Papa is quite sure he told him in one of his letters after the war. Why he would do that, God only knows." She stopped behind Aimée's chair and reached out to rub her daughter's shoulders.

"Perhaps he isn't a Nazi," Elsie went on, "but he still must follow orders, and he's in the German army. If a Nazi officer tells him to arrest Jews, you must know what he'll have to do."

"Very well, I shall write him and ask."

Elsie sat back down. "No, absolutely not. You mustn't do that under any circumstances. The danger is too great, you mustn't write him any more at all."

"Why not? Hans deserves to know why you treated him so—"

"Why not?" André resisted the urge to stand. "Because it isn't safe. The slightest reference in a letter to your being Jewish will put us all in harm's way and endanger Hans as well." Calmed, he continued. "Were you aware Hitler has declared that no Germans are to associate with Jews? He even passed a law forbidding German citizens to marry Jews. Hans is bound to know these laws. So you see, if Hans knew you were Jewish, or someone else knew he was associating with a woman of Jewish blood, as a soldier of the Third Reich the penalties for him would be severe."

Aimée searched her mother's eyes. "Then we can't just stay here, not with the Nazis deporting Jews, or whatever they do with them. Papa, what must we do?"

Elsie tried to reassure her. "Ma chère, as long as no one knows I'm Jewish, we're safe."

"But what about Claire and Papa?"

"I fear for them as well, but especially you and Claire. Even though your father is not a Jew, he's married to one, and furthermore, you and Claire look Jewish. I'm sure you never thought of that, did you? If I were arrested, you without a doubt would be as well, and Claire, and probably Papa, too."

Hans felt drained. Emptiness overcame him on the long journey back to Berlin. Even though he knew it had to be this way, at least for now, doubts nibbled at his conscious. Should I have told the Ferrands I knew Elsie was Jewish, or told Aimée at least? What does it matter to me? I'm not a Nazi. I have no sympathy with their cruel policies, no hatred for other human beings; in combat I fight because I am a soldier, trained to obey, not because I harbor hatred toward my fellow man. Would they even believe they have nothing to fear from me?

To the core of his marrow, Hans knew his sense of self-preservation had held him back. Finally, he surrendered to the fatigue and settled into his seat as the train pulled out of the Frankfurt station on the last leg of his trip. What sleep he had managed on the rocking train had been far from restful. Just as he eased his head back, out of the corner of his eye he caught a familiar movement on the platform. It was a man, walking, something about his gait not quite right. Hans sat upright. The man passed through the door into the station and disappeared into the bahnhof. With every step his right leg seemed to falter, if only for a moment.

Had he been on this train? Was he in the Nancy station? Hans didn't want to believe it. He must live in Frankfurt. That's it. The man in the dark suit lives in Frankfurt. Come now, Hans, think. Was anyone left on the platform when the train pulled out of St. Dizier? Had anyone else been waiting there for this same train?

He couldn't be sure.

CHAPTER 19

Berlin
Thursday
8 April 1943

Dear Hans,

Your mother and I both write to tell you of the sad news we received this Monday last. A telegram arrived informing us your brother Peter was lost at sea. It contained no information about the events that led to this painful communication. We regret to say there's no solace that we were able to celebrate an early Christmas with Peter when he was home in November.

After his furlough, Peter had to return to Kiel by 12 December for the U-357's next patrol. Our goodbyes at the train station were most difficult and afterwards, your mother was paralyzed with worry. When the telegram arrived, she knew it was about Peter. Nothing I can say at this time consoles her, I pray time heals this wound.

Hans, we are sorry to burden you with such news, and we wish we were there to share your grief. Promise us you will be cautious and avoid unnecessary harm. It is impossible to control such things, but it means so much to your mother and me to tell you this.

Please write as soon as you can. Perhaps one day you may understand how a parent worries about a child, despite their age.

May God watch over you and keep you.

Your loving parents

Oberst Beck offered Hans a chair. "Major Krüger, it's good to have you join us. You are one of the lucky few."

"Excuse me, Herr Oberst, but under the circumstances, I fail to see that luck has favored me as much as you believe." His distracted gaze shifted to the situation map behind Beck's desk. "I still find the loss hard to grasp."

Poor Jacob. Even if he were captured, he's as good as dead now.

"Ja, Major Krüger, we surely could use those good men now, not to mention the entire 6th Armee. If we'd been victorious at Stalingrad, perhaps the fighting would be over." Beck grunted as he twisted around to point at the map. "For now, however, Major, this is what we have to work with."

"How long will it take to get the new division operational?"

"Good question. Three months, maybe four."

"Any news of our deployment status?"

"My guess is we'll likely head south into Italy to meet the advancing Allies, unless the Afrika Korps is once more able to throw the Allies back. Recent reports, however, have not been encouraging."

Beck faced his desk again, removed his glasses, and held them up to the light. "You do realize, if the Allies cross the channel this year, everything could change?" He didn't wait for a response. "As you've no doubt surmised, that's why the 3rd Panzer-Grenadier Division is exactly where it is in the Lyon region."

"Herr Oberst, I think you give me too much credit."

"Nonsense, Major. I've seen your service record." The oberst picked up a pitcher of water from his desk and poured two tumblers full, passing one to Hans. "Now, any questions before I brief you further?"

Hans took a couple of sips and set the water down. "Thank you, sir. Just one. How likely are the Allies to attempt to cross the Channel this year?"

"Straight to the point as usual, Major. I'm just back from a staff meeting with General der Panzertruppen Fritz-Hubert Graser, who assured me of three things." He raised his index finger. "One, the invasion won't come at all until next spring, perhaps not before summer of 1944." A second finger joined the first. "Two, we shall see to it they never get off the beaches. Of that you can be certain."

Hans waited for the third. When it didn't come he said, "And the third?"

Beck leaned forward and looked first to his left, then to his right. He lowered his voice, just above a whisper. "The Allies *will* be invading Italy, probably through Sicily, by summer." He locked his gaze onto Hans'. "You did not hear that from me. Verstehen Sie?"

"I understand."

Beck studied Hans a moment longer, then leafed through Hans' service file. He looked at Hans again, seeming puzzled. "Major Krüger, have we met before? I have quite a definite feeling that somewhere our paths have crossed."

Hans did his best to appear to search his memory, frowned, then shook his head. I'd better not mention the shameful restaurant scene in Robert-Espagne, the defiant waitress, the one Beck had treated with such arrogance.

After the oberst tossed the file onto the corner of his desk, he stood up, and stretched. "No, I suppose not. I see we've never been assigned to the same unit at the same time."

Hans returned to his appropriated quarters to consider all he'd been told. After the fall of Stalingrad he knew the German forces had been altogether occupied contending with the Allies in North Africa. In command of the Deutsches Afrika Korps Panzers, in the early phases of the campaign Erwin Rommel had earned the respect and praise heaped upon him as well as his nickname, "the Desert Fox." With the success of Montgomery at El Alamein, though, the British had driven the Germans back to Tunisia. And now that the Americans had entered the conflict, after their amphibious landings in Morocco, Hans understood that the combined Allied forces did not bode well for the Wehrmacht.

Nor was it good for his own situation back in France, unable to visit Sermaize-les-Bains. Sure, he could go if he had a furlough, but it wasn't the Wehrmacht that limited his freedom. For God's sake, why did he have to break it off with Aimée? Hans, he told himself, you're a dunce. You don't even know if they're safe, or even in Sermaize-les-Bains. A complete mess, an utter Goddamned nightmare, a nightmare from which he never seemed to wake up.

To distract himself from the pain, he settled into the chair at his desk, located pen and paper, and began to write the letter he was dreading.

Charbonnières, France
Monday
10 May 1943

Dear Mother and Father,

News of Peter in your recent letter has left me saddened to a degree I did not believe possible. I cannot even begin to comprehend the profound grief that has engulfed you. Know that I think of you and pray for you often. When I visited a church here in France a while back, I lit a candle and said a prayer for Peter, something I will do more often in the days to come, along with two more candles for you. It is hard for me to remember the last time we were together, but it makes me glad to know you were able to see dear Peter in November.

I doubt I have ever told you this, but I now know I must. Thank you for all of the wonderful memories you have given me and all the joy a boy could possibly know growing up. Mother, thank you for always being so kind to my friends when they would come to play, and Father, thank you for your patience when I would cross you. I realize you did not deserve this treatment from such an impudent boy. Enough about these things.

I have just returned from a briefing with my new oberst. He arrived from the 386th Infanterie-Division, charged with helping from the new division here. I never actually met him until now, but Jacob and I did observe him in a small café north of here three years ago. I was relieved he didn't seem to remember me, although I won't go into that now.

We hear much speculation about where we will be sent. Some think northern France, others Greece, but I am told it will be Italy, and soon. Only time will tell. Our conditions here in Charbonnières are adequate for our needs, although some things are not as plentiful as they once were. The widespread rationing of food has made it difficult, but less so in the country. Charbonnières is north of Lyon and bustling with activity. The division is being reformed as the 3rd Panzer-Grenadier Division. My duties will be much the same. In that regard, little has changed.

In addition to my sorrow for Peter, I feel very grieved to have lost all my comrades in the action at Stalingrad, but the new men I've met seem worthy replacements. So far I've met no one whose company I enjoy as much as I did Jacob's, and I wonder if I ever will. Aside from the new recruits, everyone else here seems rather reserved and withdrawn, as if they have met their mortality and stared it down. They try to keep up their morale and the morale of everyone else, but something has changed. No one discusses it, but we're all aware of the difference.

In the event you wonder, I have not written to Aimée since last autumn and I feel it is best this way. As difficult as it is for me to resist writing, I think of her much of the time, even more so now that spring has come with all its glory. Nor have I received any letters from her. When I left her in Sermaize-les-Bains last October, I made it clear it was best this way. I pray Aimée believes this, but I'm afraid her mother still believes I am a threat. When I consider the options in this situation, I'm afraid I see no circumstances in which I can have a life with her, at least for now. It is the things over which we have no control that are so very hard to endure. I know you understand.

Are you still considering a move to Dresden? I agree you should, at least for the duration of the war and your reasoning is quite sound. I presume you can work out all the business arrangements to your satisfaction. And even though there have been few bombs dropped on Berlin thus far, it is just a matter of time before that all changes given the pounding the Luftwaffe has given London. I have no doubt that chubby little Churchill would love to keep Berliners up at night for a change. One thing you didn't mention as an element in your consideration is your present proximity to the railway station. I can tell you with certainty when the bombings increase, the rail yards will be prime targets. Despite the poor aim of the British, when this happens, you would be even more vulnerable.

For now, though, know that I am well. I think of you often and wish I could be there with you. One day this war will be over, and it may even seem like nothing more than a bad dream. Is it too much to hope for? I tell myself all sacrifice is worth it in the end and I pray these sacrifices will prove no different.

I give you my pledge I will do all in my power to be safe and do nothing foolish. Rest assured our officers are competent and our new general is a worthy one.

I will write again when I can.

Your loving son,

Hans

Hans walked the short distance into Charbonnières and posted the letter to his parents, still feeling awkward in his comments about Peter. Did I say too much or not enough? My God, what torment must mother be suffering, having to endure the agony of where and how Peter died? There's no solace for her in knowing he would have faced death as a gallant and courageous sailor. Hans knew a telegram from the government would do nothing to console her, for they both knew there was not enough bravery in the Third Reich to keep the tons of water from crushing him in an instant when his U-boat sank to the ocean's depths.

Hans closed his eyes to squeeze back the tears, and when he opened them, the intoxicating perfume of lilacs just outside Charbonnières filled his nose. He stopped, if just for a moment, to enjoy their wonderful fragrance. The distinctive essence carried him back to a time in Berlin when he was five years old. Wanting to please his mother, he'd torn off an armful of lilac blooms from a private garden on their street. A week later, the woman whose garden it was had stopped Greta Krüger to complain that after a cold, harsh winter, Hans had stripped her bush of its long-anticipated blossoms. Greta had apologized and taken him by the hand to go and apologize to the woman himself. He'd felt ashamed, wanting to cry, yet that bouquet of lilacs he'd picked for his beautiful mother had brought a smile to her face that he'd never forget.

And as always, whenever Hans thought of beauty and flowers, he thought of Aimée. How could anyone even know Madame Ferrand was a Jew? God knows what would happen if anyone found it out. He thought back to one of the first letters his father had received from André. His parents had gone to the neighbors to visit, leaving him to watch over his brother. While Peter napped, Hans stole into his father's study and read a few of the letters, and over the years as his command of the French language improved, many more.

He remembered how André wrote that it was the priest in Sermaize-les-Bains, Father Feuillerat, who'd approached M. and Mme. Blaisé about taking Elsie into their family. And before that, it was the priest in Revigny-sur-Ornain who'd asked him to do it.

The lilacs forgotten, Hans quickened his pace to the post office, bought appropriate stamps, and passed his letter through the slot. No trouble with the censors that time, anyway.

When he came back onto the street he saw that the building next door was la mairie, the office of the mayor. Perhaps he could have his question answered here, the question that had been bothering him for so long. It was a municipal office, anyone should be able to inquire.

Seeing several doors opening off the main hallway, he chose the first one on the front. Inside, a woman sat behind a desk working through a stack of papers.

"Excuse me, Madame. May I trouble you a moment?"

The clerk waited before setting her papers aside and regarded him over the top of her spectacles. He couldn't tell if she was annoyed or preoccupied, or both. "Yes, Major. How may I assist you?"

"I would like to know if, when a child is adopted, an official record is made of the details."

She scanned his uniform before she removed her glasses. Hans knew the French had become quite clever at learning German ranks and functions. "It depends. Why do you ask?"

"A matter of general interest." He studied the top document on the stack beside her. "Suppose I wanted to find the birth parents of an adopted child. Where would one go to find a record of it?"

"I assure you, Major, we keep very complete records." She was tapping her pencil on the desktop. "It's the law. In France anyway, all vital statistics must be maintained."

"I would expect nothing less. We maintain the same statistics in Germany. What I hope to discover though is where such information is recorded, and where it can be found."

She pursed her lips in irritation, then recited, "Date and place of birth, father's full name, mother's full name." She looked again at the stack of papers she'd set aside. "Mother's maiden name, father's profession. This is recorded for everyone."

"Naturally, Madame. I know you're busy. One last question, if you please. Suppose an adoption were carried out through a priest, then *where* would those records be kept?"

Frowning, she sighed and looked at his uniform again. "The law is the law. I would have thought you knew these things. They're here a lot lately, demanding our records without so much as a 'please' or 'thank you.' "

"They?"

"Gestapo."

"I see. Thank you very much, Madame. You've been most helpful."

Hans stepped out onto the sidewalk, and when he passed the front window of the office he'd just left, he saw the woman raise the telephone to her ear.

Well, what was done was done. He set off walking to headquarters, annoyed with himself to have aroused her suspicion. What was worse, he hadn't learned what he wanted to know. He quickened his pace. Another question—why is the Gestapo interested in vital statistics? If they're searching, they must be finding something that interests them. Why else would they keep demanding the French records?

The sight of the cattle car crammed with Jews continued to haunt him. Ever since he'd seen it, Hans scanned every train he saw, inspecting each one for the telltale cattle cars. And the more he looked, the more of them he saw. They were always pulled off on a siding either just ahead of or just after a railway station. He could no longer deny what was happening, for it was happening before his very eyes. And German people were doing it. Nazis, yes, but they were Germans all the same.

The Jewish Question he'd been required to read in officer's training only made things worse, contributing to the increased frequency of his hideous dreams. All the dreams were alike, and each would end the same. Aimée's beautiful white dress and slender figure would appear before him, then her anguished and frightened face begging for rescue would become clear. It was at this point he always awakened, drained and soaked in sweat. Any time it happened, for hours afterward throughout the day, the anguished look on her face stayed with him.

Conversations about Jews now seemed to take place everywhere. The longer the Germans occupied France, the easier it became for some of them to discuss *The Jewish Question*. Hitler had decreed last year, on 7 June, that all Jews in France over the age of six must wear a yellow star on their breasts in public. It was impossible not to be aware of the endless roundups and deportations of Jews, and now they were hearing of a place called Auschwitz. The fearsome name was spoken in hushed tones, but as more and more Jews were detained and sent eastward, the more vocal the pronouncements became. "Auschwitz," Hans heard time and again, slithering from the mouths of Nazis.

It was common knowledge that in Paris the previous March, after two Luftwaffe officers were murdered at the Carrousel, two thousand Jews were rounded up and deported—a thousand for each Luftwaffe officer. The more Hans listened, the more he heard about Lyon, eighty kilometers to the south, and Klaus Barbie, new head of the Gestapo. In the few short months since Barbie had been posted there in November, his ruthless tactics had become legendary. Before that, early in the Nazi occupation of Holland, his methods had been just as cold-blooded. Now, Hans had no difficulty believing the rumors of his sadistic and savage treatment of prisoners and Jews in Lyon.

Each day, every day, he considered the safety of the woman he loved. Waking or sleeping, it haunted him. What could he do? There had to be something, anything.

The yellow Star of David with *Jude* emblazoned in its center was now his persistent and relentless tormentor.

Oh God, please, not for my Aimée.

CHAPTER 20

"Please read the charges against the defendant."

Hans stood with his hands clasped, his face devoid of all emotion. The shackles on his wrists remained silent.

"Yes, Your Honor. Major Hans Krüger, you are charged with crimes against the Reich for violation of the Military Penal Code, paragraph 91. Further, you are hereby charged with failure to perform your sworn duty as an officer of the Reich for not reporting the presence and location of known Jews."

The presiding judge leaned towards his left, and in a hushed tone, conferred with the other officers seated for the tribunal. He did the same to his right. With a brisk rap of his gavel on the bench, he looked down at the defendant. "Major Krüger, because your crimes against the Reich are punishable by death, you are entitled to defense counsel." The judge looked to Hans' right. "Is counsel ready to proceed?"

"Yes, Your Honor."

"The courtroom may be seated. The defendant is to remain standing." The judge picked up the file before him and passed it to his left. "Oberleutnant Schmitt, your opening statement."

"Your Honor, it will be shown that Major Hans Krüger has, since June of 1940, been in a close and intimate relationship with Aimée Ferrand, the daughter of a known Jewess, and further, it will be shown the defendant failed to report the location of this family of Jews to the proper authorities."

"Major Krüger, how do you plead?"

Motionless, Hans stared straight ahead and spoke in a monotone. "Not guilty."

"Noted. Oberleutnant Schmitt, call your first witness."

"If it pleases the court, I call Major Bruno Werner."

Hans turned and scanned the courtroom. He didn't recognize a single face. No one had stood to take the witness stand. But then, with a loud creak, the door at the rear of the courtroom opened. Heads turned.

Hans froze.

The man seemed familiar. Two steps and Hans knew. In uniform this time, Major Bruno Werner, if that was his name, was the man in the dark suit from the train. That same sickening odor of his pomade wafted to Hans' nose as Werner strode past on his way to the witness stand.

Oberleutnant Schmitt began his questioning. "Major Werner, please tell the court your full name, rank, and service assignment."

"My name is Bruno August Werner and I am a major in the Geheime Staatspolizei, Berlin."

"Thank you, Major. Tell the court, please, how you came to know of the defendant's crimes against the Reich."

"May I consult my notes?"

"Please."

Werner reached into his breast pocket to retrieve a worn notepad and flipped through it until he found the relevant page. "Ja, here it is. On Monday, 12 October 1942, I traveled by train from Berlin to Frankfurt on my way to interrogate a prisoner. I found a seat in a compartment occupied only by the defendant."

"Are you saying, then, you and he were the only two passengers in that compartment?"

"That is correct."

"I see. How did you come to suspect him of the crimes of which he is charged?"

"During our journey the major fell into a restless sleep and as he slept, he mumbled. I tried to comprehend his mumblings but they were unintelligible. Once he awoke, however, he became nervous, acting in a suspicious manner."

"Suspicious how?"

"He seemed jittery, uneasy. I observed by his uniform he was attached to the 3.Infanterie-Division, and when I said I knew his division was on the eastern front at Stalingrad, he volunteered that he was traveling to Paris on medical leave. At one point during the journey we happened to see a train on a siding transporting carloads of Jews east. The defendant, seeing this, uttered the words, 'Dirty Jews.' "

Hans looked at his defense counsel and shook his head in protest. He was about to speak out when the judge slammed down his gavel in warning. His counsel also shook his head and put a finger over his lips.

Schmitt said, "Go on, Major Werner."

The witness consulted his notepad again. "I asked him about the relocation of Jews. He stated, 'Relocation of Jews is best for the Fatherland.' "

"Major Werner, did he make any other comment about Jews?"

"He did, later." Werner regarded the judge. "Your Honor, I wish to add something, if I may."

The judge looked to the prosecuting officer, who nodded, then to the witness. When Werner didn't respond right away, Schmitt spoke up. "Go ahead, Major."

Werner directed his next remarks to the judges. "When one considers guilt, often it is not a question of what a suspect says, but rather *how* he says it. Do his pupils dilate? Does he look away, unwilling to maintain eye contact? Does he fidget? It was all these things that convinced me of his guilt."

Hans brought his hands to his face in exasperation then glared at his defense counsel as if to say, You must refute this! His counsel sat unmoving, pretending not to see.

The presiding judge's voice crackled through the courtroom like an electric charge. "One more such behavior, Major Krüger, and I shall order you chained to a chair." The judge leaned forward and said in a lower voice, "I'm sorry, Major Werner, you may continue."

"Thank you. After some time, I invited the defendant to join me in the dining car. He declined, saying he preferred to rest, and when I returned to our compartment, he had fallen asleep once more. My return had not disturbed him and before long he began to mumble, but again, his mumblings were incoherent. Just the same, I was able to make out a few intelligible words. The suspicious nature of his earlier behavior prompted me to take notes on what I heard. May I consult my notes again?"

Schmitt nodded. "If you please."

Werner turned several more pages in his notepad. "Yes, here it is. 'Jews,' the defendant mumbled, at least three or four times, and one other word that sounded to me like 'Emmay.' When I investigated the matter further, I would learn he was saying a French woman's name, 'Aimée.' "

"What did you do then, Major Werner?"

"Before I got off the train in Frankfurt I informed a fellow agent of my suspicions. This agent followed Major Krüger for the remainder of his journey to Paris."

"What did you learn about his activities?"

"Two things." He held up one finger. "First, Major Krüger lied when he told me he was just traveling to Paris to see the sights. In fact, he never went to Paris at all. Where he did go was to a town by the name of Sermaize-les-Bains.

"Second," he held up another finger, "through further investigation it became known to the Gestapo that Major Krüger, while an officer of the Reich, had an ongoing relationship with a Jewess and that he was fully aware of the location of this family of Jews from Sermaize-les-Bains."

Schmitt made a checkmark on the top page of a stack of papers lying before him. "Thank you, Major. And where was this family of Jews?"

"On a farm near the town to which he traveled, Sermaize-les-Bains, in the Marne département, northeastern France."

"One final question, Major Werner. Did you acquire any other information from your investigations in this matter?"

"I did, Herr Oberleutnant. I learned Major Krüger's father, Konrad Krüger, is a book publisher who has published the writings of Jews, and that both Herr Krüger and the defendant's mother, Frau Greta Krüger, were also aware of their son's relationship with this family of Jews."

"Thank you, Major Werner. Are you aware of the disposition of these parties?"

"I am. The Ferrands, this family of Jews from Sermaize-les-Bains, were arrested and deported to Ravensbrück six months ago. Konrad and Greta Krüger have been tried by a civil tribunal and found guilty of their crimes. At this time they are awaiting execution."

"ENOUGH!" Hans shouted, springing from his place to throw his entire weight against Major Werner's chest. As Werner fell backward, Hans, locking his hands around Werner's neck, began choking him with all his might. "These people are innocent, you filthy pig! These people are innocent, I tell you!"

CHAPTER 21

"Hans! Anton! What's all this about?" The extra set of hands allowed Anton to get his breath.

"Gerhardt, thank you for your assistance. I didn't think I'd be able to get Hans off of me." Anton stretched his neck and sat up straight. "Hans was asleep, then he became quite animated. Next thing I knew, he's choking me."

"Gerhardt, what are you doing in here?" Hans said, rubbing the side of his head.

"I was minding my own business, walking back to my room, and I hear this shouting, 'You filthy pig.' Hans, I know Anton is a slob, but I had no idea how much it upset you."

Hans pushed his fellow officer away. "Funny. Very funny, but if you had the dream I just had, you wouldn't be so comical."

"Well, fine. If that's how you show your appreciation for preventing you from killing your best friend, then I'll just leave."

"Gerhardt, thank you. I do appreciate it."

"Don't mention it."

After the door shut, Anton said in a low voice, "Are you all right? You were screaming, 'These people are innocent!' I came over and nudged your arm. You lunged at me, grabbed me by the throat, and began to choke me. It was all I could do to pull you away. Then you called me a 'filthy pig.' Thank goodness Gerhardt happened by when he did."

"I'm sorry. I was having one of my nightmares." Hans sat on the edge of the bed, his palms covering his reddened face. "My God, you can't believe how real it all seemed. Tell me I didn't hurt you."

Anton stood and stretched his neck again, first one side and then the other. "No harm done. But what was it that seemed so real?"

Hans looked up, rested his forearms on his thighs, and clasped his hands in front of him. "I've been having nightmares. Before, these cursed dreams dealt with things I'd seen, maybe hint at things I've done, soldiers I've shot. Faces. Images. God." Hans closed his eyes and let out a long weary breath.

"This time I was on trial for crimes against the Reich, and a Gestapo agent had just told the court my parents were in prison, waiting to be executed."

Anton sat back down on his own bed and adjusted the collar of his shirt. "Why would you dream such a thing? Considering how much strength you put into trying to choke me to death, it must have seemed real. Shall I get you something? Coffee? Schnapps?"

"No. No, thank you." Hans stared at the floor. "I'll be fine in a minute or two." He took his time getting up, walked over to the desk then sat back down. "Do you remember my telling you about Aimée?"

"How could I forget? Especially after seeing her picture."

Hans leaned back in his chair and looked around. "You know I swore off writing to her, but now I think it's time to reconsider."

"Does this change of heart have anything to do with your dream?"

"Alles." Everything.

There was no way on earth Hans could divulge Aimée's family secret to Anton, nor to anyone. At the moment all he felt was the need of a friend's assurance.

"Because of these nightmares—I can't seem to stop them—it's clear to me any of us could die at any moment, from any cause. If something should happen to me, Aimée deserves to know how I feel. She needs to know I regret my treatment of her."

He was relieved to see Anton nod in agreement. "Can I count on you to tell her for me? I mean, if something were to happen to me?"

Anton came to him and laid a hand on his shoulder. "You know you can. But you must first tell me how to reach her. Who knows? Maybe if you write to her it will put your demons to rest."

Hans extracted his pen and paper from the drawer. "And wouldn't that be a fine thing. However, after everything I've seen and lived through, I have little faith in miracles."

Rome
Wednesday
12 April 1944

My dearest Aimée,

I cannot post this letter from our headquarters, and as you read further, you will understand. Also, you will see why this letter must find its way to you alone. Perhaps the Italians can deliver the mail better than they fought as Germany's ally, for at least Mussolini succeeded in making the trains run on time.

This letter is most difficult to write as I no longer know what is in your heart, for this I have no one to blame but myself.

I regret my actions and I cringe to think of the pain I caused. When I left your side I convinced myself it was to make things easier for you and your family, but I now see and admit I acted of my own selfishness. How it shames me to think of your sorrow. Aimée, can you ever find it in your heart to forgive me?

I love you more than you could ever know. I think of you for hours during every day and dream about a life that might have been. Do you remember the last time we spoke? You said, "Why can't we run off together?" How I have wished we had. I still believe you're the reason I'm alive today, and if we survive this war, I want us to be together always.

You know I am not a Nazi. I have never fallen under the spell of the Nazi Party, and I never will. I abhor the vile filth they spew. There is not a place the Nazis have been that one doesn't hear of terrible things they've done—Poland, Moscow, France, Italy—it's all the same. It doesn't matter where they go. Innocent people are murdered. These deeds are despicable. This is not me. Believe what I tell you, ma chérie, if for no other reason than perhaps it will give me some peace.

I'm forever plagued by nightmares. These terrifying dreams convince me I am to blame. I'm tormented by things I have done and my lack of courage to do what is right and to prevent the senseless loss of life when it's in my power to do so.

There's more. I have failed to tell you things you should know.

Until this moment, I've been unable to say what must be said. Aimée, even as I write, I find it difficult to put the words onto paper. I wanted to tell you the last time we were together, but I was afraid. What I am about to reveal is the awful truth, the truth I must share with you and it is my fervent hope you will try to understand.

During our campaign in Poland, I was ordered to shoot a helpless woman. My superior officer was behind me, shouting:

"Shoot her! Shoot her!" I had already shot the man in the room with her, a sniper crouched on the floor, at the window. I cannot tell you how much I wanted to disobey a direct order. Instead of shooting her, I wish I had shot the hauptmann who ordered me to do such a thing. At least if I had shot him, the hauptmann I mean, I would have been executed and put out of my misery. Perhaps he had his reasons for the order, perhaps he thought she would pick up the fallen sniper's gun and begin firing on our men in his place.

This is the hardest thing I shall ever have to tell you but until I do, I don't believe I will ever feel worthy to live. After I shot this woman, she slumped to the floor in a heap. When I am forced to relive this despicable thing in my dreams, the instant I pull the trigger I see the bullet depart the end of the barrel. I reach out to try to stop the bullet but I am never able to do so and as it inches across the room every spiral of the bullet takes forever. Aimée, I swear to you on my soul, it was only when she was on the floor that I saw for the first time her rounded abdomen and the movement of her unborn child.

Do you suppose God will ever forgive me for this? I pray for forgiveness every day. But beyond that, can you ever find it in your heart to forgive me? I know I don't deserve it, but it's the thing I crave with all my being.

Aimée, the truth is, I'm nothing more than a miserable coward. Yes, I have been decorated for bravery in battle, but I am, nevertheless, a coward. Please understand, I did not end our relationship out of concern for you and your family. Yes, I was concerned about you, but I was concerned about myself more. How shameful it was of me.

This war has disillusioned us all. Here in Italy we no longer fight in a country to assist an ally. Rather, we fight in a country that has joined the enemy, and the enemy is no longer just the Allies. It is no longer the Italian farmers scattered over the scarred hills of what was once such a beautiful land. This war has made me my own enemy. Over and over each night I struggle with my dreams and nightmares, nightmares I fear will never stop. This is the war I'm afraid I will never win.

In the meantime, I must do my duty as a soldier, for any of us who resists will be shot.

One of the greatest regrets of my life, as great as my regret for having murdered an innocent woman and her unborn child, is for the pain I have caused you. I love you and always have, since the moment I first laid eyes on you. Do you remember that day in July of 1940? I remember, it was the 5th. And the stroll we took together the next day? What beautiful memories they are. There is not a day that passes I don't think about the joy and freedom I felt walking with you, listening to your voice, holding your hand. And yes, I still remember the white blouse with the blue print pattern you wore.

If I should die tomorrow, Aimée, please always know these thoughts of you would be my last and your name would be the final word to pass my lips.

I miss you terribly, and I miss your wonderful letters. Can I dare to hope you will forgive me and one day when this cursed war has ended, I can cradle your face in my hands and gather you up into my arms again?

I live only in that hope.

Until then, all my love is eternally yours.

Hans

Rome
Wednesday
12 April 1944

Dear Mother and Father,

Much has happened since my last letter to you. I apologize for not writing more. We have been involved in sustained and concentrated combat against the Americans at places called Anzio and Aprilia. The Americans landed a force north of our southern flank 50 kilometers south of Rome. The fighting was as intense as I have known, with a prolonged artillery battle that served only to deplete our dwindling supplies. After the successful breakout by the Americans, we have withdrawn north. I can tell you, it will be impossible for Rome to be in our control much longer. I foresee a protracted battle in the north of Italy, but if Rommel's forces can somehow manage to repel the coming attack across the English Channel, Germany's fortunes will change.

This is the first I have written in such a tone, and it pains me to do so, but the war has made me weary. Father, I was foolish not to listen when you and I talked in Berlin and you told me war would change me. I have to ask, though, what difference would it have made? I do not believe anyone could have prepared for this war, or for that matter, any war. Those who fought in the first war and then came back to fight in this one, perhaps they were better prepared than we young fellows, but who can say? Had I listened to you, would the division have survived Stalingrad? I'm afraid nothing could have saved them.

I very much fear no new generation is prepared for the future, despite what the fathers have witnessed and what the politicians warn. But we must continue to fight for the Fatherland and secure the victory the Führer promises—so I keep telling myself.

The most difficult thing for me to accept is the destruction of the villages and towns. We fight, then depart, on to the next battle, and once we're gone the citizens come out of their hiding places and walk about staring at all that's left, rubble, devastation, want. Does war do nothing more than create yet another generation of men comfortable with such knowledge, immune to its effects?

Mother, it makes me very happy to hear you're settled into your new home in Dresden and now that you've left Berlin the fighting seems far away. I can't imagine how difficult the rationing must be at times. I long for the day I can come walking up your street with a basketful of fresh vegetables and a chicken under my arm to surprise you with my safe return. A year is a long time, but maybe when I come it will be springtime and I can pick a bouquet of lilacs along the way!

I have written to Aimée and asked her to forgive me. I am most anxious about her response, but I will not be surprised if no answer comes.

Please rest assured, Mother, that I look after myself. So far as it is in my power, I shall continue to be safe. Of that you may be sure. My thoughts and prayers are with you and Father.

Your loving son,

Hans

Hans folded the letter and sealed the envelope, then searched out his last letter from his parents to confirm the new return address. He had it right: 72 Dürerstraße, Dresden. He slid both his letter to them and their earlier one to him into his tunic, along with his letter for Aimée.

Anton was stretched out on his bed with his hands folded behind his head. "So tell me, Hans, were you able to convince your mother not to worry about you?"

Hans sat motionless at the desk, absorbed in thought, then realized Anton had spoken to him. "I'm sorry, I was in another country. I didn't mean to ignore your question. What was it you asked?"

"Honestly, my friend, I'm beginning to worry about you. Dreaming again? I asked you if you convinced your mother not to worry."

"I have nightmares, you have dreams. Nothing I could ever say would make her stop worrying about me. Maybe before Peter died, but not now. Never. Anyway, isn't that a mother's job, to worry about her children?" Hans took a worn photo of his parents from his pocket and looked at it for the thousandth time. "Father's letters hint it's been hard on her, but how she must grieve and worry. All I can do is try to reassure her."

He slipped the photo back in his pocket. "Why is it when you think back to when you were young, say eight or nine, you can't remember a single day it rained, only all the sunny days when you played outside? Have you every wondered about that?"

Anton bit his lower lip then closed his eyes. "I wonder why I can remember the first pocketknife my grandfather gave me twenty years ago, but can't remember where I left my favorite ring twenty minutes ago." Anton opened his eyes and smiled at Hans. "When I think of it, I don't know what happened to that knife either. I'd like to have it today just to cut up an apple."

"You're right, it's odd what we remember. I wonder, what do you suppose we'll remember of this war? Which memories will stay with us? And will they be memories we cherish, or ones that torment us?"

Anton glanced at his watch. "I don't have much more time for all this philosophy, but I'd say that some memories, like people, can be good ones and some evil. The so-so memories, like those rainy days, will fade away and get lost over time, while the terrible ones and the wonderful ones will stay with us. All we can do is hope the good far outnumber the bad."

Anton tossed a pair of rolled-up socks at a fly on the ceiling and caught them on the way down. "Maybe really terrible memories are like a newly formed mountain, rough and rocky at first. But then as time passes the rains and the winds wear it down till it's only a rounded hump, no longer the jagged feature it once was. That's what I think happens to our terrible experiences and how they become memories for us. At least I hope that's how it is."

Hans considered his friend's words. God knew they'd seen their share of terrible things. Ever since Anton had joined the division, Hans had enjoyed their discussions. He still missed Jacob, but he and Anton had been friends from the start of the Italian campaign, and like all soldiers, they'd learned to depend on one another. Jacob's death at Stalingrad had to be one of those jagged memories, a sharp pain yet to be rounded down. While no one could take excitable Jacob's place, Anton's modest ways and discretion were appreciated. Anton knew what certain things he shouldn't say or discuss, and he was a very good listener. He was the only person Hans felt safe to confide in about his love for Aimée.

"Do you think she will forgive me?"

"Who are we talking about, the chambermaid, your mother, Aimée? I can't read your mind. If it's Aimée, then I think a better question is, 'Can I forgive myself?' How many times have I told you she will? She loves you. I don't understand why you didn't write sooner."

He tossed the same rolled up socks at Hans. "Why keep tormenting yourself? If she doesn't write back, give me her address and I'll write to her myself." Anton looked over to see Hans grin. "I'll need her address anyway to tell her what happened to you when you're out in the field daydreaming about your sins and some American sniper wings you.

"If you want me to write sooner, then I can tell her what a pain in the ass you've been. I'll beg her to forgive you so you can stop fighting your demons and get on with fighting the Allies. She'll forgive you, my friend, but you ask too much of yourself."

Hans smiled in return. "I hope you're correct." He stood up to leave. "Thank you, Anton. Thank you for everything."

CHAPTER 22

Sermaize-les-Bains, France
Monday
29 May 1944

Honored Monsieur Krüger,

Thank you for your correspondence of 12 April 1944. I received it in the post today. I would like to inform you there has been no change in the status of your account, and the information you provide is truly appreciated and explains the circumstances of the balance due to my full satisfaction.

Therefore, please be advised that full disclosure has taken place and your future activity in this regard is greatly anticipated.

Yours with every respectful consideration,

A. Ferrand

CHAPTER 23

At 18 rue Jeanne d'Arc in Reims, one purpose remained at the Gestapo's two-story headquarters—eradication of all Jews. By August 1944 time was running out, and no one knew for sure when the trains would no longer transport cattle cars crammed with Jews to Poland.

"Where did you get this, Huber?" Major Braun held what looked like an old book, a business ledger in his hands.

Braun was known for his ruthless bearing and cruelty, traits most people believed were linked to his short stature. A Napoleon, in fact, he tried to compensate by staying seated at his desk, seldom coming from behind it to shake hands or otherwise acknowledge visitors. His notorious depravity, his indifference to prisoners and sadistic approach to their interrogation ensured continued success within the Gestapo and guaranteed a high regard on the part of his superiors in Berlin. Braun's approach to the elimination of Jews was obsessive, methodical, and absolute.

He turned the old ledger book over, then back again and rubbed its worn and smooth surface like a magic lamp as if his doing so would reveal its contents instead of a genie. Cracks in the binding suggested long and frequent use yet the cover bore no visible marks or yielded any clues to its content.

Oberleutnant Huber saluted for the second time. "We raided the priest's home in Revigny-sur-Ornain, Major."

"The one we've had under surveillance? Richard Gravois?"

Oberleutnant Huber appeared even more anxious than usual. "Yes, M-Major, he's the one. Father Gravois, that's what the Catholics call him. We suspected he was helping the

Resistance rescue downed American and B-B-British airmen. We'd questioned him before but never found enough evidence to arrest him. All the same, we were suspicious."

"Yes, go on." Major Braun turned over page after page of the record book.

"We knew there was a downed American flier from a P-38. We found the wreckage, but no pilot."

"The one two weeks ago, south of here?"

"Yes, Herr Major. We felt sure we were close to discovering the escape route the Resistance was using to save them."

"The route we haven't yet found?"

"Yes, Herr Major. When we made our arrests, one of the men we arrested broke free. I felt sure he was the link we were looking for. Unfortunately," Huber said, sounding disappointed, "he died before we could get him here for questioning."

"You don't sound terribly broken-hearted, Huber."

Huber smiled. "Well, you see, Herr Major, after he died, he led us to the priest."

Braun slapped a hand onto his desk in exasperation. "Dummkopf, how could a dead man lead you anywhere?"

Huber took a step backward. "B-but he did, I swear. I learned back in 1942 and 1943, whenever we interrogated suspects or arrested someone, they always had something with them."

"Something? What something? Oberleutnant, you are making no sense."

"I'll try to do better, Herr Major. I noticed they might have a scrap of paper, some coins, a pencil, any sort of something. But then this year I began to observe that those we arrested no longer had anything like that in their possession. No pencils, no coins, no paper. Nothing."

The oberleutnant leaned forward to rest his hands on Braun's desk.

"Stand to attention, Huber, and get your hands off my desk!"

Huber backed away and stood up straight. "I beg your pardon, Major. But you see, I concluded the maquis had become more organized, telling anyone who helped them not to carry anything that might incriminate them. Once I realized this, it only seemed logical other things might be hidden in their clothes."

"Shrewd deduction, Huber."

"Thank you, Major. So I had him brought here to headquarters, that is, his dead body, brought in through the delivery entrance." He pointed to the floor. "After we stripped off all his clothes, I went over every stitch. The belt loops seemed wider than usual, and on closer inspection I found one was stiffer than the rest. I tore this loop off and cut out the stitching. Inside was a folded piece of paper with an address *and* a date and time. The date was yesterday, 13 August."

Braun whistled, eyes open wide. "Get it over with, Huber. And pull your nerves together. You make me nervous waiting for you to get to the point."

"Ja, Herr Major. We staked out the address four hours before the time written on the piece of paper and picked up plenty of activity, but it was clear why no suspicions were raised before."

"And why is that?"

"Clever, really. The location was Saint-Pierre church in Revigny-sur-Ornain. It was before Sunday Mass, when there would be a lot of activity. Confession, you know. Before Mass was to begin, we saw a man dressed like a priest walk toward the church. Two boys were playing ball on the sidewalk, and the ball got away and rolled toward the man who appeared to be a priest. He bent over and picked up the ball."

"So?"

"This is the strange part, Major. He stood straight up, brought his arms close up across his chest, looked over his shoulder, looked back the other way, extended his arms, and threw the ball, fast, to one of the boys. Before the war, I visited my cousin in St. Louis and we went to a baseball game. The suspect threw that ball just like an American baseball player."

"That's it? Huber, really—"

"That's it, Major. But that's very important, you see, because he entered the church, so we surrounded it and went in after him. He surrendered without a struggle. It was the American pilot. The church pastor tried to say he didn't know who the man was, had never seen him before. When we searched the priest's office, though, we found that ledger"—he pointed to it—"in a secret compartment of his desk."

Major Braun opened the ledger and ran his finger along the top line of the first page.

"J N, F O, N N, G, V, D, F A slash mark R, and a plus sign. Hmm."

He then traced down the first column.

"Numbers ... I see. Dates that seem to go back well before the first war."

Huber bent forward over the book, as if eager for praise. "Yes, yes, the first one is 1896."

"This next column must be surnames. Interesting. Ah, yes, I see they are. F A slash mark R—what do you make of that, Huber?"

Huber straightened up. It was becoming difficult for him to contain his glee. "The last column should clear that up for you, Major." He walked around the desk to stand next to

Braun and look down as he scanned the column, until the major's glare sent him back to the other side of the desk like a shot.

"A plus sign again? Interesting. C, C, C, P, C, C, P, H, H, H, H."

With the fourth H the major's finger shot over to the column headed N N. "This one's a Polish name and that plus sign must be a damned cross. I'll bet it's for the birth religion." Major Braun began to rub his hands together. "These are Jews! H for Hebrew, C for Catholic, P for Protestant. Huber, this book is a record of adoptions, secretly arranged by this priest!"

"But, Herr Major, this Gravois couldn't have arranged adoptions in the last century, he's too young."

"That doesn't matter. I'm sure I'm right. The priest before him would have passed the record book on to Gravois."

With that, Braun went back over the headings of the columns again and read each one aloud as he deciphered it.

"J N, that would be jour de naissance, date of birth. F O, famille d'origine, birth family. N N, nom de naissance, name given at birth. G for genre, gender. V for ville, the town and D for Département. F A slash mark R would have to be famille adoptive, the adopting family, and R for résidence, where the adoptive family lives."

"Brilliant, Herr Major!" Huber pointed to the column of Hs. "You see, now you have a record of all of the adoptions this priest and the one before him arranged during the last fifty years. Think of it, a total of forty-eight Jews right here in those pages. Forty-eight more Jews to round up."

"Unteroffizier, bring me two glasses. Schnell!"

Braun reached into his bottom desk drawer to retrieve a bottle of cognac. When the glasses arrived, Braun poured a hefty tot into each one.

"Huber, you're a genius. Well done. Well done, indeed. I wouldn't be surprised if you might expect a decoration for this." Some insignificant one, he was thinking, but Huber didn't know that. The man was like a puppy dog, so eager to please.

Braun jotted down some numbers on his blotter and looked up. "What we need to do now is calculate how many of these forty-eight Jews could have fathered or given birth to children. Once we know that, we may have far more than forty-eight to round up." He studied the columns and made some more notes. "Huber, wouldn't you agree anyone born after 1929, even if they were a Jew, wouldn't be old enough to create any more Jews?"

"That makes sense, sir."

"Then I count thirty-five Jews that could have created more vermin."

"But Major, any offspring, especially from a Jew that was adopted, might not be a full-blooded Jew but a Mischlinge. Don't at least three grandparents have to be Jewish before they're considered full-blooded Jews?"

"Oberleutnant, do not bother yourself with details. If they look Jewish, that's good enough for me. Arrest them. I assure you, we're perfectly within our rights to do so."

Braun grabbed a red pencil and began circling adoptive family names and locations in the ledger for the thirty-five Jews adopted before 1930. "These are the ones we need to concentrate on first. I want to know the whereabouts of these individuals and any progeny." He drummed his index finger on the page. "I want this information by tomorrow morning. Now, then, Prosit. Drink up, Huber."

While Huber was polishing off his cognac Braun had more orders to give. "All this should be easy enough. I want this information encoded and sent to Berlin at once, and see to it this ledger is locked up."

Huber set his glass down, saluted, turned on his heel, and was almost out the door when Braun called after him. "By the way, be sure to thank the good Father for his assistance." After Huber left, Braun sat for a few moments relishing thoughts of the outstanding results this day's work would soon bring.

He grabbed the notes he had made, stood, and carried his red pencil to the operational map on the wall. First, he wrote a 5 next to Renigny-sur-Ornain and circled it. In similar fashion, he wrote other numbers next to four other towns and villages surrounding Revigny-sur-Ornain and circled them. With a final flourish, he wrote a 4 next to Sermaize-les-Bains, just to the southwest of Renigny-sur-Ornain, and circled it.

With that he returned to his desk, picked up his unfinished drink, and downed the rest of the cognac in one conclusive gulp.

The next morning's dispatches saw to it that Braun's jubilant mood didn't last. The Germans were still in control of the rail lines west of Paris, despite the Allies' anticipated rapid advance. Knowing Paris would fall in a mere matter of days, Braun set himself to calculate how long before the Germans would be forced to abandon Reims. Figuring an average advance of ten kilometers per day, it should give them at least two weeks.

From the file drawer to his left he withdrew Gestapo memos 71,198, 71,199, and 72,003. He looked over the memos, savoring what they predicted. They'll have to give me that promotion now.

"Unteroffizier, get Oberleutnant Huber in here at once."

"Jawohl, Herr Major."

In less than two minutes Huber stood at attention before Braun's desk.

"Huber, sit down." Braun studied the file before him, then removed his glasses and rubbed his eyes. "Huber, where are we with the final roundup?" He held up Gestapo memo 72,003. "I have just read the most recent dispatch from Berlin. It's been ordered for the 29th."

Because word had already got around that Braun was in a nasty mood, Huber did his best to avoid his wrath.

"Major, we have all necessary transport in order. The men have been briefed on their assignments. We have confirmed whereabouts of all the Jews from the ledger as well as the rest." He paused for breath. "And I have taken the precaution of posting extra guards around the railway station in Chalons-en-Champagne and extra patrols on the tracks east of town."

"Fuel?"

"I have requisitioned the fuel and vehicles we will need."

"And the thirty-five Jews born before 1930?"

"Yes, sir. Of the thirty-five, seventeen were male and eighteen were female. Of the seventeen males, four died in the war, two died of natural causes, and five could not be located."

"What do you mean, could not be located?"

Huber cringed, stammering again. "M-M-Major, we t-turned over rocks, we searched b-barns, we looked everywhere but the b-bottom of the river. They're just no longer here. But—" his face brightened. "We were, however, able to confirm fifteen offspring and their location."

"And the females?"

"We were able to locate thirteen of the eighteen females and confirm nineteen total offspring. We should be able to arrest all fifty-three and all the other Jews we know about."

"Excellent, Huber. This is excellent." As Huber's shoulders relaxed, the major leaned back in his chair to gaze at the ceiling, hands clasped behind his head. "So, your plan?"

Huber moved to the map and began pointing. "Major, if I may, we can begin at dawn on the 29th, start close to Reims. We will work south and east from Épernay. When we reach Chalons-en-Champagne we will unload our detainees and proceed toward Bar-le-Duc. Our last location is Sermaize-les-Bains, about midafternoon."

"Who has the northern sector?"

"Oberleutnant Wagner."

"He must understand he needs to be at the Chalons-en-Champagne railway station no later than 1800 hours on the 29th."

"Yes, Herr Major."

"Good. We shall all board the train. It is to be the last train headed east, and in view of the fact that it will be loaded with Jews, we shall have priority. We wait for no one, Huber."

"Yes, Herr Major. I understand."

"No one, Huber, not even you." Braun waved a hand in dismissal.

Huber had turned to leave when Braun expressed his final thought.

"Huber, I want those Jews. I warn you, all of them. If anyone gets in your way, do whatever you must. Arrest them or shoot them, it doesn't matter. I want those Jews!"

With a smart salute Huber left the room.

After Braun had Oberleutnant Wagner brought in for a similar briefing, he dismissed him as well, confident all would go according to plan. In the now empty room, Braun moved to the map again and studied the area between Paris and Reims. After fifteen minutes he barked out yet another order.

"Unteroffizier, get me the most current situation report of the front."

The report was brought, and as Braun read it and compared what he was reading to the varicolored pins and labels on the map, he refused to believe the conclusions being forced upon him. His beloved Fatherland was crumbling before his very eyes. How could this have happened?

He thought back to how things had been in the beginning, after Hitler came to power and established the Gestapo. Wherever the Gestapo went, immediate respect had followed. Or so he had believed. Until this moment he had never admitted respect was not what made people cower and comply with their orders, no matter how brutal. Fear and fear alone had impelled it. In the light of such a significant increase in resistance activities, their missions often downright brazen, he understood at last no one respected the Gestapo. He saw the motivation of the maquis for what it was, pure hatred. A blazing, impassioned hatred gave them superhuman courage. The truth of all this sank into him, no longer to be denied.

As the failure of the Third Reich became a reality, Major Braun's hatred of the Jews, ever powerful, became even more intense. They were to blame for all the problems that had plunged Germany and the rest of Europe into despair. Because Braun laid at the feet of the Jews every ounce of blame for the millions of lives lost, it was only right they should pay with their own.

In 1915, when he was twelve years old, Braun had last seen his father, a casualty of the Great War. Young Braun needed someone to blame for his loss. At first he blamed the Bolsheviks, but when he learned more about the Russian

Revolution and realized how many of those revolutionaries were Jews, he had someone to blame—the Jews. The rise of the National Socialist Party solidified his beliefs once and for all. The Jews, they were to blame, and no one but the Jews.

Without the Jews, there would have been no need for war.

Without the Jews, Europe would be a safer place.

Without the Jews, his life had little meaning.

In 1936 when he heard his Führer speak at a Munich rally, Hitler's words had inflamed and galvanized him to action. "In the battle between the races, there is no truce. If you are determined finally to defend yourselves, German people, then be pitiless!"

Braun took two new pins from a small box on the shelf beside the map. Each pin bore a small red paper tag imprinted on one side with a black Hakenkreuz, the swastika. The other side was blank. On the blank side of the two tags Braun wrote "3PG" and pushed them into the map just to the west of Paris.

He felt confident, knowing the 3rd Panzer-Grenadier Division would be responsible for stabilizing the front in the direction of Reims. He knew the American 3rd Army under General George S. Patton was on the move to the south and east. If Patton could be contained, prevented from getting ahead to create a pincer movement that would trap the retreating Germans, the planned roundup for the twenty-ninth should proceed according to schedule.

Moving away from the map, Braun resumed his seat behind the desk and picked up the ledger book to caress it. He ran his hand over its smooth surface as a master cabinetmaker would stroke a finished table. He then opened it to look again at the pages filled with those meticulous notations.

"Oh yes," he said to himself. "The beautiful twenty-ninth."

CHAPTER 24

Anton sat at the wireless set with one ear next to the speaker.

"Come on, Anton, we want it word for word, exact. Every lie that fat little bastard spews. You got that?"

"Listen to me, Friedrich, if you're jawing, I can't hear well enough to translate." Anton continued to twist the main dial, then the fine-tune knob. When Churchill's voice came over the BBC, audible in spite of occasional crackles, Anton began to translate.

"My Lord Mayor, My Lady Mayoress, My Lords and Gentlemen: When I look back over these war-time years, I cannot help feeling that time is an inadequate measure of their duration …"

One of the officers crowded around the radio shouted, "Why the hell do we have to listen to that pompous son-of-a-bitch? If you don't shut that crap off, I'll put a bullet through the wireless."

"Quiet, you assholes," Hans said. "Some of us want to hear what he has to say. Your life might depend on it."

"Come on, Krüger," another man argued. "You can't possibly believe what he has to say, can you?"

Anton continued, undeterred. "... Sometimes events are galloping forward at reckless speed. Sometimes there are long anxious pauses which we have to bear."

Another interruption. "Jawohl, we'll give you plenty to pause about before long, you fat bastard!"

"… It's hard to remember how long ago this war began. One can never be sure if it has lasted a flash or an age. I congratulated the city of London in 1943 on that memorable and exhilarating year of almost unbroken success. All Africa, Sicily and Italy has been cleared of the enemy. The Allied advance north into Italy was a long, bloody campaign. The German's defensive strategy to delay the allied advance into Italy had been an effective one, but futile. Aided by geography and weather, it took almost a full year for the combined Allies to push successfully into the underbelly of Europe. By June of this year, 1944, Rome had fallen, and the Allies had successfully landed across the English Channel. After bitter fighting in the hedgerows of Normandy, the Americans and we British are finally poised to sweep across France on their drive to force the German invader into its lair."

Hans, who found himself stirred by the man's magisterial language, took pains not to let the others know even though many were listening with as much interest.

"In Russia, Marshall Stalin's armies are rolling triumphantly forward to cleanse their native land of the German invader. The Germans have suffered one defeat after another." Anton kept his head bent and his hand on the tuning knob, making frequent adjustments. "The U-Boat menace has, for the time being—I always put these remarks in for life is full of surprises—has been practically erased. The map of Nazi Germany is contracting. My Lord Mayor, our island nation is secure and the Luftwaffe has been decimated allowing the Allies to exercise total control of the airspace and continue their relentless bombings of Germany. I can assure you we have not suffered a tenth as those who first started this merciless war."

By now some of the group had sat down, looking serious for the first time.

"But we must not slacken in our efforts. The wounded and rabid animal that was once the Third Reich now lies stretched across Europe, panting in near-agonal breaths, but it will take the full exertion of the three great powers, every scrap of strength and sacrifice that we can give to crush down the desperate persistence that we must expect from Hitler's deadly army."

The look on Anton's face suggested he might have begun to think the Wehrmacht was not the threat it once was. Well, Hans said to himself, they could believe it or not, but it was true. Near-agonal breaths, Anton had translated. Their last gasps.

"Nothing must stand in the way of the prosecution of the war to its ultimate conclusion and if we were to fail in that, we should not be worthy of your confidence, My Lord Mayor."

Anton shut the wireless off and stood to stretch. "Did you listen to those ignorant slobs clap at his nonsense? How much of that can anyone believe?"

Hans answered him. "We may not believe it, but clearly the British people do, and the man does have a point. We haven't had a successful offensive in months."

"What are you, Krüger, a traitor?" someone shouted.

"No more than you," Hans said. "But I believe there may be some hope in this, for complacency can be our best friend. You wait and see."

"So long, you two," Friedrich said, giving Hans and Anton a wave. "We'll let you both solve the problems of the German army." And with that he and the other officers left to go to their quarters.

"Good, they're gone," Anton said, while closing the door. "Hans, Hitler just might realize the war is lost. It's like that fat little bastard said, the Third Reich hasn't seen a success on the battlefield since Russia. I couldn't say it with them here, but I for one am starting to question the outcome of this war."

Hans shook a finger at his friend. "Be extremely careful whom you say this to. We both know if you said it to the wrong person you could be shot."

"Fine. Shoot me. At least I'll know when and from where it's coming."

"I know the door is shut," Hans said, "but seriously, Anton, let's find a more private place to discuss these things."

The two friends got up and walked to a secluded reading room downstairs away from the hotel lobby, went in, and closed the door. Hans placed two chairs close together before he spoke again.

"Anton, in Hitler's mind there are two wars. I'm convinced of this. The obvious one is the war we're waging, the other is his war against the Jews. And the former war, our war, is a consequence of the latter one, the war of Jewish extermination."

Anton leaned back in the chair and stroked his chin. "You may be right."

"I know I'm right." Hans spoke with more force now. "Our war, the one we've been fighting, began in 1939. Hitler's declaration of war against the Jews, on the other hand, first appeared in *Mein Kampf*, but the documents legitimizing this war were not made official until he became chancellor in 1933."

"Not so loud, Hans. Maybe you're the one who should be careful."

Fired up by his conclusions, Hans couldn't hold back. "Think of it! We've had only a little less than five years of conventional war, yet that pales beside Hitler's nineteen years of waging war on the Jews. Look at everything the German army's done in France. Every move designed to kill Jews."

Anton bent closer, almost speaking into his friend's ear.

"Hans, please. Lower your voice. Someone might hear."

Hans tried to oblige. "All right, Anton, I'll keep my voice down, but I must make you understand. Do you know why we can't get trains to transport our troops?"

"Allied bombing? The maquis?"

"No. Don't be foolish. Can't you see it? All the trains are used to transport Jews to places like Auschwitz, Ravensbrück, Buchenwald. Sure, the maquis has been a thorn in our side, and sure, the bombs keep falling, but if you look around, you'll realize all our government's efforts have been aimed at and intensified against the Jews, especially now that the Allies are on the outskirts of Paris. They have to do it now, or they'll never be able to."

"This is too much for me to digest. What about stopping in the bar for a beer? I need one after all that," Anton said.

"Fine with me. I could use a beer myself." They found a table in the hotel bar and got the barman to serve them, if not with outstanding enthusiasm. They didn't have much to say to each other by then, and as they sat together letting the beer soothe their tense nerves, two fellow officers at a nearby table were discussing the Drancy transit camp outside Paris.

"I feel sure the last convoy to Auschwitz will be leaving from Drancy," one of them said.

The other, a stern-looking chap, grinned. "In that case, there go another twelve hundred for the Führer."

Hans shivered, whispering to Anton, "My God, will they stop at nothing?"

Anton was whispering in return. "Come on, let's go. I've finished this beer, I don't want any more."

When they reached their quarters Hans held the door open for Anton to precede him. "What's the use?" he said. "We seem to grow weaker and weaker, while the Allies grow stronger every day."

Anton plopped down onto his bed and tossed his hat aside. "Come now, this is no time for despair. We have our duty to do. And I don't have to remind you, the war is far from over. We're still in France, still capable of fighting."

"When do you think Paris will fall?"

Anton thought a moment before he answered. "Soon, no more than a week or two, and then we'll be headed east. I can't see us making a stand here in France. A delaying action, maybe, but no all-out stand." He considered the prospects further. "We might dig in our heels when we hit the Ardennes," he shook his head, "but not here, never."

Hans felt as if he might be sick.

"Hans, sit down. You look ill. What is it?"

"Nothing serious. I'm just thinking about all of this chaos, what a mess it's likely to be."

"Anton, what's your guess? Will we head due east, or more to the northeast?"

"The most direct route to Germany is due east by way of Nancy, but my guess is we'll take a route northeastward to Reims and on through Luxembourg. It would make more sense because the terrain is more favorable. Why?"

"Just wondering, that's all."

Anton looked puzzled. "Are you sure that's all? Regardless of the route, you can count on the maquis causing more and more problems for us. We've seen it already. Once Paris is liberated, their boldness will surpass everything they've done thus far. It won't be pretty. They'll be bolder than ever, mark my word."

Hans felt distracted, unable to settle. He stood and put on his hat. "I have to go over to headquarters." Before starting out and closing the door behind him, he said, "I'll catch up with you later."

With every passing day, as more and more actions were taken against the Jews, the more Aimée occupied his thoughts. In all the twenty-two months since he'd seen and held her, so far he'd been unable to think of a way to guarantee her safety. That knowledge tortured him. Though his nightmares had lessened a bit, they'd never gone away. Now, with the Allies heading east, perhaps he could allow himself to entertain the possibility of a life with her after the fighting, or at least after the Allies overran the area around Sermaize-les-Bains. Realizing it might be possible, he began to formulate a plan.

CHAPTER 25

Hans was within 100 meters of divisional headquarters when he saw a cloud of smoke swirling around the entire building. No longer the usual model of organization and order, it was a disturbed beehive. Men rushed in and out with reckless abandon. Hans cleared the threshold then stepped aside to avoid being caught up in the tumult. No one paid any attention as he watched a nonstop procession of clerks carry armloads of documents out the back door to drop into fires, every record relating to the 3rd Panzer-Grenadier Division.

A motorcycle courier jumped off his machine and dashed into the building, trying without success to catch the eye of an officer from the communications room. Agitated, he stepped in front of the officer, snapped to attention, and saluted.

"Heil Hitler!"

Immersed in reading a report, the officer didn't look up. The courier reached into his leather pouch to bring out an envelope.

"Herr Hauptmann, I have a dispatch from Gestapo headquarters."

"Incoming dispatch tray." The hauptmann pointed, otherwise engaged.

"Herr Hauptmann, I have orders to personally give it to you."

"Fine, you've given it to me."

The courier stood waiting for a response.

"Dismissed!"

"Herr Hauptmann, I have orders to await a reply."

Annoyed, the hauptmann looked around the room and jerked a thumb at the corner. "Stand over there out of the way." He picked up the envelope and took out the dispatch to read.

GEHEIME STAATSPOLIZEI - BERLIN

17, AUG. 1944

MEMO NO. 72003

+BERLIN 346 482 17.8.44 09:15===

TO: HQ 3RD PANZER-GRENADIER (MOT)===

REGARDING: DETENTION AND DEPORTATION OF JEWS IN SOUTHERN SECTOR OF REIMS DEPARTMENT 29, AUG. 1944===

YOU ARE HEREBY ORDERED TO PROVIDE COOPERATION AND NEEDED ASSISTANCE TO THE ROUNDUP OF ALL KNOWN JEWS IN THE SOUTHERN SECTOR OF THE REIMS DEPARTMENT ON 29, AUG. 1944. THIS ORDER IS IN EFFECT UNTIL FURTHER NOTICE. JEWS IN THE CITIES OF ÉPERNAY, AVIZE, RENIGNY-SUR-ORNAIN, CHALONS-EN-CHAMPAGNE, SOMMESOUS, VERTUS, VERZY, GIVRY-EN-ARGONNE, AND SERMAIZE-LES-BAINS ARE TO BE ARRESTED. THIS AREA WILL INCLUDE A 100 KM ARC SOUTHEAST OF REIMS AND WILL INTERSECT WITH THE WESTERN BORDER OF THE NANCY DEPARTMENT OF THE GESTAPO. ALL ACTIVITIES WEST OF BAR-LE-DUC WILL FALL UNDER THE JURISDICTION OF THE REIMS DEPARTMENT. YOUR COMPLETE COOPERATION AND SUPPORT ARE EXPECTED. ARRESTED JEWS ARE TO BE

IMMEDIATELY ESCORTED TO THE RAIL STATION AT CHALONS-EN-CHAMPAGNE BY 18:00 HOURS FOR DEPORTATION.

NO DETENTION REVIEW DATE.===

The hauptmann laid the Gestapo dispatch on his desk and looked around. Seeing a typewriter at a vacant desk, he strode over, cranked a sheet of paper in, pounded out a reply, ripped it free, and sealed it in an envelope. "There. Your reply."

The courier stowed it in his pouch. "Thank you, Herr Hauptmann. Heil Hitler!" And he was off again on his bike.

A nearby oberleutnant said, "What was that all about?"

The hauptmann shook his head. "Unbelievable." He tossed the report he'd been reading on the desk next to the typewriter. "In the midst of all this, the Gestapo has a few more Jews to collect. They actually have a train scheduled for deportation on the 29th out of Chalons-en-Champagne."

The colleague shook his head in sympathy.

In all the confusion, Hans noticed the forgotten dispatch on the hauptmann's desk. He eased through the steady procession of clerks hauling out documents and caught the arm of one of them. The clerk snapped to attention and saluted.

"At ease. Get me the map for the region between Reims and Nancy. Now!" The clerk went away and returned in a moment. Hans took the map and laid it on the hauptmann's desk. "Is this the correct one?"

"Yes, I double-checked."

"Good." When Hans left it lying there, the puzzled clerk saluted and went back to what he'd been doing. Hans grasped the folded map, careful to include the Gestapo dispatch beneath it, and carried both to the lavatory where he could read undisturbed.

Moments later, aware of all the dispatch's terrifying content, he returned to the cacophony of the larger room to spread the map on a table in the corner. His intention was to trace possible routes the division might follow in its retreat. On the far wall he could see the Western Front situation map. He began to formulate his plan.

Maybe, just maybe … .

The situation map indicated the U.S. 20th Corps was on the move, just south of Paris. The U.S. 7th Army driving north from Marseilles would ensure that the 20th Corps drifted no further south. Seeing this, Hans knew his division's retreat would take him just south of Reims, near if not through Sermaize-les-Bains.

The only potential challenge was that Patton's 3rd Army would be part of the advance of the 20th Corps, and Patton's legendary speed might limit his own division's time in or around Sermaize-les-Bains.

Everything would depend on the maquis doing its job.

Hans was struggling to keep his approach analytical and not let emotions run away with him. He studied the area south of Reims and west of Bar-le-Duc and his gut ached when he discovered Sermaize-les-Bains was included in the roundup ordered for the 29th. He checked the map's scale to calculate the distance from the Chalons-en-Champagne railway station to Sermaize-les-Bains.

Only fifty-seven kilometers.

He refolded the map, taking care to conceal the Gestapo dispatch underneath. He laid both on the corner of the desk just as the clerk who'd gotten it for him scooted past.

"You, I'm through with the map." He pointed to it. "Right there."

After he'd walked several hundred meters from the command post Hans' pulse raced even faster than it had inside. Deep breaths failed to calm him. His anxiety rose by the minute, too great for him to control.

Fifty-seven kilometers. It could work.

With the 3rd Panzer-Grenadier Division's probable future location on the 29th somewhere near Sermaize-les-Bains, it was just a matter of timing and logistics. Trained in both, he could make it work.

What new information had the Gestapo discovered? Was one of the fifteen filed copies of some report to blame? With a little luck, he could pull it off. While he knew he still needed to devise a viable, yet flexible plan, Hans felt in his heart that Aimée was safe and would be so until the afternoon of the 29th.

The dispatch added a sense of urgency.

Hans was back in his room when he considered taking Anton into his confidence. He was talking to himself as he thought.

"What the hell can I do to make this happen? Suppose they aren't even there?"

Anton looked up, hearing his voice. "Who? Who aren't where?"

"I have something important to ask you. Do you remember my telling you I knew it in my gut the day my brother Peter died?"

"Ja, but you don't know exactly what day he died."

"I do. It was right after Christmas, December 26th. I'm sure of it. I can't prove it, but I'm sure all the same."

Hans pulled off his boots and tossed them aside to lie back on his bunk. "I remember I felt fine, but then out of the blue I had an overwhelming premonition something terrible had happened to U-357."

"Ja?"

"If you truly love someone, if you're connected to them in your heart, don't you think that same kind of communication can exist, the kind I know I felt when Peter died? For everybody, I mean, not just brothers."

"Ja, I think that might be true."

"Good. So do I, Anton. So do I."

CHAPTER 26

The wind hitting his face at eighty miles per hour was an abrupt and welcome change from the rising nausea Lieutenant Stephen Mabry had been feeling throughout the flight. He and his team, still inside the transport plane's fuselage, were about to be dropped into German-occupied France. Mabry reviewed the squad's operational orders in his mind and attached his static line just as the C-47 made a steep banking turn to the south in an attempt to deceive Germans who might be tracking their ground path.

All eyes were on the jumpmaster responsible for the elite members of the United Kingdom's 22nd Special Air Service Regiment. On his command, the group hooked up and waited for the warning light to signal they were over the drop zone. Before anyone had time to adjust to being upright, the light flashed green.

The jumpmaster slapped each paratrooper on the back as one by one, they plunged headlong out the open door.

"*GO! GO! GO!*"

Mabry was first out. After what seemed an eternity, his parachute lines jerked him upward like the strings on a marionette. Looking to the left he was comforted to see five parachutes. Four parachutes supporting his men swayed back and forth, followed by a distant fifth bearing their needed supplies. The full moon provided superb visibility, while the August night soon swallowed up the drone of their fast-departing plane.

Impressed by the vast solitude that lay beneath him, Mabry wished it would last forever. The fresh aroma of the French countryside filled his lungs as he considered the topography. Right, that must be the Saulx valley. Thank God he'd dropped us west of the Ornain River. Yes, and that must be Bar-le-Duc.

He was encouraged by the absence of dimmed headlights on the outskirts of the town. Good, no one in pursuit. Now let's hope there'll be no ambush.

As the ground rose to meet him, Mabry flexed his knees to absorb the impact. The instant he landed he rolled forward, sprang to his feet, and gathered up his parachute. Fifty yards in front of him he could see the other four members of his team. Excellent job, men. No sound. So far, so good.

With his immediate task accomplished, Mabry scanned the tree line to the north. There it was, the reception team's anticipated signal light. Dit dah, it flashed: A in Morse code. The four paratroopers, crouching low, ran to meet their reception party less than 200 meters away.

A deep but subdued voice broke the silence. "Bonjour, mes amis. Welcome to France. Je suis Yves Mirande."

Out of breath, the lead man of the British team answered. "Leftenant Mabry here, and these are my men." He rested a hand on the shoulder of the man next to him. "Sergeant Colin Hartwig, then Private Walsh—"

"Call me Wally."

"And next to Wally there, Private MacGregor."

"Mac."

"And finally, at the end, Corporal Smythe."

All four nodded in unison.

"Eh bien, mes amis."

The leader of the maquisards embraced the lieutenant and kissed him on both cheeks in the French manner, then repeated the welcome with the other four. "We are most, how do you say? Excited to receive you."

Yves Mirande went on to introduce his comrades by name. Each of the four maquis fighters offered his own version of welcome. But when they reached to take the parachutes, Mabry's men resisted.

"Not to worry, men, let them go. We'll have no further use for them."

"Merci beaucoup, Leftenant," Yves said with a flash of white teeth. "Ma mère, she desires use of the silk to sew a dress for my bride one day."

At that Wally grinned and handed over his parachute. "Well, mate, you can 'ave 'er make one for me sweetheart and I'll come and get it when this bloody war's over."

"Allors," Yves said, "now we commence." He jerked his head toward the dropped supplies and without a sound all the men set to work collecting and distributing them. With that completed, a total of ten men headed west at a brisk pace with Yves in the lead until, at the edge of a clearing, he raised his arm to bring them to a halt. He stood still and whispered, "Les boches, they will sometimes wait at the edge of a clearing with their machine guns. By the full moon they can see us enter into the open and they will begin, how do you say? shooting." When all they heard was the steady cadence of crickets he signaled for the others to follow the edge of the trees.

Mabry caught up with Yves to ask in a hushed tone, "How far do we have to go?"

"To the house of a farm about two kilometers distant. Your men will be able to repose, perhaps sleep in the barn. We can examine your orders."

Mabry fell back to join his team. "Just two klicks to go, men. We'll rest there for the night."

Smythe looked worried. "Sir, d'you suppose the bloody Krauts know we're here?"

"Doubt it. If they did, we'd know by now."

The familiar smell of manure confirmed the emerging outline of a barn and a farmhouse. A low stone wall blocking their path delineated the property. After Yves and the lieutenant conferred, Mabry beckoned the sergeant over.

"Hartwig, we'll base out of this farmhouse. Yves is reconnoitering to be sure it's safe. If a firefight breaks out, follow this wall to the left. Got it?"

"Yes sir."

The entire group gathered in the kitchen. Yves spread out a map on the table as he and Mabry took chairs while the others hunkered on the floor, backs to the wall. Mabry studied his host. Despite his slight stature, the Frenchman's forward, matter-of-fact manner, plus the fact he spoke English, made it clear why he was in charge.

"I must apologize," Yves said, "but we have no coffee. Would you like tea?"

"Nothing better," Mabry said.

Yves got up, filled a kettle with water, and put it on the stove to heat.

"While it's heating," Mabry said, "I have something here for you." He stood up to grope inside the leg pocket of his jumpsuit and produced a small, well-wrapped parcel. "Thought you'd appreciate some real sugar."

Yves looked up from the map, his face alight. "Bien merci. Silk and sugar. Ma mère will be most excited. Tomorrow is to be a good day."

The water was soon boiling, so Yves brewed up the tea to steep while he reviewed for the Brits what the maquis knew about the most recent German troop movements, suspected strength, and location. With a finger on the map he pointed south and east. "As of yesterday, 27 Août, the southern flanc ... is this the same word in English?

"Do you mean flank?"

"Oui, Leftenant, flank. This is the word. The south flank of the 3rd Panzer-Grenadier Division is here, Saint-Dizier. We believe they are at complete strength."

Mabry said, "Even after the Italian campaign?"

"Eh bien, mon ami, I see you are well informed. Oui, even after the Italian campaign. Forgive my poor English, I do my best. I tell you, do not be tricked about these boches. They are well exercised from battle, hard men, not fresh recruits. My people tell me they have excellent discipline."

Mabry said, "Shall I pour the tea?"

"Ah, oui."

While Mabry found some cracked mugs and poured tea for those who wanted it, Yves smoothed out the creases in the map. "They have—I do not know your word for this, garnison—"

"Their garrison," Mabry said.

"Oui, their garrison in the main part is around Saint-Eulien to the northwest of Saint-Dizier." He pointed it out on the map. "It appears they retreat to the east and northeast."

Hartwig said, "What about the north?"

"Yes, here are also elements of the same division. Their line marches north and south, most equal along the valley of the Saulx."

Mabry spoke up. "Our orders are to disrupt and harass their retreat and report on their location and strength. How do you suggest we proceed?"

Yves moved his finger to the northeast. "We are here, içi, about one half of the distance between Convonges to the west and Bar-le-Duc to the east. You understand the directions of the map?"

Mabry nodded. "I do. So shall we move out tomorrow?"

"I suggest we, how you say, tumble out in the morning and make a nuisance."

Mabry found it hard not to laugh at Yves's droll English. "How much opposition should we anticipate?"

"Alors, Leftenant, the American pilots tell us les boches are moving less and less during the day. And naturally the British pilots also say this. Forgive me, I don't wish to offend."

"No offense taken," Mabry said. "What about weather effects?"

"If clouds tomorrow, the Germans come out. If sun, they rest in their holes comme les lapins—like rabbits, you know, until we force them to move."

"Any readings on the weather for tomorrow?"

"We hope for much sun."

"Good, I hate a moving target."

After Yves translated with a grin for his countrymen, smiles, then a hearty laugh erupted all around. The maquisards all nodded and raised their tea mugs as if to say, to the mission's success.

Yves folded his map and checked his watch. "There will be light soon. You and your men rest, my men will guard. I will wake you when it is time."

"Righto. Jolly good," Mabry said. "Thanks. Tomorrow, or today, rather, we should have good hunting." He grabbed his Sten gun and headed for the barn, his men following after.

Morning arrived early for the SAS team. Their midnight insertion into German-occupied France provided little time for meaningful sleep. At 0600 hours, Yves was back. "Bonjour, Leftenant Mabry, I trust you and your men sleep?"

"A bit," Mabry said. "Your French straw is soft enough, but a few extra hours of kip would be nice, eh, men?"

"Bon. I regret, but we have work." Yves reached into a sack to hand out hunks of bread. "This is all I can offer, but tea is near to ready. We review things in the house when you have assembled yourselves, n'est-çe pas?"

Once again Yves had the map spread out on the table. When the last SAS man came in, he began. "I suggest we proceed south toward Combles-en-Barrois. That way we have much trees, and we may discover a convoy waiting to see what the weather brings."

Walsh said in an aside to MacGregor, "This bloke's all business," but one look from Mabry stopped further comment. "Sorry, sir," Walsh said.

Yves went on. "Très bien. We shall depart here and go immediately to the trees. There we stay in the trees as far as the road. Attend carefully to listen for motors, machines, on the road or in the air."

Mabry set down his mug. "D'accord. We accept your plan. If you will, please, lead the way." Once over the stone wall he pulled Walsh to one side. "What were you thinking, Private? We're here as their guests, and if you'd given the matter any thought, this man's a fighter who's killed more Germans in a day than you can hope to in a year."

"I'm sorry, sir, won't happen again."

"See to it that it doesn't. Now off you go."

Well within the protection of the forest, the band continued in single file. Yves, in the lead, would raise his arm to arrest their progress and listen for German activity at regular intervals. After one such stop Mabry had a question for him. "When we encounter the Krauts, how do you wish us to deploy?"

"That depends. If only a patrol, we engage them immediately. If a convoy in movement, we watch. If a convoy immobile, well, we stop and how you say? discuss. Maybe I bring in more of my men." Just then his arm went up and he whispered. "Silence. Chut."

"Did you hear something, a motor?" Mabry whispered.

Yves continued to listen, alert. Even without an order all the men concealed themselves.

Still silence.

The maquisards were the first to rise, then the Brits. Together they began to inch forward.

"I don't like this a bit," Walsh whispered. "Too quiet."

MacGregor crept from tree to tree. "Right, mate, much too quiet,"

Hartwig issued a gruff command. "Quiet, men. Want to get us killed?"

When Yves looked back at Mabry and jerked his head to indicate they should move on, Mabry gave the order. "Right, men, look sharp, follow Yves."

The mingled group of maquisards and Brits moved on through the thick trees until they fanned out at a clearing just short of a road, each one taking cover by crouching behind a tree.

Yves was the first to stand, followed by Smythe, but a flicker of light at the other end of the clearing brought Yves down again. A shot rang out, and right away the others knew by Smythe's gurgled moan that he'd taken a mortal wound. When Mabry crouched to go to his fallen team member, the man's blank stare confirmed instant death.

"Aux arbres!" Yves yelled. "Back into the trees."

Without delay, the maquisards and remaining Brits ran deeper into the forest. When they stopped to regroup, Mabry held up the dog tags he'd yanked from Smythe's neck, relieved he hadn't lost them in the hasty retreat.

"Yves," he said, "will they pursue us?"

"Non, les boches have had experience with the maquis, so they believe it is a trap. We have taught them well. But they will wait."

"Why do you say that?"

"When they find the body, they will know he is not maquis. Then they will worry about attack from the air. Non, we are safe for now, but we must move on."

CHAPTER 27

On a winding road east of Robert-Espagne and just west of the village of Trémont-sur-Saulx, the four remaining SAS and four maquisards assembled in a depression along a row of trees as the sun reached its zenith. Yves held their attention, outlining his plan on the ground with a pointed stick.

"I suggest one of your men place himself about 100 meters along the road to the northeast. One of mine will do the same to the southwest. If the Germans move, they will arrive from the southwest.

"We others, all save one, will be here on this side, the other one on the other side." Eye contact followed by a nod confirmed all was understood. "Do not forget, if they have a machine gun, eliminate it first. We only attack what is easiest. And no prisoners."

Hartwig's eyebrows went up. "No prisoners?"

"None. We shoot les boches, we do not feed them. If more than two trucks or an armored vehicle arrive, let it pass. Do not shoot before my signal." Yves stood, arched his back, and stretched his legs. "Questions?"

Hartwig had another concern. "What's our escape route?"

"Ah, a good question. If necessary, we will fall back to the tree line." Yves extended his arm and pointed north. "From there go straight in that direction, plenty of cover. Proceed to the second farmhouse, it is maquis. We will meet there. Eh bien, we go."

While Walsh headed up the roadside to the northeast, one of the maquisards headed southwest and one darted across the road. Ten minutes later they could hear a distant engine.

Yves nodded to Mabry and whispered, "Les boches. Petrol engine. Probably a staff car."

Within moments they could tell the German vehicle was almost upon them, but before it rounded the last curve Yves scanned the road to make sure it wasn't an advance element of a convoy. Still crouching, he raised his arm to indicate everyone should wait.

"Leftenant," he whispered, "do you agree they are proceeding perhaps at a velocity of seventy kilometers?"

"I'd say you're correct."

"Then we wait for them to come fifty meters closer."

The car closed the distance, and when Yves lowered his arm and stood up, a hail of gunfire blew the car's windscreen apart and ripped into the occupants. The car careened to the side and into the ditch, where it flipped over and spilled out its occupants. Moments later on the ground beside it the team counted four lifeless Germans.

The maquisard posted across the road ran over to keep watch for following traffic, while MacGregor and the other French rejoined the commandos.

Yves poked around the wreckage, lifted a leather pouch from the back of the car and handed it off. "Leftenant, this may be of interest." He then pointed to the gas can strapped to the vehicle's side. One of the other maquisards ran over, removed it, and set it aside while the rest gathered up the German guns.

Yves knelt next to the nearest body. He raised the German's limp hand and let it fall. With two fingers on the German officer's neck, he waited a moment longer, took his hand away, and said, "Mort." Dead. He did the same with the remaining three and announced with satisfaction that they, too, were as dead as the first. Then he rolled them onto their backs and examined their uniforms and insignia in detail.

Mabry, who was watching, commented, "3rd Panzer-Grenadier Division. Not bad. One leftenant colonel, one captain, and two NCOs."

Yves pulled a pistol from his waistband, confirmed a shell was chambered, and when he shot the senior officer's corpse between the eyes, the bullet's passage kicked up the lifeless head. The hole looked no more harmless than a pockmark. "Ça c'est pour mon père." He walked over to the captain's corpse and fired a second round with equal accuracy. "Pour mon frère."

Walsh looked to Mabry for clarification. "For my father, my brother," the lieutenant said.

Yves was approaching the two dead sergeants when a shout came from the road. "Plus des boches!" More Germans on the way.

Alert, the commandos made out the sound of two engines—a second car and a motorcycle. "Quick," Yves said, "hide yourselves." He spat in the direction of the NCOs' corpses and led the band to the tree line behind them before the vehicles came into view.

The motorcycle and Kübelwagen came to an abrupt stop at the ambush site. The driver of the Kübelwagen rushed to the opposite side of the vehicle and opened the door for the oberst, who walked over to the slain bodies. The maquisards and SAS group watched his face change from curiosity to the disfigurement of rage. He stood over his fellow officer's corpse, squatted down and attempted to remove his wedding band. All he found was a pale fresh furrow where the ring had been. With clenched fists and a set jaw he walked over to the motorcyclist who had dismounted to stand by his bike. Mabry was close enough to hear every word the German said.

"Unteroffizier, you are to drive back to Saint-Eulien and inform my staff of all you have seen here. Everything." His face was scarlet, his body tense.

"Jawohl," the motorcyclist said, with a salute.

"In addition, I want two fully outfitted squads of men loaded on two transports ready for departure first thing tomorrow."

As the cyclist waited for further instruction, the oberst added, "My meeting should be over by 2200 hours. Tell Major Krüger I will personally lead this mission."

The oberst returned to the staff car, reached inside to snatch up a map and spread it on the vehicle's hood. Mabry and Yves surmised he was forming a plan for revenge when they observed his finger trace a route on the map. When finished the oberst threw the folded map on the seat and cast a final glance back at the bodies on the ground before he got back into his vehicle and left the scene.

Mabry removed the leather pouch from his waistband. "Yves, I suggest we take a moment to review these documents. We may have to encode a report and transmit it to London."

"Oui, behind these trees, to rest and consider."

CHAPTER 28

Oberst Karl Beck's morning started as it always did—uniform laundered, pressed and hanging on the valet. After he shaved, washed his face, and patted it dry, he leaned toward the mirror and turned his chin left and then right, checking the closeness of his shave. Satisfied, he took another look for gray hairs, then stepped back for an admiring look and turned away.

Karl Beck never allowed distractions to interfere with his morning ritual. To do so would invite chaos, which was unacceptable. After dressing in the same methodical manner he followed each and every day—left sock, right sock, undershorts, trousers, undershirt, shirt, belt, tunic—he took one last look in the mirror, picked up his hat and emerged from his billet in the requisitioned house on the morning of 29 August. The aide who'd been waiting for him snapped to attention and saluted.

"Guten morgen, Hofmann. A beautiful day for a drive in the country, eh?"

"Yes, Herr Oberst, it appears to be."

The oberst stood outside the front door for a moment to sniff the morning air, set his hat on his head, and adjusted it with a tug on the brim. "Are the trucks loaded and fueled?"

"Just as you ordered, Herr Oberst."

"And Major Krüger?"

"Herr Oberst, he's at the command post. Shall I summon him?"

"Get word to him that I am en route to Robert-Espagne. I expect to have things wrapped up by 1200 hours." He unclasped his watch, wound it, and held it to his ear. "No, on second thought, make it 1300 hours. Either way, at the absolute latest I should be back by 1500."

With a map unfolded on the hood of his staff car, Oberst Beck retraced his finger along the road leading north out of Robert-Espagne. He visualized a convenient loop: north past Beurey-sur-Saulx three kilometers to Couvonges, then to the west and north through Mognéville. From there, northwest through Andernay and then, on to Sermaize-les-Bains. He smiled as his finger completed the circle back to Saint-Eulien.

Yes, back by 1500 hours.

Robert-Espagne was just as he remembered. Whatever scars the war had inflicted on the café, they were invisible among the welcoming tables and fresh linens.

I wonder whatever happened to that bitch. Dead by now, no doubt.

The oberst ordered his driver to proceed through the village from one end to the other ahead of the two transport trucks. Robert-Espagne was bordered on the north by the Saulx River flowing east to west while a rail line paralleled the main street, running north and south. A handful of citizens were going about their business, crossing the street back and forth between shops, pausing to chat along the way.

The arrival of German vehicles put a stop to all activities. The people on the street were eyeing Beck and the driver with suspicion. Mothers drew their children close and hurried them along, everyone avoiding being anywhere close to the car. Beck pretended not to notice.

"Hofmann, what day of the week it is?"

"Dienstag, Herr Oberst." Tuesday.

Beck glanced at his watch. "Turn around and stop in front of the post office. If I remember, that's the location of the telephone exchange. The trucks can do the same."

When Beck's car and the trucks had come to a stop, two squads disembarked from the trucks, sending citizens darting into the nearest buildings. After the oberst barked a few terse orders, four men followed him into the post-office building. His memory was correct, it also served as the telephone exchange. He strode over to stand by the switchboard, and the wide-eyed operator jumped up to back away when he began to pull cables from the front of the panel.

He turned to the soldiers. "Destroy this place."

They picked up wooden chairs from the post office, knocked over the panel of circuitry and smashed it to bits. When the defunct panel emitted a buzzing noise, they yanked the connecting wires from the wall.

"Good. Now there will be no further telephone calls."

The oberst strode back onto the street and motioned the men to follow. He stood gazing first one way and then the other along the main street of Robert-Espagne as the soldiers waited for orders.

"Half of you," Beck ordered, "round up all the men." He pointed to the railway embankment. "Over there."

"The rest of you, bring the guns." The other half ran to the truck and retrieved three machine guns.

"Set them up there," Beck commanded, "opposite the embankment. Machen Sie schnell!" he shouted. "The men, I want them here now!"

From both directions, soldiers jabbed their rifle barrels at defiant Frenchmen to move them toward the embankment.

The crowd of women and children on the opposite side of the street in front of the telephone exchange swelled in size. Heads huddled together in subdued conversation. When a woman's voice uttered a sob, someone silenced her. A sense of helplessness paralyzed the assembled citizens of Robert-Espagne.

Soldiers prodded the men to spread out in three lines along the railroad track and ordered them to turn their backs to the Germans. Evil instruments of death, three machine guns sat waiting less than ten meters behind the men's backs. Seeing that, the crowd of women erupted in wailing. One desperate woman broke from the crowd to run at the oberst, but before she could reach him, two soldiers stepped in her path and rifle-butted her to the ground. Cowed by this display of merciless brutality, the rest of the women fell silent, some embracing or clutching their children, others falling to their knees with hands uplifted in a final desperate prayer.

"Fire!"

A ferocious barrage poured out from all three machine guns simultaneously.

Up and down the line heads jolted back from the fusillade, bodies fell limp. The assembled women and children gaped in disbelief and horror as if in slow motion, their fatally wounded men fell. The instant the machine guns burst forth, a teenage boy sprinted away from the group and was halfway up the embankment before all three machine guns spat fire again to triangulate on his torso and split it in half. His chest exploded in a fountain of blood as if he'd swallowed a hand grenade. When all the bodies lay inert, lifeless, Beck ordered his machine gunners to riddle them with one final blast.

By the time the firing ceased, all that could be heard was the crying and sobbing of mothers, sisters, wives, aunts, sweethearts, and children of forty-nine male citizens of Robert-Espagne.

Still not sated, Beck ordered several houses lining the main street of the village set ablaze. The soldiers poured gasoline around before lighting the fires and within minutes the flames coalesced into a collective roar. Without another word, Beck climbed into his car like a Roman conqueror mounting his chariot in triumph. Once the trucks were loaded, the convoy pulled away from the carnage and headed north to the village of Beurey-sur-Saulx.

As the August morning wore on, temperatures rose. The occupants of the village were going about their usual activities when they heard the *rat-a-tat-tat* of machine-gun fire from the south. People milled about, scanning the horizon to point out wisps of smoke above the trees along the Saulx River. The telephone operator left her post to run to the mayor's office, concerned because she'd been unable to reach her sister in Robert-Espagne by telephone.

What could have happened? It had to be something terrible. A farmer who'd come to town with vegetables to sell reported rumors of gunfire in Robert-Espagne. Hearing that, the good people of Beurey-sur-Saulx chose to avoid the main street. The café closed its doors, and the proprietor took the outside tables off the sidewalk.

Beck's convoy rumbled into town and came to a stop in front of the deserted café. Once again, German soldiers jumped down from the trucks as the oberst stepped out of his car and issued his orders.

"Round up anybody you can."

Three soldiers canvassed the west side of the street, while three more covered the east side. When they came to the corner the impatient Nazis converged in the middle of the street to march back, having rounded up ten stumbling, frightened, and bewildered residents of Beurey-sur-Saulx.

Beck approached them as if he hadn't a care in the world. Three of the ten were women. He grabbed the first woman by the arm and yanked her hard so she stumbled and fell. He grabbed the other two.

"You, and you. Over there with her."

As the French people watched, he walked along the line of captives and counted:

"Eins. Zwei. Drei. Vier. Fünf. Sechs. Sieben..." After the seventh man he turned to the squad leader.

"Shoot them!"

"All of them, Herr Oberst?"

"Just the men."

Two kilometers beyond Beurey-sur-Saulx, before the road turned to the west, lay the village of Couvonges. Again, the three German vehicles roared into a tiny village.

"Gottverdammt!" Beck cursed. "Stop here. Now."

When the staff car screeched to a halt, the trucks that followed veered left to avoid a collision.

"Search every house. Bring out all the men."

The first house the soldiers entered was that of the village mayor. As he was being dragged out the door he pleaded to negotiate on behalf of the citizens who had placed their trust in him.

"Take me," he said, laying a hand over his heart, "but leave these people alone. They have done nothing."

Beck planted himself in front of the man. "Is it your wish to die for the sake of your village?"

"No, no!" the mayor's wife pleaded.

The mayor nodded. "If it will save my people."

With one report from Beck's Luger, the mayor staggered backward and fell dead at his screaming wife's feet. She collapsed, sobbing over her husband's lifeless body as Beck dispatched the soldiers to round up the men of the village.

In a few minutes the Germans were back with all the men they could find, young, old, in-between. The Nazis corralled and lined them up against a solid brick wall along the main street. For the second time that morning, the soldiers set up their machine guns and at Beck's shouted command, began to fire.

By the time it was over, twenty-six men of Couvonges lay murdered in the street.

The Nazis ignored the screams of the women, their anguished cries for help. Instead, they marched through the village, setting as many homes on fire as they could. It was only because they used up their supply of gasoline that six of the village's sixty homes escaped being burned to the ground.

Beck glanced at his watch. Damn it, 1245 hours. I expected to be in Sermaize-les-Bains by 1300. Indicating the direction he wanted to take with a casual flip of his wrist, he ordered his driver to lead the other two vehicles straight west. Consulting his map as he rode, he considered his options.

"Just pull over in the next village in front of the café, if there is one."

Three minutes later they arrived in Mognéville.

Like rabbits scattering at a hawk's shadow, the few people on Mognéville's street separated as the staff car led the trucks into the village on their wave of destruction. Windows slammed shut, curtains closed in defiance of the August heat. Except for three men on the street, the village was empty.

As the three huddled at the end of the block, gesturing in all directions, the one nearest the street, a man in his fifties wearing a brown shirt, turned and spat. "These filthy boches. What do they want with us?"

His companion, about the same age and dressed in a similar manner, also spat into the street, while the third turned his back on the approaching convoy.

Beck, drawn to the three men like a magnet to iron, took his pistol from its holster and shot the first one in cold blood. His victim fell like a stone to lie flat on his back, blood oozing from a single hole in the middle of his forehead. When the other two attempted to run, Beck executed them in the time it took him to squeeze off two rounds. Without bothering to confirm they were dead, he sauntered away toward the car rolling in his direction.

Andernay, six kilometers northwest of Mognéville, was an even smaller settlement that offered little to appease Beck. When the car approached the village's eastern border Beck looked at his driver, who shrugged and raised his right hand as if to ask whether he should stop. Again, Beck consulted his watch then shook his head. No. One French village spared.

"Macht schnell," Beck ordered. "Fast. Pick it up."

The driver accelerated and headed west to cover the last four kilometers to Sermaize-les-Bains.

CHAPTER 29

"Major Krüger, we've received reports of a number of French citizens gunned down in Robert-Espagne and Beurey-sur-Saulx this morning."

Leutnant Lars Koch stood rigid after imparting the information, as if Hans either knew of the events already or was capable of doing something about it.

When Hans didn't reply, the leutnant went on. "Oberst Beck took two squads out this morning at 0615 hours. You know how upset he was about the oberstleutnant. We have reports his detachments destroyed the telephone exchange in Robert-Espagne before going on a rampage."

"My God!"

With two brisk strides Hans was in front of the map. He found Robert-Espagne and traced the road north to Beurey-sur-Saulx. It took but a few seconds for him to grasp the probable sequence of events.

"Are the dispatches from Berlin still on the oberst's desk?"

"Yes, Herr Major. They haven't been read or filed."

"Get me a car, with fuel." Before the leutnant was out the door, Hans added, "And put a fully loaded pistol on the front seat."

Hans dashed into the oberst's office and grabbed the dispatches. On his way out of the building he stopped at the leutnant's desk, picked up an empty courier pouch, and shoved the dispatches inside.

Hans was on the street at the same moment his car came to a stop in front of him. "Leutnant, is it fueled? Auxiliary can as well?"

"Yes, Herr Major. All taken care of, auxiliary can, too."

The thrown pouch landed next to the pistol on the passenger seat. "Thank you, Leutnant. I shouldn't be long." Hans jumped into the vehicle and accelerated, skidding through the left turn after the sign pointing the route to Pargny-sur-Saulx. He considered his evolving plan and its chances of success. Until now he'd been unable to extricate himself from his assigned duties, and after the fall of Paris, with the Allied advance, no furloughs had been granted, not even a twenty-four hour pass.

Twelve kilometers to Pargny-sur-Saulx, six to Sermaize-les-Bains—no more than twenty minutes. It's 11:30 now. I should be able to make it in time.

When he flew past a farm wagon and the farmer signaled to someone in the trees, Hans ignored the possibility of an ambush and sped on into a curve.

He kept telling himself he'd acted out of fear and self-preservation and that he'd never been in a position to save her, until now. Meanwhile, a suitable plan continued to elude him.

What if I'm too late? What if the Gestapo acted sooner? Whatever I find, I'll make it work. I have to! What does it matter? I still love her, and if there's anything I can do, anything on this earth, I will do it.

Nothing else matters.

In the village of Maurupt-le-Montois, Hans slid through two turns, gravel and dust flying as he followed the signs to Pargny-sur-Saulx, three kilometers to the north.

Women and children scurried out of the way as Hans surged through Pargny-sur-Saulx, accelerating as he cleared the outskirts of the town.

On the open road the six kilometers to Sermaize-les-Bains evaporated in even fewer minutes.

Think, Hans. Think! What do you know? What do you need to do? Come on, you can make this work!

On the edge of town Hans ignored the citizens on the sides of the road, screeched to a halt, threw the car into reverse, and backed up, cutting the wheel to the right.

In front of the telephone exchange with the car still rolling, he jumped from the driver's seat and burst into the office.

As the other two startled women shrieked in terror and ran toward the back of the room, Aimée stood to meet him, hands on either side of her face.

"Hans! It's you!" When she threw her arms around his neck her feet left the floor. "Hans, *chéri*! Oh, *Dieu merci*, you're alive."

Breathless, he pulled her to a corner. "Aimée, you must listen. There's not much time." Careful to keep his voice just above a whisper, he said, "You've got to get out of here." He glanced at the clock on the wall. "Immediately. This minute."

With her stunned co-workers watching, she murmured, "Is it the Gestapo?"

"Yes, but at this moment that's the least of our worries. You must go home as fast as possible. Make sure your parents are there, and Claire. This is vital." He saw she trusted him completely. "Go, now, quickly."

"What are we to do?"

"Go home and wait for me there. Do not leave under any circumstances. Do you understand? You must not leave."

She nodded.

"Your friends, here, their names?"

"Yvonne," she pointed, "and Cécile."

Hans turned to the others. "Yvonne, Cécile, you two must leave. Go home, or wherever you can, but do not come back until you know it is safe."

Hans sped down the hill and positioned his car at the east edge of Sermaize-les-Bains where rue d'Andernay begins. He waited. The tranquil street scene told him Beck hadn't arrived. Hans reached over to confirm the pouch and pistol hadn't fallen to the floor. He reviewed what he would tell the oberst when he arrived, then moved on to his plan for Aimée.

He had hoped if he could do nothing else, he could at least slip away to Sermaize-les-Bains to warn Aimée and her family about the Gestapo raid. But that was no guarantee of their safety in the long run, for if the Germans managed to thwart the Allied advance, Hitler might negotiate a settlement leaving Alsace-Lorraine in German hands. That was a long-range concern, and he had to act now.

He hadn't made up his mind about what to do when Beck's convoy barreled into town. Beck ordered his driver to pull to the side of the road. Hans circled around to park in front of him in the shade of the trees lining the street.

Beck got out of his car and stood there, belligerent. "Major Krüger, what are you doing here?"

With the pouch in his hand, Hans got out of his car and walked over to Beck.

"Herr Oberst, we heard reports of skirmishes with the French. I took it upon myself to bring you these dispatches, in case you believe they require action.

"Knowing you planned to be here by 1300 hours, I felt sure I could rendezvous with you here."

"Very well, Major." Beck stared at the pouch without opening it, his eyes fixed on some distant point.

"Herr Oberst, is there something?"

"Yes, Major, there is. There most definitely is." Beck mouth was contorted as if struggling with what to say. "Major, let me ask you a question."

Hans nodded.

"If you wanted to impress these people with German superiority, to make them understand we're to be respected at all times, how would you deliver that message?" Beck was studying him, his head inclined a bit to one side. "I want the truth. The brutal truth."

"Herr Oberst, does this relate to the oberstleutnant?"

"It has everything to do with him. I want these people to understand once and for all we are in charge here!" Beck slammed his fist against the hood of the car. "Goddamn them to hell, Major. They took his wedding ring."

Hans saw the man's anger welling up in him, ready to erupt like a volcano.

"They took his wedding ring, then shot him in the head!"

Hans did his best to shape his face into an expression of sympathy. "Tell me, Herr Oberst, have you done anything about this?"

Beck's eyes gleamed with satisfaction. "I have ended the lives of close to a hundred of these pathetic French swine."

Hans felt faint after considering the oberst's words. "Women, too?"

"Not yet, but they will pay. There will be more, I assure you."

As Beck spoke, Hans began to envision the first glimmers of a plan.

"Herr Oberst, how is your supply of ammunition?"

"We exhausted our last machine-gun belt in Couvonges. I still have a few rounds in my sidearm, and the men have rifles."

"What about fuel?"

"Ah, that's a problem. We exhausted our auxiliary supply." He eyed the gas can strapped to Hans' car, then looked back to Hans.

"Empty," Hans said. "Sorry."

"Major Krüger, we need to send these people a message, and I'm almost out of time. God knows I'm out of patience."

Hans knew there was no easy way out of this dilemma. Thus far in the war he had striven to avoid the thoughtless killings, especially after the Polish campaign. He felt he'd endured enough, but now, as if choreographed, murder after murder flashed through his mind. All he could think of was a young woman in a white dress being forced into a cattle car.

"Perhaps, Herr Oberst, enough has already been done."

"Mein Gott, Krüger!" Oberst Beck threw up his hands. "What don't you understand? My best friend is dead at the hands of these animals. What do I tell his children?" Beck took up a position facing Hans. "And you say enough has been done? Oh, no, I think not. Now, I've asked you a direct question!"

Hans shifted his weight from one foot to the other. "I'm sorry, Herr Oberst, I wonder if you've considered all your options."

"Such as?"

"Nothing comes to me right away, Herr Oberst. I was just thinking out loud."

"Hmph. A lot of help you are." Beck turned away just as a gust of wind fluttered the German flag hanging in the front of the mairie. Beck saw it flap, looked away, then jerked his head back. "That's it! So simple, it's elegant! Thank you, Krüger. You're not so useless after all."

Bewildered, Hans looked around but saw nothing unusual. “For what, Herr Oberst?”

“If you hadn’t annoyed me, Major Krüger, I wouldn’t have seen it.” Looking pleased, Beck tucked his thumbs into his belt to survey the length of rue d’Andernay. “Yes, Krüger, it’s really quite perfect. They’ll pay dearly for this.”

“Herr Oberst, I don’t—”

“The lampposts, Krüger! Along the street, both sides. I’ve counted them. Thirteen.”

CHAPTER 30

Oberst Beck walked over to the first truck and spoke to the driver. "This will do, right where we are. Leave both trucks here."

The driver slammed his hand against his truck's door. Two squads of soldiers sprang onto the street while one of the two unteroffiziers stood in front of Beck waiting for orders.

"Thirteen," Beck said. "I want thirteen of these jackals rounded up."

The unteroffizier snapped off a salute.

"Men and women." Beck added.

"Women, Herr Oberst?"

"Ja. Women."

To the other unteroffizier, Beck barked, "Rope."

The man looked confused. "Rope! Now, you idiot. Get! Me! Rope!"

Aghast, Hans saw what was about to transpire, though he managed to keep his voice calm. "Herr Oberst, you don't need me any more?"

"Correct, Major." A gleeful Beck rubbed his palms together. "Dismissed. You may return to Saint-Eulien."

With a heavy heart, Hans headed west as if returning to Saint-Eulien. But once out of Beck's sight he went a block further and made a right turn taking him to the church. After hurrying up the walk, he was about to grasp the handle of the ancient heavy wooden door when it opened to reveal a stout old man in clerical black on the threshold, looking alarmed.

"I'm sorry, Father. I didn't mean to startle you. I'm here as a Catholic." When Hans offered his hand, the priest took it to steady himself. "I'm in search of Father Feuillerat, if he's still here."

"I am Father Feuillerat, my son. How can I help you?"

"Father, may we go inside?"

The priest looked along the street in both directions, then said, "Of course, this way."

While they were entering the church Hans murmured, "I'm here on a matter of life and death. Is there somewhere private?"

"Come into the vestry. No one will bother us there."

He led Hans around the altar and into a small room at one side, leaving the door ajar. There was little inside. Vestments hung on pegs next to a cupboard above two wooden chairs. Hans looked around then closed the door.

The priest took a seat and indicated the other chair. "My son, please."

Hans sat down in the second chair and spoke in his quietest voice. "Father, I don't know where to start, but we have very little time, and I've a promise to fulfill."

The priest cupped a hand behind one ear. "My hearing is not what it once was. Can you speak up? There's no one else in the church."

"Very well. We have very little time, and I must keep a promise."

The old man nodded, wary. "Now, I hear you. We, you say? A promise?"

"Father, I know you arranged the adoption of Madame Ferrand."

The priest glanced to the closed door, then back at Hans. "And how do you know this?"

"I'm sure my uniform frightens you, Father, but you must believe me, I'm here as the Ferrand family's friend. I know Madame Ferrand is a Jew."

The priest was still regarding him with suspicion.

"I assure you I'm neither SS nor Gestapo. I'm not here because I want to arrest Madame Ferrand and her daughters, I'm here to rescue them."

The old man looked at Hans with sad eyes. "I'm sorry, my son, but do you expect me to believe this of a German officer?" He began to finger the crucifix on his chest. "Yes, I can see you're only Wehrmacht, but I must ask why you would undertake such a thing and endanger yourself in the process."

"I'm in love with Aimée."

Hearing that, Father Feuillerat leaned forward, hands between his knees, palms together.

"You see, her father and my father have been friends since the Great War." When Hans spoke, the clock on the church tower struck the hour, so he raised his voice to be heard. "That's how I know about the adoption."

The priest folded his hands, ready to listen. "I want to trust you, but you must understand, I have doubts."

Hans un-holstered his sidearm and offered it to the priest. "Then hold this as my pledge of sincerity. You must believe what I have to tell you."

Father Feuillerat was shaking his head. "This is most irregular."

"Never mind, take it until I'm finished. You must not doubt me. For you see, Father, at this very moment the Gestapo are rounding up all Jews in the area around Reims." Hans made certain he held the old man's attention. "Including Sermaize-les-Bains."

The priest stiffened. "Reims? Has this anything to do with Father Gravois in Revigny-sur-Ornain? We heard the Gestapo arrested him, and no one's seen him since." The fingers of one hand strayed back to his crucifix. "Not only that, the Gestapo tore his office apart. They found the ledger, my son, the one listing all the adoptions."

"May God have mercy." Hans forced himself to take deep breaths. "There's so little time, I can't tell you the whole story of our two families now, only that I gave a solemn promise to my father I would do anything I could to help the Ferrands." Hans slid forward to the edge of his chair. "Now the situation's desperate. This morning in the Saulx valley, my superior officer slaughtered countless innocent French people. Murdered them in cold blood. And the Gestapo will be here soon. I must act quickly."

Father Feuillerat handed Hans' pistol back to him. "You've convinced me, my son, but you must have a design."

Hans let out a sigh. "God bless you, Father. I have an idea I believe will work. It must work."

By the time Hans explained his plan, Father Feuillerat's eyes were moist with tears. The old man crossed himself and bowed his head.

A few moments later when the priest looked up Hans spoke again. "Father, I haven't been to confession since the war started, and I've done things I can no longer live with. Horrible things. Will you hear my confession?"

"Yes, indeed, my son." The old man got up and opened the cupboard to take out his stole. He held it to his lips, kissed the cross at its center, arranged it around his neck with the ends draped on his chest, then sat back to wait.

Hans swallowed and began with the familiar words, "Bless me, Father, for I have sinned. It has been five years since my last confession."

Neither man spoke. The priest, used to such silence, sat without moving.

Hans swallowed hard and went on.

"Father, when we were in Poland, we stormed a house, and I was ordered"—he licked his lips—"you see I was given a direct order by my superior officer to shoot a woman who posed no threat to me. Father, please believe me when I say I didn't do this of my own free will. I was ordered to do it. I knew it was wrong, but I did it all the same. I, no one else."

With the back of his hand Hans brushed a tear from his cheek. "It was only after she fell that … only then tha—"

The priest waited. "That what, my son?"

Hans' voice broke. "That I saw she was with child. God help me, I can't rid myself of her image. I can't. I've tried, but I can't do it." He bent over, hugging himself, his body shaking with sobs.

"I hear you, my son." The old priest resisted the temptation to reach out, letting Hans embrace his pain. At last he spoke. "I'm certain you had no choice in this matter. In spite of the right intention in your heart, this wicked thing happened. My son, this is not your fault. You are merely a pawn, as we all are pawns in this terrible war."

Hans couldn't raise his head, staring at the floor, hypnotized. "I could have refused this order." Silence. "But I didn't."

"Yes, you could have, but then you'd have been shot for refusing. No, you lived. Can you see, perhaps, it was for a reason?"

"I wish I could, but I can't. I only know I suffer greatly for this sin. I try to push it deep down inside me, but still I find no peace."

"That may be how it appears to you, but perhaps God has plans for you."

Hans shook his head. "Father, I was a coward. I shot a helpless woman ... a helpless woman who would soon have borne a child. I killed her, and I killed her child." He shifted position, trying to find ease. "I was also a coward in another way. I knew Aimée was in danger, yet I abandoned her. I am a coward. Even worse, I've done murder."

Finally Hans could meet the priest's eyes. "There can be no forgiveness for me, because I've done nothing to help the woman I profess to love. Nothing. Another sin for God to punish, along with all the rest."

"But you're here now, are you not? Confessing your sin?"

The consoling words failed to soothe Hans' heart. "As you see, Father, but at this very moment my oberst is rounding up more citizens to avenge the death of his friend. He's on a rampage, I saw it and I did nothing to stop him."

The priest stroked his chin. "You say this man is your superior officer?"

Hans nodded. "And is he alone?"

"No. He has soldiers with him."

"They're armed, are they not?"

"Yes, they are."

Father Feuillerat's face relaxed. "Then I fail to see how you're to blame. He's your superior officer, you're not his. Having knowledge of what he intends doesn't make you responsible for it, no more than it makes you responsible for that madman Hitler.

"My son, this is none of your doing. You haven't abandoned Aimée, nor has God abandoned you. Your intentions are correct, and you're here today to do what you know to be right."

"But Father, you've heard my plan. What I propose to do makes me no better than the Nazis."

"It's true you're a German, but you're not a Nazi. Under any other circumstances what you're proposing would be despicable, but these are hardly normal circumstances."

Father Feuillerat patted Hans on the shoulder. "Sit up, my son. I'm certain God knows your heart and will forgive you. You couldn't restrain your superior's madness, for had you done so, you'd have been shot yourself. Just as you'd have been shot earlier had you disobeyed a direct order. Evil thrives in this world, and you are not to be blamed for the evil others do."

"But Father—" Hans found no relief. He buried his face in his hands, his anguish welling up in tears. In the end he choked out a few more words. "Father, I don't deserve to be forgiven."

"My son, I can't take these painful memories from you. I would do so if I could. But I can assure you, God's mercy knows no bounds, on this you may rely."

Father Feuillerat laid a hand on Hans' bowed head. "Give thanks to the Lord, for he is good. Te absolvo. Your sins are forgiven, my son, now go in peace."

Hans crossed himself. "For His mercy endures forever." He recited the Act of Contrition from long-buried memory and looked straight into Father Feuillerat's eyes. "Thank you, Father. Thank you."

The priest stood, and stepped over to the cupboard. After taking off his stole, folding it, and putting it away, he pulled the bottom drawer all the way out and set it aside. He reached into the dark space, removed a white cloth and handed it to Hans.

"My son, I want you to have this. It may be of some benefit to you." Father Feuillerat gauged Hans' response. "I had forgotten about it ages ago." He was relieved to see Hans unfold the cloth, lift the object up and nod in agreement. "It was years ago, twenty, maybe more. I discovered it with the blanket and a baby someone had left on the steps of the church."

Hans finished unwrapping the object and put it in his pocket. "Father, you keep the cloth. I've no use for it."

"As you wish. Now, young man, if your fears are correct, and I'm certain they are, we must act."

"*We*, Father?"

CHAPTER 31

To this point in the war the inhabitants of Sermaize-les-Bains had been sheltered. Though they had heard of the Nazis' atrocities and most believed what they were told, none could have predicted the depths to which the Nazis would go to demonstrate their utter depravity and moral degradation. So it was on the morning of August 29th, the citizens of Sermaize-les-Bains were unaware a bloodthirsty beast was stealing from town to town through the Saulx valley.

The moment Beck and his minions departed, surviving citizens crept out of the buildings where they'd taken shelter to a sight that defied belief.

The lifeless bodies dangled from thirteen lampposts like chickens in a butcher's window, necks bent at a stomach-turning angle. Of the thirteen bodies, five were women. Townspeople wept in one another's arms. One woman who screamed, then collapsed, was being tended to by her friends. Upon seeing their priest, most of those in the crowd began to wail.

Father Feuillerat knelt at the foot of each corpse, clutched the cross on his chest, and moved his lips in a silent prayer. After blessing the last of the thirteen victims, the priest noticed the mayor walking behind him, consumed in speechless grief.

Father Feuillerat rose to his feet to take the mayor's hands. The mayor looked up and down the street to ensure the Nazis had left.

"May God have mercy, Father, what are we to do?"

"Monsieur Pfleiger, we must cut these bodies down. Have you a truck?"

"Yes, Father."

"May I borrow it?"

"I didn't know you drive."

"I assure you I can drive. May I borrow it?"

"Of course, Father."

"Then please bring your truck and we'll begin to cut these poor bodies down and accord them some human dignity."

Hans wasted no time driving to the Ferrand's. Seeing what was about to happen on rue d'Andernay had sobered him beyond anything he'd ever experienced, worse than the worst of the fighting in Russia, worse even than Poland. Yet at the same time his heart seemed light, for the burden that had lain for so long on his soul was at last relieved.

After he arrived and sprang out of the car, Aimée and her parents ran from the house to meet him. They all looked scared, and Aimée was wringing her hands. "Hans, what has happened?"

"Yes, my boy, please tell us." André seized his arm. "We've been so afraid!"

Hans rushed to tell them of all of the morning's events, and before they could begin to recover from the horror of it, he blurted out, "Madame Ferrand, they know you're Jewish."

"Oh!" Elsie gasped and reached for her husband, while Aimée and Claire stared at Hans.

He went on. "The Gestapo arrested Father Gravois in Revigny-sur-Ornain, and they have his ledger listing all the adoptions. It's true, Madame, they know about you. At this very moment the Gestapo are arresting all Jews in the area around Reims, including here." He looked at his watch. "They'll be here very soon."

A panicky Elsie began twisting her apron between her hands. "How long have you known?"

"Madame Ferrand, I've always known. I know you thought I was a Nazi, but I'm not and never have been. I despise what those people do."

At that her face softened, and she closed her eyes. She let go of the apron to curl one hand into a fist and press it to her mouth, groping for her husband with her other hand.

André put an arm around his wife and looked first at her, then at Hans. "You see, my dear, it's all right. Hans, what can we do?"

"We must act." Again Hans consulted his watch and looked around the property. "Is there a farmhouse close by where you'd be safe, somewhere you can run to quickly?"

"The Pelletier's," André said, "our nearest neighbors."

"But, André," Elsie objected, "the Gestapo might follow us there."

Hans said, "No, they won't. You may take a few things with you, but leave your identity papers. It can't look as if you've fled."

The Ferrands were struggling to take in these instructions when Hans added something more. "And before you go, bring me a change of clothes for each of you."

Claire frowned. "A what?"

"Clothes, just outer garments, no underwear. I need a dress and a scarf from each of you, a shirt and pants from Monsieur Ferrand. Hurry, time's running out."

They rushed upstairs to collect the clothes and brought them to Hans, who placed each set in a separate pile on the kitchen table.

"Now, after you collect what you need to take with you, I want you, Madame Ferrand, to take Aimée and Claire to the Pelletier's and wait for Father Feuillerat. Do not leave under any circumstances. Monsieur Ferrand will join you there soon."

"Father Feuillerat?"

"Trust me."

Elsie began to cry and reached for her husband again. André embraced her, and after he released her so he could embrace his daughters, Elsie came to stand before Hans, her eyes full of tears. He wasn't sure what to do until she took both his hands in hers, and when he bent toward her, hopeful, she kissed him on one cheek and then the other.

"Hans, our dear, dear friend, how can we ever thank you? I know God sent you here to save us. I only pray someday you can find it in your heart to forgive my unkind thoughts."

After one firm shake of their joined hands Hans eased his hold. "I have. Go. Now."

Aimée, who was crying, pulled Hans close and looked up into his face. "Hans, chéri, no matter what happens, I shall always love you. You know it, don't you?"

He nodded. "I do." He kissed her on the lips, then the forehead and cupped her face in his hands to gaze into her eyes for a long, long moment.

"God keep you, Aimée. I will come back. I don't know how or when, but I will."

The Ferrand women were already running through the field behind the henhouse when Father Feuillerat drove up in the mayor's truck and hobbled to the house, where Hans let him in.

"It took me some time to find a large enough piece of canvas, but the house painter had one."

Coming downstairs, André looked shocked. "Father, what are you doing here?"

"I'll explain when there's time. For now we must hurry. Those poor despairing people in town, they thought I was taking these bodies to the church."

André's eyes widened. "Bodies?"

The priest indicated the front lane. "In the truck, under the canvas."

Hans took charge. "Monsieur Ferrand, questions later. Come with me and help move the bodies into the kitchen. Father, please bring the gas can from the side of my car."

All three men hurried outside. When Hans released the truck's rear gate and threw back the canvas, André turned white as snow and seemed to lose all his breath. Oblivious to the man's distress, Hans was already climbing into the back of the truck.

Father Feuillerat took hold of André to keep him from collapsing. "I know. I know it's terrible. These are four of the thirteen people the Nazis murdered today in Sermaize-les-Bains. Believe me, Hans had nothing to do with it, and he couldn't stop it. You must trust us, André, trust Hans and me. Is your family still here?"

André shook his head. "Gone, to the Pelletier's."

"Good. You must follow them. But first we take these bodies into the house. Hans will tell us what to do."

André was still trembling. "Hans, are you sure the Gestapo will come?"

"They will, Monsieur. According to the dispatch I read, they should be here by 1500 hours. They're under orders to transport all Jews to the rail station at Chalons-en-Champagne by 1800 hours. We need your help."

André nodded and straightened up. "Tell me what to do."

Hans began shifting the corpses, with André's help, and once all four were on the ground Hans said, "Father, do you think their clothes will pass?"

The priest inspected them, though he avoided the faces of the four people he had known so well, some he had given communion.

"The women should be fine, but the man's clothes I would change. Monsieur Lefevre"—he crossed himself—"was a banker, not a farmer."

Between them, Hans and André managed to carry all four bodies to the kitchen. Then the priest watched Hans strip the clothes from the banker's lifeless body and lay André's shirt and pants on the floor beside it.

"Father Feuillerat, while I'm doing this, please gather up all the unused clothes and take them with you. Leave me only the three women's scarves."

The priest did as he was told, collecting all the clothes and carrying them to the truck. He was back by the time Hans had the last button fastened on André's shirt. "Done," Hans said. He stood up to look again at the four bodies. "Father, now please drive André to the Pelletier's. I will finish here."

Before he left, André grasped Hans' right hand and pulled him close. "Your father would be proud of you. I'm proud of you. For all of us, thank you." He kissed Hans, first on one cheek, then the other before taking up a position to wait for his priest.

Father Feuillerat was supporting himself with the back of a chair. "I'll join you shortly, André. Please wait for me in the truck."

As Hans stood by, breathing hard, Father Feuillerat made the sign of the cross in front of him, then embraced him. "Bless you, my son. You're a brave man." He drew back to look into Hans' face. "You *will* be forgiven. God knows your heart."

"Thank you, Father."

"Ah, but we thank you, these good people and I. After the Gestapo leave, I shall come back here and return the bodies to the church. No one will know."

"I will know, Father. I will know."

CHAPTER 32

Once Hans heard the door shut and the truck's clutch engage, he hoisted the limp body of the older woman into one of the chairs at the kitchen table. The head kept falling back until Hans pushed the chair against a cupboard. From the three scarves he chose the one that seemed to suit the corpse's clothes and placed the other two on the counter. He then tied the scarf around the neck in such a way it didn't look suspicious and at the same time, concealed the mark of the noose. He folded the hands in the lap and took from his pocket the gift Father Feuillerat had given him, placed it in the corpse's clasped hands and closed the barely pliable fingers around it.

He stepped back to observe. There, that looks natural.

Next, he dealt with the man's body, hefting it onto the chair André often sat in. This second body's head fell backward as well. The gaping mouth was dry, the open eyes appeared fixed on a crack in the ceiling. Hans assessed the rope marks on the neck and tugged the shirt collar up satisfying himself it hid any evidence of a hanging. Adjusting the chair so it sat at an angle to the table, Hans gave the collar one last upward tug.

Perfect.

Hans looked out the window before he turned his attention to the corpses of the women on the floor. He dragged the younger looking one to the threshold of the adjoining room, rolled it face down, and stretched out the right arm. The left arm he tucked under the torso and turned the head to one side. Then he reached down to lift the hair and released it so it looked natural as it fell over the neck, leaving no visible skin.

The last corpse, that of a woman about Aimée's age, lay close to the table, its serene countenance a repudiation of the agony that must have defined the final struggle. Rather than pulling, Hans lifted the body and carried it to a point just in front of the other corpse on the floor. Gently rolling this body over too, he extended both arms above the head in a posture of surrender. He then slipped his index finger under the hair and removed the ribbon binding it. The tresses of hair were distributed to cover the neck. Not satisfied, he rearranged the hair a second time until it was the way he wanted it. He stood and surveyed the room. After a quick check of his watch, he looked out the window again to the north.

No one in sight. Good.

He returned to the more distant of the two corpses on the floor and took his pistol from its hip holster. Hans positioned the weapon, held it with both hands, and, with eyes shut, fired one round into the center of the corpse's back. Startled when the lungs expelled a little air, without stopping to think, he put a second round into the back of the other prone corpse.

Going back to the center of the kitchen, he took a minute to observe the seated female body. From less than an arm's length away he put a shot through the left temple. When the neck didn't jerk in reaction to the bullet's entry, he figured it was due to rigor mortis.

Hans thought to check his tunic for splatter, perhaps change uniforms when he got back to Saint-Eulien. He then moved to the angled chair and knelt in front of its burden. Taking care to crouch a bit lower, Hans positioned the pistol barrel in the corpse's mouth and pulled the trigger. The bullet blasted out of the back of the skull leaving a void the size of an orange, splattering gelatinous chunks of tissue and blood in a circle where the wall met the ceiling.

His work almost complete, Hans ran to his car and retrieved the extra pistol and auxiliary fuel can. After scanning the horizon for Gestapo, he first fired four rounds into the field, then took both the fuel can and gun inside where he set the can on the floor and laid the gun just beyond the reach of the male corpse's dangling hand.

Grabbing a copper saucepan from a hanging rack, Hans poured gasoline into it and flung it to the corner, sprinkling more gasoline from the can on the tile floor.

Not too much, it must look like a failed arson attempt. The Gestapo must see the bodies have been shot.

From the safety of the back door Hans was about the throw a lighted match onto the gas when he spotted the scarves on the counter. Damn. He grabbed them both, bounded up the stairs and into the bedroom where he flung open the top drawer of the dresser. The folded scarves were pushed into the back corner of the drawer before closing it.

Hans dashed back down the stairs and into the kitchen. He stepped into the doorway, lit a match and threw it onto the shallow puddle of spilled gas. Just as he hoped, the fire burned very little and came nowhere near consuming much of anything.

Hans stood back. The Gestapo will be sure to blame some idiot Frenchman for not knowing how to set a house on fire.

He was finished. Wondering if he would ever see this house again, the place where he'd spent some of the happiest hours of his life, after one final inspection, Hans picked up the fuel can and sprinted out to the car.

CHAPTER 33

The Gestapo staff car and trucks skidded to a stop on the gravel outside the Ferrand's farm and one of the trucks unloaded its cargo of soldiers. According to their orders they surrounded the house, the barn, and, most important of all, the other truck packed with Jews—mothers, fathers, daughters, and sons. Major Braun and Oberleutnant Huber went around the house to enter through the back door.

Braun went in first, then roared, "Gottverdammt!" at the scene confronting him.

"What is it, Major?"

"This fire. It's no coincidence, Huber. Not in the least."

The fire Hans set an hour earlier petered out without disfiguring the bodies or destroying much of the house. The acrid smell of smoke and scorched flesh hung in the air. Flames had licked at the clothing of the two corpses on the floor but failed to burn it away. Bullet holes were visible in both bodies.

Braun inspected the man's corpse. When he turned to look behind him, his mouth widened in a sadistic smile at the dried, brownish stains of blood and gluey gray matter stuck to the wall.

Huber was also nosing around. "Major, the gun there on the floor, it looks like a German model. Shall we take it with us?"

Braun stooped for a closer look. "We have no use for it. Anyway," he said, then smiled, "it has already served the Führer quite well."

He spat. "These French and their Jews!" Careful where he stepped, he moved away from the table. "You mark my words, Huber, only an animal would do this to his own family, then do away with himself. Murder *and* suicide." He shook his head. "I tell you, they all deserve to die. Jews"—he spat again—"and the bastards who consort with them."

Huber followed Braun as the major stepped over the corpses to inspect the rest of the house. Clomping upstairs to the first bedroom, he pulled a drawer open. Seeing just undergarments, he inspected the closet. When the second bedroom revealed nothing either, Braun pounded back downstairs to the kitchen with Huber at his heels.

After one more look he waved a dismissive hand over the gory scene.

"We go, Huber. There's nothing here for us."

"Jawohl, Herr Major." Huber saluted and hurried away.

Before Braun left, the female corpse in the chair drew his eye. He stood to stare at her lifeless remains. With clasped hands, she must have been praying when the bullet ripped through her skull. Just before he turned away, he caught a glimpse of something in her lap and reached for it with caution, avoiding contact as if her body were contagious. He pinched the object between her hands and pulled it free. When he recognized it, he flung it away like a snake had bitten him.

A Star of David fell to the floor and skidded toward the feet of the dead women lying nearby.

"Gottverdammt Yids!"

Braun then pulled out his sidearm, aimed, and shot the disgusting corpse in the chest. The bullet rocked the body backward out of the chair onto the floor.

Finished, he slammed the door, hard, and stormed out.

CHAPTER 34

Paris
Friday
December 23, 1983

André Ferrand walked to the podium with precision, his steps slow and deliberate. Upon reaching it, he gripped its sides as he surveyed the gathering of family and friends. The banquet room was decorated with roses, and red ribbons adorned the edges of the tables. At each guest's place was a folder of cream vellum paper with the menu printed inside and the cover featuring a wonderful color photo of Paul and Christine, taken the previous year in Paris by the Seine.

The photographer had done a superb job of capturing the loving feelings that bound the engaged couple to each other. But neither their smiles in the photo nor the ones they wore now reflected the strain of the forty-eight hours leading up to this rehearsal dinner.

At the head table, seated with André, were Christine's parents, Hans and Aimée Krüger, as well as Steve and Rachel Rosenbaum, parents of the groom. The Rosenbaums had flown from Chicago and were houseguests of the Krügers.

André reached into the breast pocket of his jacket to extract his reading glasses and the remarks he had prepared with such care. He arranged his speech on the podium, adjusted his glasses, and looked down with a beneficent smile at the head table.

"Since I've had a year to prepare these remarks, I've made certain they are translated properly, especially for our honored guests from America."

He cleared his throat and, with a mischievous grin, leaned into the microphone. "How long can you stay?"

Christine and her mother laughed, while guests at the other tables smiled. Paul turned to his mother and father to explain.

André waited for the room to grow quiet, then began his speech in earnest.

"A year ago, perhaps a little more, Christine brought Paul to Sermaize-les-Bains to meet me. It was then they both learned the whole story of the Ferrands and the Krügers, and afterward Christine decided she wanted to marry on Christmas Eve." He hesitated a moment and looked out at the faces.

"If you know Christine, then you know it would have been useless to try to talk her out of it!"

Christine's mother smiled and looked over at Paul, pleased to see him caressing Christine's shoulder.

"Before their visit to me, all Paul knew of our two families was the little Christine had told him. But before I get ahead of myself, I wish to take a minute to remember those loved ones who are not here to celebrate this marriage with us.

"I miss my dear Elsie so much, along with all of you who knew her. She would have loved to be here today, and I know she is watching."

Twice he cleared his throat, not wanting to weep. After Aimée brushed away tears, Hans took her hand and held it.

"And let us not forget Konrad and Greta Krüger, Christine's father's parents. Some of you know Konrad and I were friends. To my regret, I never had the pleasure of meeting Greta, and another of my regrets was I only met Konrad once, during World War One, which we called la première guerre mondiale. Both Konrad and Greta died, tragically, late in the second war. But I'm certain they, too, are here in spirit. The three empty places at our table are there to honor Elsie, Greta, and Konrad."

The old gentleman shifted his weight and adjusted his grip on the lectern, glad he was being listened to with such interest.

"When two people are about to enter into a marriage, they will be wise to reflect on three simple truths: love, sacrifice, and forgiveness. To explain, I ask you to let me tell you a little story about Konrad Krüger, Hans Krüger, my Elsie, and Aimée. If any of you have heard it before, don't stop me. It's a good story."

Frank laughter filled the room.

"First, to consider love. I begin my story with World War Two, toward the end of the German occupation of France. I tell you frankly, I view all the murders and atrocities as a tragic failure of civilization, a failure most of us felt helpless to prevent. But one person in this room did what he could do and he did it in the name of love."

A few knowing heads turned to Hans. At an adjoining table, Claire whispered into her husband's ear. Aware of the attention, Hans shook his head a bit, as if to minimize the importance of what he'd heard.

André went on. "Hans Krüger was a German soldier, and a loyal German officer. But he was not a Nazi. One terrible day, August 29, 1944, close to one hundred innocent people in the Saulx valley were murdered in cold blood. That day Hans risked his life to save ours. He did so, but not because of his promise to his father that he would help us any way he could. No, he did so because of love—a deep and selfless love for Aimée Ferrand."

André looked to his family for a moment, affection beaming from his face.

"The second truth about marriage for us to reflect on is sacrifice. Hans was willing to sacrifice his own life to save the lives of three Jews he knew were about to be arrested by the Gestapo."

The room echoed to gasps in several throats.

"And forgiveness is the third. Yes, forgiveness is important in a marriage. We may believe the ability to forgive and to accept forgiveness comes automatically to those in love. But if one harbors mistaken or uncharitable thoughts about another, those thoughts can make it hard either to ask for forgiveness or to offer it. Forgiveness comes easiest when we see our own selves clearly and do our best to see others in the same way."

André was speaking of how difficult it had been for Elsie to see Hans' true self before she could accept him as Aimée's chosen one and her family's protector.

When he saw Aimée smile at Paul, who had his arm draped over Christine's shoulder, and saw Paul look back and nod, André felt sure that between them all was forgiven.

"To continue my remarks, Konrad Krüger and I were friends. During the years between wars Konrad and I exchanged many letters and photographs, all a result of the famous Christmas Truce. It was the first year of our war, you know, 'the war to end all wars.'

"By the autumn of 1914 it was clear the war would not be over soon. On Christmas Eve, my regiment was entrenched opposite the Germans. Some of you may have heard there was a spontaneous celebration on Christmas Eve and Christmas Day all along the Western Front, between the Germans, French, and the British. It became known as the Christmas Truce."

Across the room not a single person stirred, rhythmic breathing was all that could be heard.

"This truce was less a celebration of Christmas than an opportunity to bury our dead. During the lull in the fighting, I met Hans' father, a German soldier, in No Man's Land. In the spirit of Christmas I gave him some wine and sausage my family had sent me. We exchanged addresses and a promise never to let our nations go to war again. Idealists, yes, but we truly meant what we said.

"After the war we corresponded as often as our busy lives allowed. Letters mostly about our families, our dreams, the state of affairs in France and Germany. But by the end of 1938 Konrad saw it was no longer safe for him to write to us in France, especially as he knew Elsie was Jewish.

"In November of that year, just after Kristallnacht, the Night of Broken Glass, Konrad had business in Paris and had planned to visit us in Sermaize-les-Bains, but because his publishing house had considered the writings of some Jewish authors, the Gestapo were watching him. So Konrad cancelled his visit, wrote to tell us why, and that he no longer felt it safe to write. He also told us he had destroyed the photographs and letters I'd sent, to protect me and my family should Germany invade France. I believe he knew it was coming."

André stopped for several sips of water, shifted his position and inhaled.

"Despite all this, during the summer of 1940, Hans, who was in the German army, paid us a visit. We welcomed him into our home, and soon he and Aimée fell in love. But by autumn of 1942 events were such he thought it best to break off the relationship. Hans did this, you see, to protect us from the Nazis.

"As the war raged on, we often wondered about the Krügers, especially about Hans. Aimée couldn't forget him, and we all prayed for this fine young man to be safe amid all the fighting."

André paused for effect. "Then, in June of 1944 we received our last letter from Konrad."

When Hans' head jerked up and his back stiffened, Aimée tightened her grip on his arm. André removed an old, creased letter from his coat pocket, and after adjusting his glasses and taking another sip of water, began to read.

"The letter is headed Dresden, Friday, 19 May 1944.

My dear and cherished friend André,

This savage war has taken a toll I am afraid will be impossible to overcome. Our dear Peter has been killed and we know none of the details. Just a telegram. My Greta is inconsolable.

As you can see, we're in Dresden. We moved here to avoid the bombing that's sure to worsen. I believe it is a good thing. In Berlin, Peter's room was just as it was the day he left for U-boat duty. I couldn't bear to cross the threshold, but Greta sat in his room for hours without stirring. There was nothing I could do to reach her.

At night now I can't sleep, and if by chance I do, all I see is a vast ocean and a sailor floating on the water, face down—nothing more. I wake up thrashing.

There was no reason for us to remain in Berlin, absolutely none. Perhaps the change will be good for Greta, but I have yet to see any improvement. I'm sorry to burden you with such sad news. Forgive me for doing so.

Hans is well, but I'm afraid this war has taken its toll on him. We fear for him every day, especially now that Peter's gone. But we feel no guilt about these things for we've always known Hans and Peter were ours only for a few short years before they went off to lead their own lives.

Hans has been fighting in Italy and his letters seldom come. Every day we dread another telegram. He doesn't mention

Peter, but I know he misses him terribly. He told us he finally wrote to Aimée after not having done so for so long. We hope she can forgive him. André, don't believe for a moment he no longer loves her. The anguish he feels was evident in his last letter. Please hasten to reassure her he thinks of her each and every day and that, for now, he is safe.

What he writes causes me to believe your and my experiences in the trenches pales next to what he has witnessed and done. He speaks of the sorrow and guilt he carries. Something terrible happened to him in the Polish campaign, but he hasn't told us what burdens him so.

The last time I wrote, I told you of my concerns for your family. I don't know whether I should continue to worry, but I believe further caution is prudent. Please be safe.

We think of you and your family often. It gives us much joy to know our Hans is so taken by your Aimée and that he has written her again. Perhaps things will be different one day. For now, you must know if it were in my power to do so, I would assist you in any way I could.

I remain, your devoted friend,
Konrad

"And there the letter ends. Six months after this letter was written, Dresden, along with almost forty thousand of its inhabitants, including Konrad and Greta Krüger, was destroyed by Allied firebombing."

Throughout the room handkerchiefs were being produced and put to use. Quiet tears had been shed by almost everyone. Hans, head still bowed, picked up a linen napkin to mop his eyes as a sob caught in his throat. When he raised his head Aimée reached out to draw him to her. After he composed himself, Hans looked up to André and mouthed four brief words: "Merci. Merci mille fois." Thank you, a thousand thanks.

The waiters had long since ceased their activities, spellbound by what they had seen and heard. Blocking the kitchen's double door were two of the cooks, out of the kitchen to hear for themselves what the waiters were murmuring about.

"As everyone knows," André was saying, "we failed in our original pledge to see our countries never again went to war. Yet Konrad, through Hans, fulfilled his pledge to assist my family, and for that, we are all eternally grateful."

When André finished speaking and turned to his granddaughter, his audience sensed the shift and looked to Christine as well. From a shelf underneath the lectern André brought out a small box, opened it, and beckoned to Christine.

"Christine, chérie, please rise and come to stand with me."

Christine looked at Paul. He shrugged as if to say, Don't look at me, I haven't a clue. Similar puzzled glances passed between her, Hans, and Aimée. Tentative at first, she stood, then went to her grandfather with the poise of a confident bride-to-be.

"Christine," he said, "your Grandfather Krüger, whom you never knew, gave me this gift during that Christmas Truce sixty-nine years ago. It's a brass button from his uniform." He held it up for all to see. "I had it mounted and made into a unique necklace for you."

"Grandpère!" She'd brought her hands to her cheeks, her mouth agape in surprise.

He arranged the necklace around her throat and let it settle, then placed a loving kiss on her forehead. He motioned to Paul to join them, concluding his speech with one of the couple on either side of him.

"There will always be good and evil in this world, but good will triumph if each one of us follows the promptings of our conscience, that inner voice that knows right from wrong, and if necessary, risk our own safety, even our lives, for the benefit of those we love.

"I say to you, Christine, and to you, Paul, always be guided by the best of motives. Never hesitate to make promises if they will bring about good. And above all, fulfill those promises, especially to those you love.

"To create your world around each other, you must follow these simple rules: Love each other, sacrifice for each other, and above all, forgive each other.

"In other words, embrace the spirit of the Christmas Truce in all that you do."

When André finished speaking the whole audience rose to their feet and began to clap.

"Come, Aimée and Hans," he said. "And Steve and Rachel, please come too."

A bit hesitant at first, in a moment the four parents made their way forward to stand with their children, and as André stood beaming among them, the room seemed to echo with distant voices, and a tremendous awareness swept over him that many unseen others had joined them—Konrad and Greta Krüger, Elsie Ferrand, M. and Mme. Blaisé, Father Gravois, Father Feuillerat, and a whole host of others whose names he would never know.

AUTHOR'S NOTE

All locations and depictions of military actions in this book are factual. The Christmas Truce has been thoroughly researched and documented, both in print and in the cinema. By no means limited to the small section of No Man's Land outside Foucaucourt-en-Santerre between the German 20th Bavarian Regiment and the French 99th Regiment d'Infanterie, it occurred up and down the trenches of the Western Front on December 24, 1914.

References to this memorable event include articles in the lay press of the time and military archives. Downplayed by British and German leaders when it occurred, the Christmas Truce was nonetheless a highlight of a war that ravaged the population base of all combatants. The sheer numbers speak for themselves: 8 million lives were lost by all combatants combined, and when prorated on a daily basis, 5,100 men died each and every day of World War One from August of 1914 to November 11, 1919.

In 1915, a similar attempt was made to revive the magic of the 1914 Christmas Truce, but with limited and isolated success. Interested readers are referred to Stanley Weintraub's wonderful history *Silent Night: The Story of the World War I Christmas Truce.*

The 3.Infanterie-Division, having been decimated in the battle of Stalingrad, was later reformed in May 1943 in Lyon, France, as the 3rd Panzer-Grenadier Division to include elements of the 386th Infanterie-Division. Both divisions actually fought in the theaters depicted and at the times mentioned. After May 1943, the 3rd Panzer-Grenadier Division fought in the Italian campaign (battles of Salerno, Cassino, and Anzio Beachhead) prior to being transferred to the Western Front. In August, 1944, the 3rd Panzer-Grenadier Division was transported by rail from Verona, Italy to St. Dizier and Bar-le-Duc, France, however, for purposes of plot advancement, I depicted the division near Paris before the city's liberation.

Elements of the 3rd Panzer-Grenadier Division were in the Saulx valley during the last week of August, 1944 and are alleged to have been involved in the Saulx valley murders. Additional deployment of the division north and east in response to the Allied advance across France brought about continued fighting until the end of World War Two in Europe, when the entire division was captured in the Ruhr Pocket on April 16, 1945 along with over 300,000 soldiers of the Wehrmacht.

The atrocities perpetrated by the Nazis against people of Jewish heritage before the outbreak of hostilities on September 1, 1939 all the way through World War Two are well known. The examples depicted in this manuscript do not come close to scratching the surface of all of the known atrocities committed between 1936 and 1945.

Further, the deportation of French Jews to the death camps is well documented, as is the accelerated persecution of French Jews following the successful landing at Normandy in June of 1944 but prior to the Allied advance. An excellent and thoroughly cited Internet source for further study, by Thomas Fontaine, "Chronology of Repression and Persecution in Occupied France, 1940–1944," is noted below.

Winston Churchill's speeches, "Review of 1944" and the "The Fruits of 1944," at the beginning of Chapter 24 were actually given on November 9, 1944 and November 23, 1944. In the novel's timeline, I shifted it to August 1944, again for reasons of plot advancement. While some passages of the speech are quoted verbatim, I did find it necessary to exercise some liberties with the text.

The cold-blooded murders of ninety-eight Frenchmen in the Saulx valley by soldiers of the 3rd Panzer-Grenadier Division on the 29th of August, 1944, were indeed sparked by the ambush the day before, August 28, 1944, of four Germans—two officers and two noncommissioned officers—by members of the British Special Air Service and local maquisards.

As a lasting tribute to the twenty-six Frenchmen murdered on the 29th of August in Couvonges, the main street of that village is now "rue du 29 Aoüt"—literally translated, the Street of August 29th.

While thirteen Frenchmen were murdered in Sermaize-les-Bains on that same day, August 29th of 1944, the events depicted here as related to those murders are fictional.

The names and events of the principal characters are also fictional.

Not fictional are the timeless themes of good and evil, love, sacrifice, forgiveness, and redemption.

As background resources, I consulted the following works:

Aubrac, Lucie. *Outwitting the Gestapo*. London, 1993.

Churchill, Winston. *His Complete Speeches: 1897-1963, 1943-1949, Vol. II*. New York, 1974.

———. *The Gathering Storm*. Boston, 1948.

———. *Their Finest Hour*. Boston, 1949.

———. *The Hinge of Fate*. Boston, 1950.

———. *Closing the Ring*. Boston, 1951.

———. *Triumph and Tragedy*. Boston, 1953.

Groom, Winston. *1942: The Year That Tried Men's Souls*. New York, 2005.

http://archive.org/details/Winston_Churchill

http://www.massiveviolence.org/Chronology-of-Repression-and-Persecution-in-Occupied-France

http://www.uboat.net

Overy, Richard. *Why the Allies Won*. New York, 1995.

Stracham, Hew. *The First World War: A New Illustrated History*. New York, 2003.

Weintraub, Stanley. *Silent Night: The Story of the World War I Christmas Truce*. New York, 2001.

Winter, J M. *The Experiences of World War I*. New York, 1989.

ACKNOWLEDGMENTS

I would like to thank all those who made *The Ledger* possible:

James Markert for his insight and encouragement in all things literary.

Steve Langan and the Seven Doctors' Project for setting me on this path.

Betsy Tice White for her kind words, sage advice and editing expertise.

The early readers for lending an ear and providing honest feedback, Patricia Zahn, Kirsten Caskey, Andrew Holm, Greg Holm, Paul Veit, Bob DeGregorio, Norm and Pam Staniszewski, Lisa and Jesse Veit, Kathy Veit, Bob and Fran Crow, George and Meda Fulton, Janice Golka, Tovah Connealy, Pam Billmeier, Linda Varney, Bill Baker, Dawn Davis, Betty McClure, Linda Six, Ann Weber, Hank Cupp, Patty and Randy Ross, and Lori Mostek.

Gretchen for her love, selfless support, numerous ideas along the way and unwavering belief in *The Ledger*.

And no acknowledgment would be complete without thanking the reader; I hope your journey was a pleasant one.

GLOSSARY

Archduke Ferdinand – Royal Prince of Hungary and heir to the Austro-Hungarian throne. Assassinated in Sarajevo on June 28, 1914.

Bahnhof – German. Train station.

Bastille Day – French national holiday commemorating the anniversary of the storming of the Bastille which took place July 14, 1789.

Black Wound Badge – Decoration awarded by the German army for wounds sustained in battle. Equivalent to the Purple Heart in the U.S. military.

Boche, boches (plural) – Derogatory French term for German(s).

Boeuf – French. Beef.

Choucroute garnie – French. Dressed sauerkraut.

Confinement – Obstetrical term for delivery of a woman's baby.

Dieu – French. God.

Dropsy – Old term for congestive heart failure.

Enceinte – French. Pregnant.

Fille – French. Daughter.

Fils – French. Son.

Fräulein – German. Single girl.

Frère – French. Brother.

Führer – German. Leader. Title Hitler gave himself.

Geheime Staatspolizei – German secret police, commonly known as the Gestapo.

Gestapo – See above.

Grandmère – French. Grandmother.

Grandpère – French. Grandfather.

Grenadier – German soldier.

Gymnasium – German school for secondary education.

Hakenkreuz – German. Swastika symbol.

Hauptmann – German rank equivalent to U.S. and British captain.

Huns – Derogatory term used in World War One for German soldiers.

Independent Social Democrats – Short-lived German political party, also known as the USPD. Active during the Second Reich, or Weimar Republic.

Iron Cross – German military decoration awarded in World War Two. The Iron Cross 2nd Class was the first decoration awarded, followed by the Iron Cross 1st Class if the soldier did something else meritorious. The rough U.S. military equivalent to the Iron Cross 2nd Class is the Bronze Star, the rough U.S. military equivalent to the 1st Class Iron Cross is the Silver Star.

Jawohl – German. Yes or certainly.

Jumpmaster – Person charged with organizing paratroopers for jumping from the aircraft.

Kilometer – Metric measurement of length. 1 kilometer = 0.62 miles.

Kit – Knapsack used by British and French troops in World War One.

Klick – Military slang for kilometer.

Kriegslazarett – German. Field hospital.

Kriegsmarine – German. Navy.

Kübelwagen – Utility vehicle used by the German army, similar to the Jeep used by the U.S. Army in World War Two. Identical to a vehicle produced in 1975 by the Volkswagen Corporation known as The Thing.

Knight's Cross – German military decoration awarded in World War Two, roughly equivalent to U.S. Distinguished Service Cross.

Kommandant – German commander, as in a prisoner-of-war camp.

Law for the Protection of German Blood and Honor – Legislation enacted September 15, 1935 intended to ensure the purity of German bloodlines by prohibiting marriages between German nationals and Jews. It further forbade Jews from hiring German nationals or Jews from hoisting the flag of the Third Reich.

Leutnant – German rank equivalent to U.S. and British rank of 2nd lieutenant.

Luftwaffe – German air force in World War Two.

M. – French. Abbreviation for monsieur (see below). Equivalent to Mr.

Madame – French. Polite form of address for a married woman. Equivalent to Mrs.

Mademoiselle – French. Polite form of address for a young lady. Equivalent to Miss.

Mairie – French. Municipal office of the mayor or town hall.

Major – German military rank equivalent to U.S. and British major.

Maquis – French. Undergrowth or underbush. The term came to mean the French underground or armed resistance movement.

Maquisard – French. Member of the maquis. Resistance fighter.

***Mein Kampf* –** Autobiographical book written by Adolph Hitler while he was in prison. Published in 1925, it outlines his political ideology.

Meter – Metric unit of length roughly equal to three feet.

Mischlinge – Person of partial Jewish ancestry.

Mme. – French. Abbreviation for Madame (see above). Equivalent to Mrs.

Mon général – French. My general.

Monsieur – French. Polite form of address for a man. Equivalent to Mr.

Nazi – German political party led by Adolph Hitler. Active in Germany from 1919 to 1945. Also known as German Worker's Party. Acronym for Nationalsozialistische Deutsche Arbeiterpartei.

NCO – Noncommissioned officer.

No Man's Land – Area between entrenched combatants in World War One.

Night of Broken Glass – Also known as Kristallnacht. Anti-Semitic pogrom sparked by assassination of Ernst vom Rath, which led to the murder of nearly 1,000 Jews, the arrest of 25,000–30,000 Jews, and the destruction of 267 synagogues by the Hitler Youth, Gestapo, and SS on November 9–10, 1938.

Oberleutnant – German rank equivalent to U.S. and British 1st lieutenant.

Oberst – German rank equivalent to U.S. and British colonel.

Oberstleutnant – German rank equivalent to U.S. and British lieutenant colonel.

Parapet – Protective area above entrenched troops, usually of dirt and boards.

Père – French. Father.

Poilus – French soldiers in World War One.

Pot-au-feu – French. Stew-like soup with boiled beef.

Potée – French. Soup or stew cooked in an earthenware pot.

RAF – British Royal Air Force.

Röntgen – Discoverer in 1895 of x-rays, Wilhelm Röntgen. Name applied to early x-ray films.

SAS – Special Air Service. British paratroop branch of military. Comparable to U.S. Rangers.

Sauerbraten – German. Dish similar to a beef roast, after marination with wine and spices.

Sharführer – German SS rank equivalent to U.S. and British sergeant.

Shul – Synagogue or Jewish house of prayer.

Silver Wound Badge – German military decoration awarded to an earlier recipient of a Black Wound Badge for a second wound sustained in battle.

SS – German. Schutzstaffel. Originally founded as personal bodyguard corps for Hitler, the SS expanded to become the military police force of the Nazi Party. The SS ran the concentration camps and was notorious for ruthless behavior in World War Two. Also known as Waffen-SS.

Sten gun – Compact automatic weapon used by British paratroopers.

Stubenrauch-Krankhaus – SS military hospital in Berlin during World War Two.

Sturmbannführer – German SS rank equivalent to U.S. and British major.

Tu, toi – French. Intimate second person singular pronoun.

Tutoyer – French. To use tu or toi in conversation, denotes being on intimate terms.

U-boat – German. Submarine.

Unteroffizier – German rank equivalent to U.S. and British rank of sergeant.

Waffen – Combat arm of the Nazi Party. Notorious for ruthless behavior in World War Two. Also know as Waffen-SS.

Wehrmacht – German. Army.

CPSIA information can be obtained at www.ICGtesting.com
Printed in the USA
LVOW080227271212

313351LV00006B/7/P